I0574513

ARES ASCENDING | BOOK TWO

LOSING ARES

KIM CONREY

Black Rose Writing | Texas

The author grants the final approval for this literary material.

First printing

ISBN: 978-1-68513-293-4
PUBLISHED BY BLACK ROSE WRITING
www.blackrosewriting.com

Printed in the United States of America
Suggested Retail Price (SRP) $23.95

Losing Ares is printed in Calluna

*As a planet-friendly publisher, Black Rose Writing does its best to eliminate unnecessary waste to reduce paper usage and energy costs, while never compromising the reading experience. As a result, the final word count vs. page count may not meet common expectations.

DON'T MISS THE BEGINNING OF
ARES ASCENDING

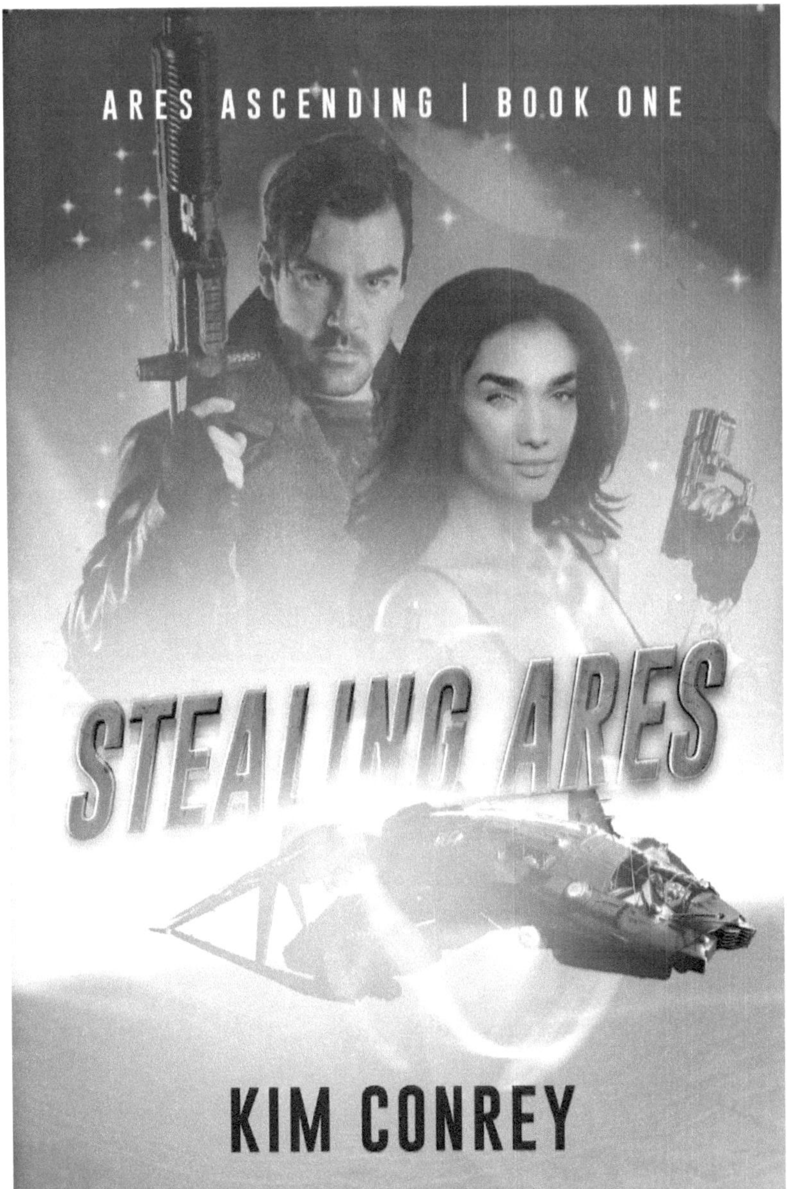

PRAISE FOR

LOSING ARES

"*On the heels of the wonderfully engaging* Stealing Ares *(Book One), this series continues with fierce characters, steady pace, and strong emotions in a journey that is woven together like a beautiful concerto. Highly recommend - This is an author not to be missed!*"

– McKinley Aspen, award winning author of Praesidium (Shadows in the Wind, Book One)

"Losing Ares *is an exciting read set in an engrossing world. It'll have you saying, 'Just one more chapter!' over and over again as you get swept up in the passion of Carlos and Safia's story.*"

– Meg M. Robinson, author of The Immortal Love series

"*Conrey's* Losing Ares *compels readers to join her on a journey where Safia Asfour must find a way to reclaim her power or lose everything, including the man she loves.*"

– Katherine Nichols, author of *The Unreliables*

For Finn, from one proud Mama Bear

ACKNOWLEDGEMENTS

I didn't get here alone, and gratitude is everything. How did I manage to be surrounded by such beautiful people?

As always, I am thankful to the Atlanta Writers Club for the years of knowledge, learning, and camaraderie. Not only has it brought me to this place in my journey, but it's allowed me to meet some of my closest friends, and one damn fine husband. The Roswell critique group has been a great help in nearly everything I've written. The Wild Women Who Write Take Flight Podcast has been the supportive bunch of writing women I wish everyone had. Thank you, Kathy Nichols, Gaby Anderson, Kat Fieler, and Lizbeth Jones. To my beta readers, Cherie Lawley and Liz Bailey, I honor and appreciate your time and suggestions. Thank you to my military consultants, Phil Fasone and Sean Conrey.

A good publisher can make all the difference in the world. Thank you to everyone at Black Rose Writing for your help, patience, and marketing efforts. There's some consistent hustle going on over there!

Without a doubt, I also wish to thank my readers. I know how much a good story means. They've gotten me through my share of dark days, rainy days, and every day. I truly hope you enjoy your time aboard the *Ares*.

LOSING ARES

CHAPTER 1

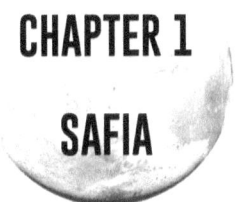

SAFIA

Safia Asfour bit the tip of her thumbnail as she watched the surface of the lake. She pulled her jacket collar higher over her ears, still not believing that the crisp fall weather of Mars, and even colder water, didn't bother her daughter, who was now five in Earth years. Even though the planet had been terraformed long ago, it was still a cold place, only reaching about seventy degrees Fahrenheit at its warmest and well below zero for long spans of time in the winter.

Safia startled as Carlos Gonsalves's footsteps crunched on the stones lining the shore. "How long has Bella been down there this time?" he asked.

"Almost fifteen minutes. Maybe I should go in. What if she's caught on something?" She began unzipping her jacket.

"She's fine. We've both already been under there with her. Of course, we had to have heat enclosure units and Aquair converters to stay down that long." He put his hand on her arm. "We know every inch of that lake. There's nothing she could get caught on. Besides, she's free dived for twenty minutes before without taking a breath."

She zipped her jacket back up but shifted her weight from foot to foot as Carlos hugged her shoulders.

Finally, Safia exhaled like air being released from a balloon as Bella's dark hair broke the surface of the lake, and she slowly walked toward them as water cascaded over her goggles and down her face reminding Safia of the legend of the selkies rising mysteriously from the water. Because of the heavy weights she wore around her ankles, she could walk in and out of the water and explore the bottom. Safia still couldn't believe how strong her daughter was.

Bella smiled broadly as she took her first breaths in twenty minutes. They were deep, but she didn't gasp for air.

Carlos held out a huge towel like a matador as Bella shook off the ankle weights, dropped her goggles, and ran into it. "That's my girl!" he said as he wrapped the towel around her and gave her a big hug.

"Are you okay, sweetie?" Safia asked.

"Of course, she's okay," Carlos said as he tickled Bella while she giggled. "Why wouldn't she be?"

Bella reached into her pocket. "I have a treasure for Mommy." She held out her hand. Inside her small palm was a lime-green peridot.

"Thank you, sweetie. It's beautiful!"

"Show Uncle Jack and Auntie Harlow," Bella said referring to their long-time friends.

Safia led them over to where Jack, Harlow, and their daughter, Selah, and their guards walked along the shore. Since Jack had gone rogue from both crown and coalition, the need for security had gotten even more necessary, and Evelyn and Devante had kept their allegiance to Jack. Like many who ignored the call to come back home and denounce the Mars rebellion, their decision would make it difficult for them to ever return to Earth. But with Evelyn having a wife onboard the *Ares* and Devante marrying a girl in the village, the choice to stay was clear.

Selah crouched at the edge of the lake and froze the water with her touch. She stomped on the ice and laughed as it crunched beneath her feet.

Jack leaned over and picked up a chunk of ice. "This one is shaped like the *Ares*."

Bella laughed and held up a large chunk. "This one looks like daddy's nose!"

Jack smiled. "What? Now you're telling porkies."

Safia held up the green stone. "Bella wants you to see her treasure."

"It's a lovely stone!" Harlow said. "Good job."

Jack gave a thumbs up and a smile.

Safia placed the gem in her pocket. "I've never seen a peridot on the bank. How far down did you find my treasure?"

"All the way down. At the bottom." Bella smiled, clearly proud of herself.

Jack asked, "Did you bring an Aquatraveler to light the way?"

Bella said, "No need. I see good down there."

Safia exchanged a look with Carlos. "Are you warm enough?" She placed her hands on her daughter's small face. It certainly didn't feel like the face of a child who had just spent twenty minutes immersed in frigid water.

"She's fine. Better than fine. She's Super Bella!" Carlos picked his daughter up over his head and spun her around.

Safia loved the way Carlos acted with Bella; he was an excellent father. She never thought of him as Bella's stepdad. The two were so natural together that she swore they were even starting to look and act alike. Seeing her family together made the terror of Bella's conception a distant memory that couldn't rob the joy they brought her. Still, she worried about Bella's gifts and what they might mean.

Carlos put Bella down and tried to wrap the towel around her again, but she shrugged it off. "I want to go get a treasure for you, Daddy."

"Okay—"

"No, we need to get going, baby," Safia said. "You'll get chilled with those wet clothes on."

"She won't get chilled. You know that." Carlos looked down at his daughter, who was already trying to pull free and head back to the water. "Go get Daddy's treasure and come right back up, otherwise no game time tonight."

"Be right back," she said as she turned around and placed a small fingertip on Carlos's nose. "Boop!" She giggled, put her goggles and weights on, then went back into the water. Harlow invited Safia and Carlos to continue walking with them, but Safia said she wanted to wait until Bella resurfaced.

After Harlow, her family, and their bodyguards resumed their stroll, Carlos said, "If someone has to go in after her, I'll do it. You don't have to get soaked."

"That's not the point." Safia took a deep breath.

"What is? Our daughter has built-in survival mechanisms that the rest of us don't have. She's smarter, stronger, more adaptable, heat resistant, cold resistant. She was born with night vision, for goodness' sake! My eyes had to be modified for that when I went into the service. She came equipped with it from the start. Every parent worries about their child. We've been given the gift of not having to worry so much."

Safia remembered her time at the compound on the now-abandoned research outpost on the other side of Mars, where former *Ares* Chief Science Officer Aldric Perthshire, the person she thought she could trust, had been experimenting on her child in utero. "They tampered with her while she was in *my* body, without my permission, to fulfill someone else's agenda. I don't care if she gained special abilities. There may be scary long-term consequences."

"Doc doesn't think so," Carlos said.

"Doesn't *think* so. We don't know for sure."

She watched Carlos close his eyes for a second, take a deep breath, and exhale before speaking. "What's the endgame here? If you try to keep her from doing what feels completely natural to her, she's going to resent you for it. Why do you continue to suppress what you can't change? It's who she is."

Safia felt a lump threaten to choke off her next words. The lake before her became blurry as she blinked back tears. "We don't know who she would have been. All we have is this altered version of her. They took who she *would* have been from us."

"Safia, my God! Stop. She's our daughter, and there is nothing wrong with her as she is."

"What if you and I have a child someday, and they have no enhancements? They likely won't."

"Then that's who they are, and it'll be okay."

Safia felt Carlos's gaze on her, and she tried to relax.

Bella broke the surface of the water and made her way to the shore.

"Daddy's treasure," she said with a smile, displaying a small, milky-blue opal shot through with iron veins.

"*You* are Daddy's treasure." Carlos took the gem from Bella and put it in his pocket before once again wrapping her in the large towel.

She kicked off her ankle weights and handed Safia her goggles. That was one vestige of normality that still held true; opening her eyes underwater for that long irritated them just like it would her parents' eyes.

"I'm hungry!" Bella proclaimed, as she always did after being submerged. Of course, it wasn't just that. The five-year-old ate nearly as much as her father, which amazed everyone on board the *Ares,* except for Harlow, Jack, and the parents of the other children who went through the genomic tampering. It was a common trait among them. Doc said it was because of their supercharged metabolism.

Carlos, Safia, and Bella walked over to where Harlow and her family stood with their guards.

Bella dug into her pocket. "Got you a treasure too," she said, before handing a small peridot to Selah.

Harlow leaned over to admire the gift. "Oh, that's a nice one. We'll take it back to the *Ares* and put it in the tumbler until it's all shiny."

The little girls held hands as the two families and Jack's guards headed to the ship. On the way, Bella told them about all the various things below the surface of the lake. "Fish, little ones, big ones, crawlfish. They call them that because they crawl, right?"

"You mean crawf—" Carlos began, but Jack gently smacked him on the shoulder and smiled.

"Yeah, I haven't thought about that," Carlos said. "Sure, why not. Because they crawl."

Selah laughed and repeated, "Crawlfish."

Safia watched Carlos and Jack stifle laughs. The girls had talked early for their ages, walked early, and they learned more about their unusual abilities every day, but silly moments emerged that, thankfully, reminded the parents that they were still their little girls.

They were halfway up the ramp leading into the back entrance of the ship when they were all knocked from their feet, and Safia's ears rang. She looked for the two girls, terrified for their safety, but they were already getting up. A quick sweep of the group assured her that no one was injured. Safia locked eyes with Carlos for a moment, then watched his gaze shift to a spot just over her shoulder as his jaws clenched and his eyebrows knit together. She turned to glimpse what he was seeing.

Someone had blown apart two of the huge shipping containers waiting to be loaded onto the *Ares* for the next delivery to Spain. In the last several hundred years, mining iron ore on Earth had become more dangerous as it became necessary to dig ever deeper. Natural resources had become increasingly depleted and costly, especially after the ash known as the Gray Death from the Yellowstone caldera eruption crippled production worldwide. Transportation from Mars had opened up now that the *Ares* was making regular trips. But Mars was a divided colony, with half the populace loyal to the old coalition and half fiercely backing the rebellion, incidents like this were becoming more common.

Evelyn and Devante helped Jack and Harlow to their feet.

Carlos turned back to Safia and said, "Take Bella inside."

Carlos, Jack, and his guards went racing toward the debris and the screams and shouts of dockworkers. Harlow held out her arms, and Selah snuggled close against her. Safia knew the look of worry on Harlow's face mirrored her own as her best friend watched Jack leave with his guards—they had learned long ago not to argue with him. They couldn't keep him from danger. They could only protect him in the midst of it.

Harlow moved off to the side with Selah. "I hate not being able to go with them. I hate having to—"

Safia put a hand on Harlow's arm. "I know." They both felt the helplessness. Safia knew it was worse for Harlow. She'd heard the stories of how Jack and Harlow had met. How Harlow had thieved, schemed, and done anything else she had to do to help the colonists survive. Some of those things were familiar to Safia as well, from her time living on the streets of Toledo, Spain. They were doers, but as mothers, they had to get their children to safety, not run toward danger. More personnel raced past them on their way to the wreckage.

Safia kissed the top of her daughter's head as she watched the flames lick at the twisted cargo containers and whispered a Muslim prayer from her childhood that no one was injured or worse. "O Allah, protect us from our front, behind us, from our right and our left, and from above us. We seek refuge in Your Magnificence from being taken unaware from beneath us." She looked up and locked eyes with Harlow. So far, three colonists had been hurt in such incidents, but this was the biggest explosion yet. If anyone had been over there...

Safia whispered to Harlow, "What have we started?"

CHAPTER 2

FALLEN PRINCE

Former Prince James Eadred Windsor, known to the colonists now as Jack, and the Ares army as Marshal, though certainly not back home where he'd been stripped of the title because of his rebellion, took a deep breath as Harlow attempted to rub some of the soreness from his shoulders. Someone was trying to send him a message, and now Colton Chang was missing a leg because of it. Jack rubbed his eyes to banish the image he saw in the wreckage. It wasn't the first time he'd seen something like that. When the Royal Air Force had gotten involved with riot duty—as all branches of the military had to when the Gray Death was at its worst—he'd seen that kind of thing and more, but this was different. He felt personally responsible.

When he first returned to Mars after defying his parents, he'd naively thought the colonists would accept him as one of their own. After all, he'd given up a life of luxury and privilege to live rough among them and demand fair prices on behalf of the people. He also counted on the colonists being united in viewing the Chinese on Enceladus as a common enemy and understanding the threat of the

Brotherhood. Though in all fairness, the entire Earth Coalition had given the colonists "the finger" to coin an old Earth phrase.

The Brotherhood had become a catch basin for many disgruntled factions, but especially those who believed the less fortunate were left to die when the ash came while others were allowed to breathe—via advanced air filtering technology only the wealthy could afford—and now had designs on using Mars as a base from which to terrorize Earth. While many saw it from his perspective, there were plenty who didn't and were furious enough about his "betrayal" to the Earth coalition to create problems. He was just glad Air Vice Marshal Miller had set him straight four years ago when he'd first returned home from exchanging his crown for a life among the colonists. Her advice didn't stop him from rebelling against the coalition, but at least he wasn't taken completely by surprise when things went pear-shaped.

• • •

He'd been home for only a few months when Spain, India, and the Palestinian-Israeli United State or "PIUS" started outbidding each other and driving the price up for materials coming from Mars. He sought counsel from someone he knew could advise him.

Air Vice Marshal Miller walked in wearing the uniform of the Ares army: cargo pants with practical utility pockets, and a form fitting breathable shirt that showed this woman was as fit in her fifties as Jack was in his thirties. Her dark bobbed hair bore a few strands of silver that only added to the air of intrigue around her. She'd flown with Colonel Hanson, Harlow's father, since the day the *Ares* first entered the embrace of the cosmos and she'd been through hijackings, riots, and survived the recon mission that Colonel Hanson never returned from. The years had refined, hardened, and paradoxically softened, where needed, this remarkable warrior. When she entered a room, you knew it before she uttered a word.

"You needed to see me, Marshal?"

He'd tried to get her to stop calling him that after he came home from London for the last time. They'd all been stripped of their ranks and titles, but Air Vice Marshal Miller insisted ranks kept order and discipline intact. Over twenty years his senior and with a deep knowledge of interplanetary politics—and human nature—she wouldn't try to please him. She would shoot straight every time. That was exactly the kind of advice he needed.

"Yes, thank you. Please have a seat." Jack motioned to the chair in front of his desk. "Since these are off-duty hours, could I pour you a drink? First Sgt. Gonsalves has been dabbling in home brew again. I must warn you it's hit or miss, and this will be my first go at this batch." He smiled as he poured the amber liquid into his glass before looking at AVM Miller for the go ahead.

"Fill 'er up. There's no one else I'd rather rot a gut with," she said with a smile.

"Brilliant." Jack poured another and handed it to her. "I'd like your advice. We've talked about how Spain, India, and PIUS have been outbidding each other and driving up prices, but now Nigeria and Sierra Leone are in the fray. What I'm thinking of doing is forming a new coalition in order to stabilize prices for everyone, but I don't want this to be perceived as a threat."

Jack watched Miller's eyes grow wide, and she took a drink as if trying to make the news go down easier. She swallowed and looked into the glass of home brew with a little nod of appreciation before speaking. "Not bad," she said. "But as to your pricing problem, it will absolutely look as if you are gathering allies against the original coalition and be bad news for our sovereignty vote in the Galactic Nation States."

"Well, I'm not. It's simply an attempt to stabilize prices. I just need to make that clear to them."

"It won't matter what you say."

"Well, I can't do nothing. These prices will get so high that it will start to harm our reputation. A coalition is simply a way to make prices reasonable for everyone, not a declaration of war. That's preposterous." He waved a hand in the air.

Miller moved to the edge of her chair and sat her drink down on Jack's desk. "Sir, if I may speak freely?"

"Of course. That's why I called you here."

"Okay. In case no one has laid the reality out to you as it truly is, I will. Here are some things you must accept about yourself, or you will be at risk of making errors that might get us killed. You know you have my full support because I believe you did the right thing, but these are the facts. You stole a ship that has no equal. It may have seemed like yours because it belonged to your family, your country, and your coalition. Everyone abandoned it except you after it went dormant, but you declared yourself a rebel to the crown, stole the *Ares*, and refused to return it."

Jack leaned forward and gave Miller an incredulous look. "Return it? So they could turn Mars into a slave colony? This ship and its firepower are the only things that guarantee our freedom."

"We all know that's true, but if you form another coalition, it will be tantamount to raising allies against the Crown. It does not and will not matter what your intentions are. It will be an excuse for those looking for a reason to come after you. You are guilty of treason. You need to let that sink in all the way down to your bones. Understanding that is the safest thing you can do for this colony right now, at this moment. I don't think you're there yet, and you need to be."

Jack looked at Miller for a long, sobering moment. Too sobering. He gripped the glass of home brew, lifted it, and said, "Here's to those who don't mince words."

She picked up her glass, nodded, and drained it as he did the same.

"Thank you," he said.

"Anytime," she said. "Sir, if I may?"

"Of course."

"You're doing a fine job. Just keep in mind that everyone is looking for an excuse to think the absolute worst of you right now. Don't let that tie your hands, but don't forget it either. You may be Chief Military Advisor and Head of Trade on the Martian council, but these are titles that can be taken from you. You aren't a prince anymore, either."

He nodded and looked out the window. "I never came here to lead a colony. I only wanted to wake a sleeping ship."

"Perhaps fate puts us where we need to be at the right moment."

Jack looked at Miller and felt thankful that fate had placed her on the *Ares* decades ago. "Indeed, it does, Air Vice Marshal. I'm glad it placed you here."

He only hoped he didn't get her killed along with everyone else who backed him.

CHAPTER 3

BROKEN GOD

Carlos felt Safia's arms slide across his chest and the warmth of her kiss on his cheek as he sat in the ratty chair he'd owned long before they moved in together. "You're doing the best you can," she said.

"It isn't enough." His exhaustion sank in as deep as the discouragement after the explosion. "These bombings are starting to feel personal."

"They aren't. It's just that you, Jack, and the council are seeing things are they are, and the loyalists are seeing things as they think they ought to be. They can't accept that the people, the planet that gave them life, are taking advantage of them, treating them as slave laborers. If you all hadn't kept the *Ares*, there would be no medical treatment here. The Earth coalition would hold our transport hostage. We would sit on this planet at the total mercy of the Earth coalition."

"But we seem to be powerless to make them see."

"You're not a god. There's only one of you." She stood behind him and rubbed his chest, then undid several buttons and placed her hands inside his shirt. He relaxed into her touch as she made slow circles over his skin. Warmth radiated from her palms. Her breath against his face and neck made him forget his worries for a few seconds. She brought moments of grace when he'd searched his entire being and found none.

Safia removed her hands from his shirt and pulled him to his feet and toward the bed. Bella was asleep in her room. Though their daughter was superhuman in many respects, she mercifully slept as deeply as most five-year-olds.

He wanted to forget, believe, and maybe even somehow be... redeemed from the war he feared he, Jack, and the other rebels had started and didn't yet know just how bad it might become.

Carlos tried to guide her onto the bed, but she pivoted and shoved. He ended up on his back, sprawled across the coverlet, as she climbed on top of him.

"Hmm?" He gripped her hips.

She leaned over and kissed him long and lazy, then rose to her knees with her palms braced on his chest and rocked back and forth on him while they were still clothed. She looked into his eyes. "Let me take your worries away."

"You don't have to ask me twice." He attempted to roll them both over.

"No," Safia said with a smile. She pressed his shoulders back onto the bed.

"What?" After four years, he knew what she liked. More than that. He *really* liked what they did together. Tonight, he wanted comfort, sameness, while everything around him was changing.

She unbuttoned his shirt the rest of the way, removed it, and unburdened him of his pants. She ran her hands up his legs, along his taut abdomen and chest. "You're mine."

"Always," he said. He unzipped her pants while she slid her shirt over her head and tossed her bra to the floor.

He watched her, feeling fascinated and, truthfully, a little worried. It wasn't as if she'd never been on top before, but something felt different this time. There had been a distance between them, and now she wanted something else in bed. Maybe he wasn't pleasing her. Maybe... *You're making more out of this than it is. It's been an insane day. The most beautiful woman in the colony is seducing you. Get over yourself.* He reached up to cup her breasts as she lowered her mouth to his neck. She kissed him with an energy that made him more than ready to be inside her when she reached down between them, wrapped her fingers around him, lifted herself, and then lowered onto him with a throaty growl.

He closed his eyes, groaned, and arched his back. "Dear God, woman." He took her wrists, wanting to lock her in place and get a good look at her. He felt curious about this goddess atop him. She had changed so much since that day he'd found her at the compound on the other side of Mars, grieving for a baby she thought dead. She'd looked so fragile then. He remembered how long it had taken to gain her trust. People changed. They grew. He suddenly felt conflicted about that.

She whispered, "I love you," then shook the bed with the intensity of her rhythm. She wasn't fucking around. Well, she was, but...

"I love you, too." He was so taken by what she was doing, he could barely answer.

She continued rocking on top of him with a ferocity he seldom experienced from her. When she cried out, he let go as well and felt his muscles relax for the first time in days.

He lay in bed awake long after Safia's breath had settled into the soothing pattern of deep sleep. He wondered, for the first time, if she were discontent with their life together, if he were doing something wrong. She was his touchstone. When the colonies were one enormous challenge after another, and he constantly worried if he did enough for Jack, his other friends on the *Ares*, and the people of Mars, he'd always felt confident he was enough for her. Now, he couldn't be sure.

He wondered why one night of phenomenal lovemaking left him feeling so confused.

CHAPTER 4

SOJOURNER

The breakfast rush at the Sojourner's Retreat was underway. As the smells of coffee, bacon, and eggs filled the air, Safia and Judith ran back and forth with plates of food. Things had gotten much busier since the formation of the new coalition called the Nexus. The *Ares* brought supplies and people to and from Spain, India, PIUS, and the other countries under the Nexus, and they ended up at the only decent restaurant in Colony Six. The Indian starship *Vijayee* also brought in more people, and as Earth recovered, corporations were building their own transports and requesting permission to enter the colony.

Customers from the larger Earth cities weren't used to being waited on by actual people. Even through the riots of the Gray Death, waitbots were so plentiful that their parts were never in short supply. The restaurants that went out of business during the food shortages had plenty of bots lying around. So, if one managed to keep their business afloat, they still had their bots—but not on Mars.

The colonists had been so supply poor that they no longer had functional bots and now, when they could get supplies, they all agreed they didn't want the waitbots, and were enjoying conversing with an actual human. And waitbots would've taken jobs away from the colonists.

But they did not impress one loud and disgruntled visitor to Mars, as he scolded Safia for her service. "Dear Lord, just get some waitbots in here already. I could've eaten my breakfast and been back on my ship in the time it took you to get this order out here."

From a couple of tables away where Carlos sat, his conversation with some crew from the *Ares* stopped, and a deadly look passed over his face. He placed a hand on the table and started to get up when Safia shook her head at him. He complied but kept a sharp eye on the man.

Safia turned to the visitor and spoke. "On Mars, we have a saying. It started when we first realized we were abandoned, and no one was coming to save us. 'Blessed are the hands that grow it, the hands that protect it, the hands that prepare it, and the gratitude of those that receive it.' Do you know how hard it is to protect crops from a Martian dust storm? If you have no gratitude, I can take it away and give it to someone who does."

The man's breakfast companion snickered at him from behind a cup of coffee.

"It's fine. Thank you," he replied.

"You're welcome," she said with a smile.

Safia walked over to where her husband and his friends from the ship sat.

McNamara, former RAF but now AWOL like the others, teased Carlos. "Maybe your woman doesn't appreciate your interference, mate."

Carlos was quick to defend his girlfriend. "Hey, she's a strong woman. It's not that she doesn't appreciate it. It's—"

Safia stretched an arm over the group of men and sat a plate full of eggs down in front of one of them as she spoke. "Oh, she appreciates his interference, all right. She just doesn't *have* to have it. That's all." Safia gave Carlos a wink and a kiss on his cheek.

Judith spoke from where she wiped off a table nearby. "She's not the only one perfectly capable of taking care of herself. Harlow once broke a man's wrist for grabbing her ass at the bar one night."

"That's harsh!" McNamara said.

"Well, keep your hands to yourself, and it won't be a problem," Safia said.

"That's it." Judith raised her hand.

Safia smacked it on her way to the kitchen, exclaiming, "Damn right!" as their palms made contact.

• • •

After the breakfast service, Safia packed up the leftovers to give to Harlow's sweet little friend from the village, Piper, who was golden eyed because of a natural mutation. She and her mother struggled to make ends meet and despite the splinter between the rebels and loyalists, the colonists still tended to take care of their own.

Safia felt her fingers tingle with the urge to create. She took out her paints and went to work on the mural she'd been creating in a nearby storage room for almost a year. She hummed as she uncapped the linseed oil and mixed it with a dash of turpentine and crushed dandelion powder to make more yellow. The scent of springtime on Earth filled the room as contentment filled her heart.

Painting transported her spirit to a place where she felt free. The more tense things got between the loyalists and the rebels, the more she wanted to create something beautiful in the colony. The mural was a Martian sunrise, as she'd seen it the first morning she woke up next to Carlos. She thought of the curve of his shoulders as the light came in through the window of his room that morning and kissed his body. Dandelion yellow with a bit of cinnamon echoed Carlos's skin tone. It ensured there would be the very essence of him in her art. As she remembered their time together, she smiled.

She'd lived on the *Ares* for six months by that point, and Carlos had been courting her, making her dinner, telling her about his family, finding opportunities to conveniently be where she was. She laughed out loud at the memory. The *Ares* was enormous. There was no way coincidence could have put him in her path *that* often. He played with Bella and connected with her like she was his. Family was everything to him. His eyes lit up when he talked about his relatives back on Earth. Now, she worried he'd never see them again. Throwing in with Jack and the rebel colony meant he was AWOL, couldn't return home without risk of severe punishment, and had to accept the meager wages the Martian council could afford to pay him and the others on the ship.

Still, he spoke with his family and saw their faces over the Rapid Message. His mother, aunt, and sister appeared holographically and told him all the things they wanted him to hear in an excited rush of English, Spanish, and his grandmother's Portuguese slang, and when they were done with the clan gossip, questions, worries, exclamations, and updates on various medical maladies and his sister's failed recipes, they'd send the message and wait for Carlos, Safia, and Bella to reply. Each RM took a second to convey. Once in a while, a solar flare or other interference created a choppy delivery but mostly, it worked well. She couldn't imagine the old days when it could take as long as twenty minutes for a message to reach Earth and back. The energy his family brought made her smile every time. She loved being part of his world.

That feeling warmed her and called for more yellow. She scooped up extra dandelion powder on her brush and brightened up the golden reflection on the slopes of Elysium Mons.

Judith passed the mural on the way to the kitchen. "Looking good!"

"Thanks," Safia said.

What she painted now, even with the colony in the middle of a rebellion, it was so different from the midnight blues, violets, grays, and blacks she'd composed back at the shelter in Spain after her assault. She wondered what had happened to those pieces. Hopefully, someone trashed them. She knew they were depressing and didn't want them bringing anyone else as low as she'd felt when she created them. Her dark inspiration was on another world entirely. As much as she wondered what it would be like to be with Carlos's warm, loving family, she didn't want to be on the same planet with the man who'd brought such a depth of sorrow into her art, her life.

She hoped to never visit that dark place again.

CHAPTER 5

MARCUS

Marcus sat by his father's bed as the old monarch took one ragged breath after another. He knew the signs. He'd watched his mother succumb to the same thing: ash pox.

If you lived in the city centers and had the means, you no longer needed to die of that, let alone a heart attack, diabetes, most forms of cancer, and many other diseases. However, after Britain's beloved son, Jack, had made a break with his royal family, most of the public's sentiment had gone with him. The Crown had a PR nightmare on its hands, and they knew it. A trip to the most blighted areas of the realm was in order, at the behest of the king's advisors, so that the family might appear caring and sympathetic, a bit of a twist to Jack's preoccupation with Martian affairs. The Crown could be portrayed as the family that takes care of its own, here at home, while Jack ran off to Mars, abandoning his people. So off Marcus's parents had gone, to prove how much they cared.

They arrived in Northern Ireland to the filthiest air they'd ever experienced. Depending on the jet stream, the sky above a district could almost be blue again while a mere shift in track and pressure could mean gray skies and breathing problems for weeks on end.

The community nanobots swept through once per week, but it was but a fleck in the dustbin compared with the ash still making a continuous circle around the Earth. It wasn't surprising that the Brotherhood had sympathizers when he thought of those conditions.

Nonetheless, the family had something to prove. Marcus remained at home, happy to have a break from the constant, albeit unspoken, message that he was not the man his brother was.

The palace physicians had assured the King and Queen whatever damage done to their lungs could be mopped up once they returned home to the finest care on the planet. And it could have if their visit hadn't coincided with the emergence of the ash pox. No one could air out their homes when the atmosphere outside was worse than the atmosphere inside. Filters couldn't keep up. Whatever diseases were brewing in the community used their homes as viral replicators.

By the time the royal couple returned to Buckingham Two, they were coughing continuously. Their physician believed it to be simply that they weren't used to the unfiltered air, but as the weeks wore on and samples from their lungs grew in the lab, it matched the samples from the people in Northern Ireland. Ash pox had taken hold, and even the greatest minds had yet to engineer a cure or a vaccine to prevent it, but so far, people could recover as long as their lungs weren't already riddled with the thousands of tiny cuts that the ash delivered. Despite every healing treatment available, the Queen's lungs could not repair. She passed away a year after her trip. The King was still hanging on six months later, but as with his wife, the inflammation never ceased.

Even though Marcus had never been close with his father, it was a terrible thing to observe. He wasn't keen on watching anyone suffer. On the one hand, the King's impending death would bring freedom to Marcus. No one would judge his every move. *Just an entire kingdom.* Yet the judgement of millions somehow felt less daunting, less utterly oppressive, than that of his father. He could rule as he saw fit. On the other hand, he had no idea what he saw fit to do. Most of his life had been spent wondering what his parents wanted him to do, how to please them, and then speculating what Jack would do.

His lips curled, disgusted with the knowledge that he was a grown man who had allowed everyone else to determine his path. He glanced up to realize that the nurse had caught the look on his face and likely thought it was directed at his dying father. How could he explain to her it was pure *self*-loathing? She looked away. *Damn it.* He knew it was one more reason for the people to have no confidence in him.

A coughing fit seized the King, making him convulse, and Marcus helped to steady him as the nurse rushed over. She spoke her credentials to the med comm and increased the oxygen saturation in the surrounding area to help him recover. Marcus felt lightheaded from the enriched air as he made room for the attendant to work.

His father lay there a while before he slowly opened his eyes and looked at him. He seemed to have something to say. It was nearly sunset, the first time he had been alert that day. These moments were becoming increasingly rare.

His father looked at him with red, watery eyes. Marcus felt a lump form in his throat. Why? The man had rarely approved of anything he'd done. Was it even possible here at the end that he could finally have some faith in him, some word of encouragement for the uncertain road ahead?

"I'm here, Father."

The King took a shaky, ragged breath as he attempted to speak. "James?" he asked.

The name cut through Marcus like a serrated knife. "No, sorry. It's just me."

"James?"

"No, he's still on Mars, Father."

A sound of frustration and anguish came from the King's throat, which led to gasping. The nurse bent over him once more.

At the moment, Marcus wished he were on Mars as well. Anywhere but where he was, watching his father die while the man asked for someone else to be by his side.

Marcus remembered his last trip off-world.

• • •

As the transport rode along smoothly in its EM bubble, making it possible to traverse space in a fraction of the time by putting the craft in an electromagnetic sphere such that space and time flowed around the ship and kept it from being subject to its constraints, he contemplated why he was even doing this. He wasn't sure. The first thought that came to mind was how his brother had strutted down the vast hallway of the palace without looking back while his father fumed, and his mother cried. Jack was sleeping with a woman they hated, while Marcus had been dating the same parent-approved, pretentious witch for the last two years, during which time she'd tried to control every aspect of his life and constantly threatened to break up with him if he didn't propose soon.

Even worse, sex with her was as exciting as steeping tea. He was too afraid to marry her, too afraid to call it quits. But his brother... *that* mighty bastard had bollocks to spare. He knew what his father would never say aloud: the old man loved Jack for his dissent. That's why Jack was the only one worthy of the crown, but also the only one their father would keep it from. He couldn't control him. Yet he didn't think a true king *should* be controlled. Damned definition of irony.

Marcus grabbed a package of food labeled "The Ultimate Steak and Kidney Pie," though he doubted the contents would deliver on the label's promise. He thumbed the button at the bottom of the pack, and the whole thing heated in an instant. He sniffed it first. It smelled just like the real thing. Snagging a fork from his pack, he took a bite. It was like a copy of a copy of a copy and could never compare with the genuine article. Was that how his father saw him? After a few more bites, he threw it in the recycle.

He put his feet up on the console. Jack would be surprised to see him, even more surprised to learn that he had defied their father. Marcus had told the old man he was headed to Mars after Jack left, that he wanted to see firsthand what kind of rebellion they were dealing with and report back to Parliament, but his father's reaction was...

"No, absolutely not," the King replied.

"And why not? My presence is least likely to escalate matters, and he's more apt to trust me with what is truly happening there. He will be honest with me."

The King laughed. *Laughed.* Marcus felt heat rise around his neck. He looked at his father with barely contained rage but controlled his voice when he spoke. His father would use his anger against him. "You believe Jack has no more faith in me than you do."

"Son, it isn't personal. Just leave matters of treason to those with more experience."

The comm device on his father's desk began chiming.

"I need to answer this. We can talk more later."

Marcus walked out of his office and straight to his room to pack a bag, grabbed a few provisions from the kitchen, a precious few fresh, mostly replicated and thus tasteless, since the Gray Death, then on to the hangar to punch in the coordinates for Colony Six on Mars. His father wouldn't have given the hangar personnel any instructions to ground their transport—he would never believe Marcus would defy him. That was more Jack's territory.

Every time his transport dropped out of the EM bubble, there was another furious message waiting for him. He pictured the communique hurtling through space toward him, fueled by his father's pompous, self-righteous rage. Being in the EM bubble had gotten him some respite before they began reaching him. He'd ignored them all. Until he found the rum rations...

"Well, bugger me!" he said as he spotted the bottle of rum after leaning down to stow a couple of extra food packs. Though the rations ended hundreds of years ago, now and then someone would bring a bottle along in the name of "tradition." The rations were a testament to a bygone era that he both loved and loathed. His father wielded tradition like a sword, pinning him to the wall with it.

Marcus laughed. "Here's to bygone rituals," he said as he unscrewed the top and turned it up. He had nothing to do until he made it to Mars in a few days, anyway. After drinking enough to gain the courage to break up with his girlfriend, he recorded a Rapid Message to her: "See here, I'm my own man now. I dress as I please. Anyone who wears a dickie looks like a dolt, by the way. Oh, and we're through."

After sending the RM, he praised himself for finally cutting her loose. "I'm free. It's done!" He held the bottle high in celebration, staggered sideways, caught himself before he fell over and bragged to the empty cabin about the size of his newfound bollocks before deciding to listen to a few of his father's messages. He replied to these, "I might be your second choice, but I'm all you've got, you wanker." There was no one on the ship to hear the bravado, but it felt good all the same. "What are you gonna do? Live forever out of pure spite? Jack's gone." While deleting his father's third angry rant, he felt a surge of defiance and freedom.

As he approached the Martian atmosphere on the fifth day, he dropped out of the EM bubble, hailed the *Ares,* and drank the last of the rum. Jack came on the comm a few minutes later, sounding surprised. Marcus wasn't shocked to find the *Ares* scanning his shuttle for other life forms, weapons, etc. Jack was no fool.

Marcus stepped out of the transport and wobbled a little before being greeted by Jack and Aunt Mary. He knew he was deep in his cups but felt he was doing a fine job of holding it together.

Jack looked at him strangely. *Don't blow this. This is official business. Sort of.* "Sorry, my legs are a little wonky from being on ship. You know how it is."

"Oh, of course. Good to see you, brother." Jack hugged him.

No sooner had Jack let him go than Aunt Mary wrapped her arms around him. He returned the embrace as he heard her make an exaggerated sniffing noise. "You found the rum rations." She laughed. "Did you save any for me?" She put her hands on her hips, as if to pout, and smiled at him.

Marcus laughed and simultaneously cursed himself at the unexpected heat that gathered behind his eyes. *What the hell is wrong with you? Maybe you are as weak as Father thinks.* But he realized the cause of his reaction was likely that his father wasn't as genuine as Jack, and his mother had never been as warm as Aunt Mary. He thought, for the first time, that it was a shame she hadn't had children of her own. Now that her nun's habit was gone, after she'd broken the seal of confession to keep an innocent woman—his sister-in-law, Harlow—from spending her life in prison, and her wavy gray hair fell about her shoulders, he could see her in a different light. How strange it was that an article of clothing changed the way he'd seen someone for decades. It seemed wrong somehow that he hadn't really "seen" her before.

Jack said, "I didn't think I'd be seeing you here after the way I left home. How in the galaxy did you convince Father to let you go?"

Marcus had a rush of adrenaline as he answered. "I didn't. I just left. His furious messages reached my transport en route. It's best to establish early on that the second choice will not be his puppet." He looked from Jack to Aunt Mary, wondering what he hoped to find there. Respect? Admiration?

Jack nodded in approval. "Fair enough, but I wouldn't want to be in the hangar when you arrive back home."

"Hell, I don't want to be there either. I'm in deep shite, to be sure."

The three of them walked down the hallway, talking as Jack showed Marcus to his guest quarters. Jack placed a hand on Marcus's shoulder. "I'm glad you're here."

Marcus walked beside a brother who was entirely different from the man he knew back home. This Jack wore his military attire—cargo pants, boots, and a t-shirt—he wouldn't have done that at home. He would've had an image to maintain. Even the way he greeted people differed from his persona at the palace or when he was on duty in the RAF. But there was more to it than that. Marcus struggled to put his finger on exactly what it was. Then it hit him with shocking clarity. The man was happy! How in the hell was that so? They had stripped him of his royal title and rank—something Marcus knew bothered him far worse than losing the claim to the throne—and yet, the damn fool was happy. He wondered if Jack realized the change. His aunt had given up her lifelong calling as well, but there was also a contentment about her that calmed him.

Jack introduced him to one shipmate after another. There was a hesitancy Marcus sensed in most of the people he met. They knew he was part of the coalition that had abandoned them. He still didn't know how he felt about the whole thing—he had a fleeting thought that perhaps it was part of the reason he was there. Jack never seemed to waiver in the pride he took when introducing him. *He's naïve. That's what it is.... Jesus, are you so barmy that anyone who is proud of you must be a fool? Now* that's *fucked up! Pull it together, man.*

Jack startled him from his thoughts. "You all right, mate? You're looking a little pale."

Marcus scrubbed a hand across his face. "Yeah, I'm right chuffed to be here. Just a little knackered from the trip."

Aunt Mary winked at him. "And the rum, I suspect."

Marcus held up a thumb and forefinger in front of his eye. "Only a little."

"Hmm, well, sleep it off, nephew. We're going out tonight."

"Where are we headed?"

"O'Malley's. Best brew in town," Jack said.

Marcus held his head and groaned.

Jack spoke to the ship to reprogram a room for Marcus, motioned for him to swipe his palm across the door, and it opened for him. Jack chucked Marcus on the shoulder before heading back down the hallway, and Mary gave him a kiss on the cheek. "I'll have the kitchen send up some soup."

Marcus walked in, and the door shut behind him. He laid down on the bed and marveled at how strange it was that it could be so much more confusing when people treated you well than when they were total wankers.

"What in God's name is wrong with me?" he whispered.

• • •

That evening, Jack, Harlow, and Aunt Mary sat with Marcus in Mike O'Malley's pub, listening to a woman from the village named Isla sing and play guitar in a duet with a man playing violin. Marcus listened to the words that sounded for all the world like they were a longing for somewhere on Earth. The song described oceans, meadows... it sounded like an old Irish ballad. *What did that even mean? The Martians were fiercely loyal to Mars. But if they sang songs of home? Did they want to go back? Could both be true at once?*

"So, what do you think?" Jack said.

"Lots to take in."

"Yes. Well, it's been a while. You haven't been here in, what? Over a decade?"

From across the bar a man looking to be roughly his brother's age and a woman of maybe Harlow's age made their way to the table. Jack smiled and introduced them when they stopped at their table. "Marcus, please meet some friends of ours. This is Carlos Gonsalves and Safia Asfour. Meet my brother, His Highness, Marcus Windsor."

Carlos smiled. "Hello. Pleased to meet you, Your Highness." Carlos said cordially.

"Hello," Safia said, but Marcus couldn't help but detect a bit of an edge in her voice that made him nervous. "We're all thrilled that your brother and Harlow have gotten the *Ares* up and running again. Going back to Earth to resupply has already saved lives. Just two days ago, medical finally synthesized the enzymes that repair the pancreas and cause it to regulate itself and they were also able to get the genetic scanner going in sick bay again. No one is dying of heart attacks now."

"People were dying of heart attacks?" Marcus cringed. Even during the worst of the Gray Death, the genetic scanner was still going and those prone to heart attack were warned, diagnosed, and nearly always corrected.

"Yes, they were. Dr. Nakamura, who assists Dr. Hagen on the *Ares,* is a good friend of mine. She was telling me all about it."

"Father didn't mention this."

"Did he know Dr. Nakamura's son died of tetanus?"

"What is—?"

"It's something we don't have a vaccine for here, but everyone in a city like London still does. You don't have to give it a second thought because there has been a vaccine for so long. Hinata stepped on a rusty nail. He was two, and that was it." Safia moved her hand in a flat slicing motion.

Marcus looked at Jack. He'd introduced him to this woman who was now attacking him as if it were his fault. He wanted to punch him. No doubt his brother knew at least some of this. Jack didn't seem at all rattled by what the woman was saying.

Jack leaned over and whispered, "A good king listens to the people both at home and abroad."

Marcus knew Jack was testing him. He took a deep breath before looking at Safia again. "Okay, what else?"

"Nakamura's husband is suffering from lung disease. He's been an engineer in the mines for many years. We need more respirators."

Marcus watched the man Safia had come in with place a hand on her arm, but he didn't appear to want to stop her. To Marcus's horror, he may have even been offering support. Marcus took a deep breath. "I understand. When I return, I will do my best." He knew his next words wouldn't be well received, but he didn't want to make promises he couldn't keep. After growing up at court, he was a realist when it came to knowing what could and couldn't be done, even if he were king someday. "Please understand that the reply to anything I ask for will be that they will not want to lift a finger until the *Ares* is returned as a coalition ship."

Marcus watched Safia take a deep breath. An earful was coming. He broke in before the onslaught began. "Rest assured, I will explain to my family and the Prime Minister as well that this is something that has been owed the colonists long before now, and the goodwill can only help matters and reflect upon the Crown's benevolence."

"Hmm, well, okay. If that's what it takes, I'll accept a lie of benevolence. Thank you... Your Highness."

"Of course. Would you two like to join us?"

"We don't want to intrude on a family gathering," Carlos replied.

"Please. You all *are* family now," Jack said.

Carlos and Safia sat down with them and quickly became engrossed in conversation with Harlow and Aunt Mary. Jack gave Marcus a quick slap on the back, leaned in, and spoke. "Sorry to put you in the hot seat, Bro, but I don't think it's the worst idea for you to get to know these people. It's one thing to hear reports back to Earth, but until you've been here, met them, talked to them, you don't really know or understand what's happening to them."

Marcus nodded but said little. The musicians finished their song, and the crowd clapped and shouted encouragement.

A few songs later, Harlow was yawning, and Jack announced to the table that they were ready to go. "You're welcome to stay, but if you do, I think it would be best to leave Evelyn and Devante here with you."

"I can hang around too, boss," Carlos offered.

"Thanks, mate," Marcus said, "but I'll head back as well." Everyone from their table said their goodbyes to Mike O'Malley behind the bar and began heading toward the door. Marcus thought about how he didn't get to do much of this at home. He couldn't just come and go in this way. Of course, he noticed the ever-watchful eyes of Jack's guards. They could certainly count Carlos among them, even though he wasn't technically responsible for Jack. There was an allegiance that went beyond obligation. It was... sincere? Real. Nothing like his own so-called friendships in London. It made him wonder if he perceived his entire life as fake. *Was it?*

As they stepped out into the cold Martian night, Harlow spoke to Marcus while Jack was occupied speaking to a couple from the village. "Is everything okay?"

"I'm fine. Thank you," Marcus said.

"People tend to unload on the first mark they see when they've been holding things in for a while and—"

"And other than my father, they'll never find a better target? I get it."

"Well, I just... You know, they're good people. They want to be heard, but I don't want you to feel constantly attacked, either. You're family."

"I guess I am." He suddenly felt ashamed, and it took several moments for his mind to catch up to why he felt that way. He realized he hadn't thought of her as family because his parents had found the idea ludicrous. He looked down at her protruding belly that carried his niece, due in just a couple of weeks. Harlow was indeed family. A shocking, yet pleasing, sense of warmth enveloped him. "Thank you," he said.

Later that night, Marcus fell into a fitful sleep with his mind spinning on more than unregulated beer. He was coming undone with no idea how the pieces might fit back together.

CHAPTER 6

THE LURE OF FREEDOM

After more than a week, he knew he needed to get home. At any rate, he'd sent his father a message that he would return soon and, no, he wasn't looking to form a rebel alliance with his brother. *But*, he didn't add, there was freedom here, and he was beginning to like it... too much. For one dangerous moment, he let himself consider the possibility of staying on Mars, freeing himself of expectation and his father's wrath, but there was no place for him here. Even if Jack were to pass away or put him in charge, the colonies were terrifying. The government consisted of a divided, floundering council. Half supported Jack, half wanted to slit his throat.

Marcus drove off from the village and slipped the watchful eyes of Jack's guards, who'd taken it upon themselves to ensure his safety since he'd not arrived with his own security. He cut the engine of the sputtering old buggy and held his arm out in the setting rays of the sun. His skin gave off a faint pinkish orange glow here. He liked it. He liked the smaller room he occupied on the *Ares*. It was soothing, somehow. He liked... *It didn't matter*.

He turned his hand in the orange-pink glow once again, letting the last of the Martian day slip through his splayed fingers. There was a buggy in the distance. This one hummed, a nicer, solar-powered ride with a newer battery, though new was a relative term on Mars. The vehicle was coming from the Mars "outback" as many had referred to it because of its relatively untouched, underdeveloped regolith. There wasn't much there except a couple of research centers. Marcus grabbed the standard phase-modulated weapon he'd brought with him and tucked it into his back pocket as he got out of the buggy. He stood to face whatever this might be. It was one man, alone.

The vehicle stopped roughly four meters away, and the unknown person got out and leaned against it. "Your Highness," the man said with a Russian accent as he bowed slightly.

Marcus watched him warily. The man must have had him under surveillance and knew he'd be out there alone. He no longer felt clever for slipping past the guards. He saw flashes of his body lying in the Martian desert, baking beneath the sun, left there for a search party to find the next day. *Why do you jump straight to defeat? Jack doesn't do that. Does he?*

"Good evening," Marcus replied.

The man didn't come any closer but spoke from where he was. "You finally know I did not betray your family. Yet I have spent many years freezing in exile for it. Aldric is paying for his crimes now."

"Mikhail?"

"Yes."

"What are you doing here?" Marcus knew better than to trust the man outright, despite Aldric's confession of murdering Jack's late wife and child.

"Perhaps the same as you. I'm not sure there is a place for me on Earth currently, but under the right circumstances, there could be."

Marcus let the silence hang in the air between them. He'd spent far too many years trying to fill the tense gaps between Jack and their father with words; he wouldn't do it for this man now. Let other people be responsible for their own conversations, feelings, awkward pauses. Exhaustion and liberation drove his newfound revelation as he waited in the silence for Mikhail to speak.

"You love your brother. I loved mine, too. He died while I was rotting on Enceladus." Mikhail took a hard case from his pocket, opened it, and put what looked to be a hand-rolled cigarette between his lips. He removed a vintage finger-torch from the other pocket, lit it, and inhaled deeply. The glow of the cigarette created an orange cast on his thick silver beard as he blew smoke into the air. "I remember when the two of you were little."

Marcus recalled Mikhail's family visiting. It didn't mean he owed the man anything.

"This colony will eat your brother alive. It is already beginning. They plot against him. It will only get worse. Everybody wants revolution until they have one. Revolution is glorious in theory. Is hell in practice. They will turn on him. I know this. I lived this. If you want to protect him, the best thing you can do is get the *Ares* back... by any means necessary. Form an alliance with the colonists loyal to the coalition. You will be king soon. Ensure fair trade with the colony. In time, Jack will come to understand this is best for everybody."

"Jack won't just give me that starship. I didn't spend seven years working on it day and night. It isn't mine."

"And it isn't his either," Mikhail said. "And I never said he would just give it to you. "You will have to take it. If you love him, you will. This place is crawling with loyalists. Jack is a big, powerful man but will be no match for one well-placed bomb." Mikhail blew a large plume of smoke from his nose and mouth and looked for all the world like a dragon. He then threw what little remained of his cigarette onto the red-orange dirt and ground it with his heel.

Marcus shook his head at the absurdity of what Mikhail was suggesting. He was sure everyone on Mars adored Jack just as Harlow did, just as his father and mother did. They would never turn on that charismatic bastard.

"Mark my words. The day is coming." Mikhail lit another cigarette and inhaled. "The *Ares* will save Jack's life when it is gone." He abandoned his casual stance of leaning on the vehicle, stood up straight, and pointed at him with the cigarette caught between two fingers. "Better still, it will gain you utmost respect in your father's eyes, and to the people, you become known as the king who took back the most formidable weapon in our solar system."

Marcus's head swirled with everything Mikhail was placing before him. These were things only a king did. *Things only a king did.* He was to be a king now. He needed time to think, to get away from this man. Time alone without all the thoughts bumping into one another was what he needed—what he'd come out there for before Mikhail arrived. He turned to get into his buggy without another word before one phrase, one question, rose to the surface among all the others, and he spoke it before he had a chance to think it through or second guess it. "What's in it for you?"

Mikhail's face broke into a sly grin that Marcus saw now only in the eerie last rays of the faint pink-orange sunset.

• • •

Even years later, he still thought about his time on Mars almost every day. He reminded himself that he was likely romanticizing the whole thing. It was one thing to visit, quite another to live there. Those people did without so much.

The days spent by his father's bedside were strange. He didn't feel he owed it to him when his father made it clear he would rather have Jack by his side. Regardless, he felt paralyzed as to what else he should be doing.

When he wasn't there, he was dealing with Jacob Worthington, the king's long-time advisor, who lay in wait outside his door like a vulture. Worthington used every opportunity to bend his ear to "what your father would want," and what he wanted was for Marcus to continue his campaign to press other countries to avoid doing business with the colonists until, *Ares* or not, Mars would welcome back the old coalition. They would have to be *controlled.* It was no longer politics. Controlling the colonies might have been what half the world wanted, but it was also their father punishing Jack.

He knew the advisor took him for a pliable young fool, and he knew there was more than a little truth to it. He was thirty-three and had spent most of his life assuming his father or brother would lead, and he would never bear such a burden.

The other frightening component to conversations with Worthington was that he was starting to make sense. The bombings on Mars had gone from small sporadic things a couple of years ago to bolder, more destructive acts of terror in the last few months. Just two days ago, the largest explosion yet had taken place on Mars. A huge storage container blew apart outside the *Ares.* A man had nearly bled to death and was lucky to escape with only a lost leg. No doubt they would have liked to plant that bomb under the *Ares*, but it was designed to withstand asteroid hits and missile strikes. But how long was it until someone snuck on board with one?

He thought back to his conversation with Mikhail years ago during his visit to Mars. He'd said something that Marcus had been sure would only benefit Mikhail, but it too was starting to make sense now. The Russian had said the best thing Marcus could do for Jack was to take the *Ares* back. But that was crazy. Wasn't it?

• • •

He'd thought his father would pass deep in the night while the rest of what remained of Great Britain slept, leaving him alone to deal with his grief. Instead, sunlight streamed in through the massive windows as dust motes danced in the bright rays of light, and he heard the buzz of transports going about their business outside the palace walls. A dog barked in the distance, and the faintest conversation carried from the street when Marcus noticed a stillness beside him. His father had not spoken in days, but somehow the stillness filled the room and became a presence unto itself that could not be ignored. Before he waved away the holo book he'd been reading, he knew. Before he turned his head to look, he knew. His father was gone.

The city was awake, and that made the mantle of death worse. Life carried on as a soul passed from one realm to the next and, with it, any chance that his father might finally approve of him. *You aren't mourning him at all.* Marcus didn't want to dismiss the book or turn his head to the side to confirm what he already knew and what it meant: he had to figure out how to lead.

He had no idea where to start.

CHAPTER 7

CARLOS & SAFIA

Carlos straddled Safia. The sounds of others grappling on the mats faded into the background as he concentrated on a jiujitsu hold called the Americana. His right elbow held firm by her left ear as he gripped her right hand and hooked his right leg around Safia's left. Even though he'd taught the *Ares* crew members the art for years, when he'd first began teaching her, the close contact had been distracting… well, he had to admit, sometimes it still was, especially with the smoldering way she was looking at him right now.

She slipped free of the hold and wound up above him with a smile. She pulled her mouth guard out. "Stay frosty, Gonsalves," she said. A few long, dark locks slipped free of her braid, and she flashed a playful yet wild smile at him.

His family was part Brazilian, part Colombian, and his father's side had a long tradition of teaching jiujitsu. He knew the moves in his sleep and never felt restrained or self-conscious about the closeness the moves required. After all, unlike other martial arts, jiujitsu demanded the practitioner to be body-to-body: on top of, underneath, and basically all over the other individual. But as he always said, "Better get used to it now, unless you think your attacker is going to let up because you feel 'uncomfortable.' Get over it."

Safia had acclimated quickly, and the training seemed to help with her nightmares. When she first moved into his quarters, there had only been a few nights when she woke him up with night terrors. He remembered them well. It sounded as if she were trying to speak but couldn't get the words out. Then it sounded as if she were trying to scream, but it came out like a moan. She usually woke herself up doing it. One thing all the night disturbances had in common was fear. After a couple episodes of this, she explained that she often relived the experience of her assault, the night Bella was conceived.

He would pull her into his arms after she woke, fearing if he pulled her close before she opened her eyes, she might believe he was the attacker. He couldn't stand the thought of that. Other nights, he heard her wake from one of the dreams and go sit in Bella's room, keeping watch over her crib like a sentinel, as if she believed someone might come for her. Shortly thereafter, he offered to teach her jiujitsu. It was the perfect martial art for a woman. It gave her a recourse once she was on the ground, which is where many male attackers wanted, and often managed, to get their female victims.

Safia was a quick and determined study. She often surprised him when he let his own guard down and assumed she wouldn't remember what move to use in a given situation. It reassured him that she could take care of herself if he wasn't there to rip the nuts off anyone who might harm her. He hoped that day would never come again.

Under her, his back to the mat, he felt the heat coming off her, became a little too aware of the rise and fall of her breasts above him, and...

"Oof!" he cried, as she fell into a straight arm lock, first dropping her weight onto his chest with one hand on top of the other, then sliding off to the side to immobilize his right arm.

"You okay?" she asked.

Words failed him as he tried to catch his breath. Carlos felt the back of his head scrub against the mat as he nodded then laughed. "Yeah, you got me."

• • •

Safia watched Carlos drop the towel from his hips and hang it on the hook. No one wasted water on Mars doing unnecessary laundry. It would be the same towel he would use for the rest of the week. She rubbed her legs together and thought about the time they'd just spent in the bed where they'd shared a room for the last three years. Bella's room was on the other side of the wall, but she was currently in Harlow and Jack's quarters, playing with Selah.

She could look at Carlos for the next hour, but looking wouldn't be enough. No one had ever made her feel like he did, and she knew no one ever could.

Carlos smiled and looked over his shoulder after he'd put his pants on. "You're a bit of a voyeur, Safia Asfour."

She propped up on her elbows and her long dark brown hair spilled over her shoulders. A bit of water trailed down his hard chest and she watched mesmerized as it made its way lower still, over his muscled abs and below... Her mouth went dry, and she wanted him again. The need for him never stopped. After what happened to her on the streets of Spain, she thought she'd never want this kind of relationship again, but Carlos caused her to feel things she didn't think possible. She never felt like she was giving away her power to be with him. Only when he asked her one question—but he'd stopped asking her to marry him over a year ago. She was pretty sure he wouldn't ask again.

She licked her lips as the water soaked into the waistband of his pants. He slipped on his unbuttoned shirt, obscuring the view of his chest. She started calculating how she might get him back in bed.

"You look like a cricket over there with the way you keep rubbing your long legs together." He dipped his head and looked up at her. Total sin written in his dark gaze. God help her. The man knew exactly what he was doing. "You want something?"

"Is it that obvious?" she purred.

Carlos braced both palms against the door jambs leading to the bathroom as if restraining himself from coming to her. "Yes," he said. His shirt hung open, and his bare chest accentuated the hungry look in his eyes.

"Bella's with Harlow for the evening. What's our hurry?" she asked.

"I was going to help Daniel work on the mechanical component—"

Safia had already crossed the room and stopped, his words short with her mouth on his. She unbuckled his pants, slid them down, and he stepped out of them, and shrugged out of his shirt. He wrapped a large, warm hand around the back of her head and pressed her against the wall. She lifted a leg and reached down to touch him as he bent his knees and pushed his hips against her. "Take me to that stool in the bedroom," she whispered into his ear.

"The one where your legs hang off the side?"

"Oh, yes."

Carlos walked backwards into the bedroom, never letting go of her hand. He sat down on the stool and placed her on top of him. She got lost in him every time. The world faded away, the troubles brewing on Mars, what she wished she could give Carlos but couldn't... but most of all, the past faded away. She pulled, pushed, and ground him into her. He planted his hand on the stool beneath them both to brace himself, arched his back, lifted himself, and pushed up the weight of her.

Her feet left the floor as she sucked in a breath. "Carlos!" A tremor ran through her body and a moment later, she felt him throb inside her.

His breath came in ragged gasps. "Thank you," he whispered. He looked at her with half-lidded eyes, tucked a strand of her long dark hair behind her ear and ran his fingers down her neck.

"Here, let me get off you before your legs go numb." She started to rise before he grabbed her around the waist and locked her in place.

"No, stay." He wound his fingers through her hair and kissed her again. His tongue was demanding. He finally pulled back, gasping. "I love you." His breath was warm. His lips swollen from their kiss, his tan complexion, everything about him was like a spell she couldn't, didn't want to escape.

"I love you, too. With all my heart," she said as she rested her forehead against his.

"So, I haven't asked in over a year... and we've been together for three years now. Marry me, Safia."

Damn it! Why? Breathe. Don't hurt him. "Carlos, you know I love you. There's no one else in the world, the galaxy for me."

"But."

"Yeah." She shifted her weight and swung her leg off him, walked over to the bed to grab her robe, and wrapped it around her.

Carlos didn't say another word but got up, strode over to where his clothes lay on the floor, retrieved them, and got dressed. She knew he wouldn't even look at her before leaving the room. She knew he didn't want her seeing the hurt in his eyes.

She sat on the bed and tried, for God knew how many times, to picture herself marrying him. It made her angry every time. It felt as if something were being taken from her. *Why?* It would require weeks to repair this. This was the third ask in as many years. They would argue now. She often wondered if it weren't for Bella, whether he would have already broken up with her, but it was clear he loved being Bella's father. Turning him down hurt him deeply. Family was everything to him and marriage seemed to hold a permanence in his mind that living together simply didn't, no matter how many times she tried to explain to him the depth of her commitment.

• • •

"He asked again," Safia said as soon as Harlow came to the door.

"Oh, boy. Come on in. Jack's out. Things have gotten even more tense since the king died. He probably won't be back for a while. You want to have some tea and talk about it?" Safia looked at the picture hanging on the wall that she painted for Harlow after she'd come to live on the *Ares*. On the bottom of the canvas, a hand reached out of water while, above, a hand reached down from the sand. The two grasped in the space between. "Sure. I'd love to."

A few minutes later, the aromas of lavender and peppermint—some of the easiest herbs to grow in the Martian soil—drifted from their steaming cups and scented the air. They sipped their tea and watched Selah and Bella play in the kitchen. Selah's hand hovered over the wash water in the sink and froze it. After that, she smashed it with her fist and the two giggled. Bella then placed both her hands over the ice chunks to melt them and the process repeated.

"I know it's crazy. I love him. It shouldn't be such a problem for me, but when he asks me to make that sort of commitment. It just feels like... I just... Somewhere in my head, I panic."

"What word comes to mind?" Harlow asked. "What's the first word that comes to mind when you think about this whole situation?"

"Trapped. I feel trapped. Like I was at the compound. Trapped like I was when I was..." Safia sat her tea down and leaned over, trying to get a handle on the wave of nausea and dizziness that washed over her. "Trapped like I was in that alley. When I couldn't get away from... that other man."

"But you feel safe with Carlos?" Harlow asked.

"Always. Completely, but the idea of being forced to marry him—"

"You realize you just used the word 'forced,'" Harlow said.

"Shit. I did. Why would I say that?"

"I think that's what you need to figure out. As soon as you do, maybe you'll be free. That's why I think you'd be the perfect one to take my place. Have you thought anymore about it? There's been a gap since I left. I can't do any of that now that I married Jack. We have to keep everything straight. It's boring as hell," she grumbled. "Anyway, Maricopa's father-in-law is on the council. You know damn well that's why Colony Six security hasn't hauled in her husband yet from when she showed up in *Ares* medical last week with that broken nose and cracked ribs."

"I confess it would feel good to dispense a little justice on her behalf."

"Hell, you'd be getting some for yourself while you're at it."

Safia tilted her head and looked at Harlow. "How so?"

"I don't mean to overstep, but did it ever occur to you that maybe some of your problem with Carlos is related to what happened with your attacker?"

"I don't see how. Carlos is nothing like him."

"Of course not, but you used the word trapped to define a commitment to him. You're the one who still needs to have an escape route. All I'm saying is there's something to being able to get your power back. Maybe you get justice for Maricopa and some of this stuff with Carlos works itself out."

Safia felt herself oscillating between hostility and intrigue toward her friend. It was a strange confusion of emotions.

"You know jiujitsu better than anyone on this ship. Jack said so."

This was news to Safia. She'd been training faithfully for three years and loved it, but didn't realize anyone else noticed, especially someone she respected like a big brother. "He did?"

"Yes. Not only that, but I could also teach you how to get in and out of places undetected. We could derail some of these terrorists. Just don't go in alone. I had O'Malley with me most of the time. You could take Seraph, Evelyn's wife. She has almost as much combat training but isn't an official part of the Ares Army and was never Jack's guard. So, if she were to get caught, it wouldn't be as big of a problem."

"Hmm," Safia watched a few peppermint leaves float around in her teacup. She remembered the wrinkled face of an old Spaniard lady reading tea leaves for her and her friends when they were kids. The woman had entranced her and made her wish for such a talent so her life wouldn't feel beyond her control, but maybe it was time she took command over the situation. She looked up at her friend, who was watching her intently. "I'll definitely consider it."

"Please do. I think once you get your sense of power back, this feeling of being trapped won't be an issue, and you can marry him, if you like, because you *want* to. Not because you feel you have to."

"I hope so. I'm scared I'm going to lose him if I don't." Safia looked at Bella and asked herself if she could just push past her fears and marry him for Bella's sake. "There's no one else I'd rather be with. Why can't that be enough for him?"

"Family is everything to him. I guess he thinks marriage makes you officially part of it," Harlow said. "It also might be worth considering that he's feeling vulnerable now that he can't get back to Earth to see his family. He's considered AWOL since the US called their troops back and declared the colony a rogue state. Maybe marrying you keeps him from feeling adrift, you know? He needs this."

He was adrift, and she was withholding something from him when he needed it most. Safia wrapped her arms around her midsection, leaned over, and started taking deep breaths. When she sat back up, tears streamed down her face. "I should be able to do this for him. What the hell is wrong with me?"

"Nothing." Harlow sat her teacup down and reached across the small table to place her hand on Safia's arm. "We all have our stuff."

Safia wiped her cheek and cocked an eyebrow at Harlow. "C'mon, not the great Harlow Hanson. Woman, you got your shit together. Mind melded with a spaceship, married to a rogue prince, mother of a superhero daughter—well, I'm one of those, too, but you know what I mean."

"Hey, I've got my issues. Since I've become a mom, I'm always the one who has to go hide with Selah when there's danger in the district. I never had to do that before. Being a mom, as amazing as it is, as much as I love it, has taken something from me. When the cargo container exploded, I would never have been able to hand Selah to Jack and tell him to get her to safety while I go deal with the explosion. It was a given that I would go hide with her. I get it, he's the best equipped to deal with this particular situation; when he was in the RAF, they were trained to handle that sort of thing, but it's hard to be the bystander. This is my district, my colony, my damn planet, and I have to hide while it all goes to hell. That has been taking something from me for a while now."

"And we're so lucky to have these two amazing people to turn to while the world is falling apart around our ears. I feel guilty that it isn't enough for me. That I still have some issues," Safia said.

"You're not ungrateful. You're just human."

When Harlow spoke like that, she reminded her so much of Harlow's mother, Judith. Harlow didn't have Judith's fiery red hair, but she possessed her knack of heading straight to the heart of the matter. If someone were looking for sugar-coating or half-truths, they wouldn't get them from Harlow or Judith. Safia loved them for it.

As true as Harlow's words were, Safia couldn't help but wonder how much longer Carlos would keep holding on.

• • •

After Safia had gathered up Bella's backpack, thanked Harlow for the tea, and headed out the door with her daughter, all she could think about was getting back to Carlos. What Harlow had said about him wanting to marry her because he'd lost touch with his family and felt adrift rang true. She wanted to wrap her arms around him and assure him that despite her hang up about marriage, whatever was at the heart of it, she was there for him, no matter what.

The Indian ship, *Vijayee*, was bringing along supplies and a couple of counter-terrorism experts to help with the increasing amounts of destruction in the colonies. There were even rumors that the Brotherhood was living among the population and working with the loyalists to plan the bombings. One expert was catching a ride from her native Spain. Apparently, he was the best and thwarted several plots that would have resulted in thousands of deaths near her hometown of Toledo. If he saved just one life in the colonies, it would be worth it. It might be good to see someone from home and ask him how things were there.

She'd been born amidst the Spanish Muslim war. On her fifteenth birthday, Spain had ceded nearly half its territory. She knew Carlos would be busy with Jack, meeting the visitors, but thought maybe she and Bella would catch him during a break. Having Bella with her might help her reunion with him.

Holding Bella's hand, she rounded the corner to the hallway where the central command was located. As she did, she saw Carlos and smiled. Their eyes met, and her mind replayed tender moments: every encouragement, kindness big and small, caress, trembling breaths and moments of heat that made her heart race. For the briefest of moments, she thought she could be okay if she married him. She almost gasped to find that the fear had receded. He didn't look angry like she expected but seemed happy to see her. He cleared his throat, as if he'd experienced the same avalanche of feelings. A man in a different type of uniform, one Safia recognized as the

Spanish Armed Forces, stepped up beside Carlos, who said, "I'd like you to meet Alvaro."

Safia felt the blood drain from her face, and she struggled to make her voice work, her feet move. *He's just a man. Not a god, not a demon. He can't hurt you.*

Shards of recollection from the alley in Toledo replaced all the loving memories of Carlos. She remembered Alvaro yanking the hijab from her head, exposing her hair. She'd not worn it since and always believed he'd taken it from her first thing to show his dominance, not only over her as a woman, but over her as a Muslima. He beat her until she lost consciousness and dragged her into an abandoned warehouse where he'd raped her.

She didn't return home to her strict, aging aunt and uncle after it happened. Her father had died in the war, and her mother succumbed to lung congestion during the Gray Death. She didn't want her aunt and uncle to have to deal with what had happened to her, and they might even believe it was her fault. She was almost an hour late coming home from her friend's house and had promised she wouldn't be on the street without a chaperone. But waiting another half hour for her friend's parents to escort her would have made her later still, and her relatives would've been furious with her and likely wouldn't have let her out for months. Walking home alone had seemed like a risk worth taking.

Until the end of the second trimester, she'd lived at a shelter and found work where she could, while telling the lie that the baby's father had died in the war. She prayed the lie was true. One evening, the director announced they had received grim results from some tests the welfare department had run on the pregnant women at the shelter. He told her the only place that could help her baby was a research lab on Mars and explained how lucky she was that they had room for her there—and would transport and house her at no charge. That's where they tried to take Bella from her. If it weren't for Jack, Carlos, and the rest who came to rescue Harlow and by default her, she might have never seen her daughter again.

For a second, she thought she detected a flicker of recognition cross Alvaro's face. Either way, he was certainly coming off more naturally than she was. "Pleased to meet you," she said with a forced smile. *The man is key to rooting out the people harming the colonists. He won't dare hurt you with Carlos around. But what if he takes Bella away? Oh, God! He doesn't know about Bella!* Her first instinct was to move in front of Bella so he couldn't see her, but it was too late.

He was looking straight at his daughter.

CHAPTER 8

MIKHAIL

Mikhail moved through the darkness of the village as he thought of his good fortune to live in such times. The dream was within reach at long last. The king was dead. Jack's death was only a matter of the right blast in the right place, and Marcus, well, he was looking like a wild card, but he could be handled, too. All those years on that freezing rock Enceladus were worth it to be so close to realizing the dream.

He crept around the side of the building, rapped gently on the basement window four times, waited a few minutes, then opened the door.

Rupert Whitlow ushered him in.

"Welcome, friend," he said with an English accent.

Mikhail was grateful for a leader who understood loyalty. Though their reasons for wanting to take Jack down differed, the end goal was the same. "Is everything ready?"

"I'm more than ready to blot out that gormless traitor to my country."

Mikhail heard Rupert's accent thicken when he talked about home. His own accent did the same when he spoke about the history of Mother Russia.

Rupert said, "I've been making the glass bottles for O'Malley's for decades. He won't question what I bring in there. I deliver them in the afternoons. The explosives will be in the false bottom of each of the crates. I'll detonate them after Jack's cronies follow him inside, so we take out as many of them as possible, too. With Jack gone, it will become easy for the loyalists to move in, with the help of the Brotherhood, of course."

"Oh, of course, we only wish to help. What if O'Malley orders fewer bottles than usual for that evening and there aren't enough explosives to do the job? We will only get one shot at this. If we fail in our attempt, Jack will never go in there again."

"Whenever I drop off a shipment, there are always at least two or three crates of bottles left from the last resupply. This is the way it has been for twenty years. He always over-orders because he never wants his supply to run out."

Rupert walked over to a chest of drawers and retrieved a box. "I have a gift to celebrate our impending victory." He reached into the box, pulled out two cigars, and snipped off the tip from each. "We shall have a smoke to celebrate the death of a king who couldn't hold on to his kingdom, to the power of the people, and to an *English* pub on Mars."

"I'll order the very first drink, comrade. We will drink to victory, the end of foolish monarchy, and the rise of the people." Mikhail lit his cigar and blew smoke rings into the air. "Is our contact inside the Bastille de la Terra Rouge still well?"

"He is. Perhaps better than you were on Enceladus."

"Still, our brother Aldric deserves his freedom, and he shall have it soon. He will be out for blood when he is released. After he took such wonderful care of all those women, Harlow, Safia, and those others who betrayed him and went with the usurpers who stormed the compound, even after he granted their children the gift of miracles."

"Then perhaps they deserve his wrath. Ingratitude is such a tragedy," Rupert said. "They were provided everything, rescued from a life on the streets, and they abandoned him. And after we take out Jack and his hangers-on?"

"We return the *Ares* to the people. Marcus is still useful in that regard."

"But how do you get him here?"

"He hasn't returned to see his big brother in over four years. I think the death of their father, along with a younger son trying to figure out how to be king, is the perfect time for a visit, don't you?"

CHAPTER 9

READ MY MIND

Safia pushed a couple of peas around her plate with a fork. She'd brought the family's food into their quarters so they could have dinner together at their own table, away from the noise of the mess hall—something she normally didn't mind. The residents of the *Ares* were family, but when personal matters needed discussing, a noisy cafeteria wasn't the best choice. Bella had made a hasty retreat to her room after eating the required amount of green peas and making a resentful face at her parents to go along with it.

Safia's appetite had vanished once she began talking to Carlos about Alvaro. "Are you sure you can trust him?" Safia asked. She wondered for the thousandth time why Alvaro had attacked her. Especially now that she'd seen him in daylight. He was a good-looking man. If she set aside her fear and hatred for a moment, she had to admit most would consider him gorgeous even, but to her, he was hideous. It made her question why someone who could have any woman he wanted would only want those who *didn't* want him.

"What?"

"How well do you really know him?" Just saying his name sent waves of adrenaline and nausea through her body, so she tried to avoid it.

"He's solid. I'm an excellent judge of character. Do you realize we've made eight arrests since he's been here just based on him reviewing and connecting the dots on intel we've already collected? Those arrests then led to searches that uncovered bombing plots that were prevented because we rounded those people up before they could act. His presence here has already saved lives."

Safia gave no reply. He was the best at what he did, and that was why she wouldn't say the truth outright. Yet, she wanted the man she loved more than anything to somehow, magically, *just know* Alvaro was trouble. It was too much to ask, and she knew it.

"Honey, I've been doing this job for a very long time."

"Sure. It's just that we don't know who to trust these days. I mean, you're nice and expect that he will be as trustworthy as you are and maybe he isn't who you think or—"

Carlos shoved his chair under the table and the edge smacked against it, causing Safia to jump. "You don't have faith in me as a warrior or as a partner." He stood with his palms pressed against the back of the chair as he looked out the small window, not making eye contact with her.

"That isn't it at all. Not at all," Safia said. "When I was living in Toledo and the war was going on, I—"

"Oh, shit. I get it now. You don't like him because you're Muslim, and he had to kill a lot of Muslims when he was hunting down the bastards planting the bombs and—"

"No, it's more complicated than that. Give me a little credit for being able to do more than boil it all down to some reductionist rant about good guys and bad guys, and why must you jump to thinking I have no faith in you? Why do you do that?"

"We've been through this before. It's wearing me down. You can't commit to me. Now you're criticizing what I'm trying to do to save this colony. Our home."

"I still don't understand why we couldn't just bargain with the coalition that we had. We didn't give it a fair chance."

"The old coalition was going to turn Mars into a slave colony. Jack gave up everything to prevent that."

"The military of the coalition showed up when I was trapped in that compound where Aldric and his Brotherhood psychopaths lied to me and took Bella away."

"No. Jack ordered the raid on the compound. He didn't need the coalition to do that. He can and would do the same thing right now if we needed it. You don't have the coalition to thank for it."

"All I know is this rebellion is tearing everyone apart."

"The rebellion isn't tearing *us* apart. You are doing a fine job of that all by yourself." Carlos shoved his feet into his shoes and headed out the door.

She wasn't sure what she'd hoped to get out of the conversation but wasn't prepared to tell him all about Alvaro. The man was outstanding at what he did, a genius even, and might be able to help them before another bombing happened. It was a miracle no one had died yet. She guessed she was hoping he'd say something was off with Alvaro, and she would feel less alone, but if Carlos believed in him, and she wouldn't tell him the truth, then she had to do something else. She knew she couldn't live on the *Ares* as long as that monster did too.

After Bella went down for her nap, Safia took out the purple paint that she'd made from the grape hyacinth flowers, one of the easier and sturdier flowers to grow amidst the Martian sandstorms and dipped her brush inside the jar. On half of a canvas already filled with sunshine, she drew an approaching storm. Heavy clouds rolled in across the "outback" heading toward the village.

There was no escaping it.

• • •

Judith hung the last pot on the rack to dry as Safia put the broom away.

"All right. Let's lock up and get out of here," Judith said.

"Before you go, do you have a minute?"

"Of course." Judith gestured to a table.

Safia sat down and took a deep breath. *It's not too late. You can just go tell Carlos everything.* "You told me that if I ever needed anything, you'd be there for me."

"I did, and I will."

Safia liked the direct way Judith spoke. Despite the difference in hair and eye color, she could see so much of Harlow in Judith. There was a candor and truth when they spoke that made you feel safe. "I need a place for Bella and me to stay for a little while, but I'm not yet prepared to talk about why." *Don't cry. Be strong.*

"Done. Let's head by the house now."

"I don't want to intrude on your time with Eoghan, so just let me know when the two of you need your space, and Bella and I will make ourselves scarce."

"Oh, don't worry about that. I can go to Eoghan's place whenever."

"I'll help with rent."

"I'm sure you'll do what you can. I'm not worried about it. When will you two be moving in?"

Safia surprised herself by laughing and crying with relief, all at once. She took a shuddering breath and wiped her eyes. "I'll grab our things and be over tonight."

"You and Harlow are close. Does she know you're leaving Carlos?"

"No."

Judith reached her hand across the table and placed it on top of Safia's. "If you haven't told Harlow then you must be completely alone in this."

Safia nodded as her eyes clouded over with tears, and she looked away, unable to speak.

"Carlos hasn't hurt you, has he?"

"No, of course not. He wouldn't."

"Did he ask you to marry him again?"

"Yes, but it isn't about that either. I just need a little time to figure some things out."

"Okay. I understand. Well, let's get out of here. I'll head home and make sure Harlow's old room is ready for you and Bella."

"Thank you. I'll be back within the hour."

As they stepped out into the cold Martian night and Judith headed in the opposite direction, Safia kept an eye on every shadow and a firm grip on the phaser weapon tucked inside her jacket.

CHAPTER 10

CARLOS UNDONE

Carlos walked into the room he and Safia shared, sat down in the chair by the bed, and removed his shoes, as he usually did. A heaviness settled in his chest before his brain could trace the feeling to its source. He looked around. *Something feels off.* The hologram projector containing a photo of Safia's mom that she kept on her bedside table was gone. Bella and Safia's extra jackets no longer hung on the coat rack by the door. "No, no, no," he whispered into the silence. He got up and went through the drawers and closets to find them empty of all but his belongings.

On the easel by the window stood one of his favorite paintings of light. It always made him feel better when he'd had a shitty day. Now Safia had painted thick, ominous clouds over half of it. *Why would she do this?* He ran his fingers across the dark clouds and wet, purple paint colored his fingertips. *She knew I loved this painting. I've told her that.* Finally, he stood by Bella's door, his breath shallow. He didn't want to go in but felt some masochistic urge to confirm the worst and get it over with.

Bella's belongings gone as well. He always thought in a situation like this he would feel anger. Instead, he curled up on her bed and sobbed.

. . .

He woke in the same spot before dawn, numb. It was time to flush out the Brotherhood terrorists planted in the populace. He got a quick shower, ate a breakfast he couldn't taste, hit the armory, and was waiting on Alvaro and the rest of the men and women of the Ares Army—as they'd taken to calling themselves now that "coalition" no longer felt right—long before anyone else arrived.

Alvaro led a group of twenty, including Jack, into the conference room where he'd already outlined the village in 3D holographic glowing detail. The soldiers tapped a spot on the left side of their helmets to save the hologram for future reference.

Alvaro pointed to a building on the outskirts. "Unfortunately, they've planted themselves dead center of the village, but it's still going to make the most sense to throw a couple of Knock Out Discs in there and just drag them out unconscious. Of course, they may have blocking tech, in which case we need to plan this from start to finish."

"We haven't had Knock Out Discs for years," Jack said.

Alvaro looked shocked. "You gotta be kidding me. If I'd known that, I would've brought a case of them from my personal stash. I have them just sitting around in my basement."

It was the first time Carlos had felt angry with Alvaro. He could think of twenty different places on Earth that could desperately use that kind of tech to defend themselves and Alvaro was hoarding it."

"You can't have your engineering wizards retrofit a few of those Rescue Waves to work like a Knock Out Disc?" Alvaro asked.

Carlos knew Jack well and could tell he was getting irritated with him too but was doing an admirable job tamping it down. "We can't ruin the precious few Rescue Waves we've got and have someone die the next day, and in the months after, while we beg to have one sent from Earth. These are the very reasons we broke away from the coalition."

Alvaro huffed out a frustrated breath before continuing. "Okay then, we've already dropped eyes in the place," he said, referring to the nanobot cameras that had crawled beneath the terrorists' windowsills undetected. "As of a few minutes ago, they're still active. McNamara and Wong will roll a simple smoke grenade in. We should be able to see that the house is clear when they come out. No one gets stuck inside with them."

"They'll come out armed. This is right in the middle of the village. Civilians are going to get hurt. I'll go in after them." Carlos said.

Jack looked from Carlos to Alvaro and back.

"You'll go in after them? *You'll* not be doing anything alone. We'll send a team in," Jack said.

Carlos felt Jack's eyes on him. He knew he'd be asking questions later. He'd tipped his hand with that cowboy comment. *Shit.* He wasn't ready to talk about it. It was all way too raw.

Alvaro pointed to Carlos and six others and told them they'd be going in. "I hope your teams have kept up their training. It's my experience, with units outside my control, that they rely far too much on the Knock Out Discs and have no idea how to react when confronted by serious danger."

Jack smiled. "No force in the galaxy has had to train with so little and make do. This is Mars. Hell, we thrive on it."

Alvaro conceded, giving instructions. "There are two windows leading to a basement. Carlos and Lafferty head through there. Rawlings and Tate will take the side entrance. We can see where they are the whole time. If they come near you," he said, pointing at Carlos and those with him, "Rawlings and her team will create a distraction. Between your two groups, you'll have them boxed in. We're not seeing anything visual or on the infrared that indicates a trap." The soldiers who weren't already seeing the same image tapped a spot on the left side of their helmets and a hologram appeared in front of them, showing them the same thing as Alvaro.

A half hour later, the buggy the loyalists had been using went up in flames, a simple distraction to have them run to the front window while they snuck in the back. Several of the Ares Army watched on the feed as the men inside ran to the windows, talked among themselves, but chose not to come out as expected.

Alvaro looked at Carlos and Lafferty and murmured, "Now."

Carlos crouched and ran silently to the window, with Lafferty a couple of feet to his left. Finding the windows locked, they shattered them with the butt of their weapons. Meanwhile, the other group broke down the side door.

After Carlos cleared the window, he hit the floor and took cover behind a chest of drawers before heading around the corner with his weapon in front of him. He arrived behind the loyalists in time to see a target raise his weapon at one of the Ares Army coming in through the side door. Carlos shot him in the leg before he could open fire. The other three turned. The men were old enough for any of them to be Carlos's father. It occurred to him they likely remembered Earth as their home, a place that couldn't be anything but eternally on their side. Carlos had lived on Earth as well but came from a different generation that didn't see the world in the same black-and-white way.

A sense of futility washed over Carlos as he shot another of the men and saw that Lafferty was in his periphery and had the best shooting angle, but Carlos kept pushing forward and fired before Lafferty could. The first man, gritting his teeth against the pain from his leg wound, took aim at Carlos. *Damn it!* Carlos mourned having to kill the colonist. A man who just wanted the world to be the way he remembered it, when everything made sense. He wanted that, too, but he eliminated the threat with a headshot. Behind him, he heard a grunt as a weapon fired. He turned in time to see Lafferty hop sideways, favoring his left foot, and shoot another assailant.

By the end of the assault, two loyalists were dead. One was seriously injured but would likely survive with treatment. The last one surrendered after the others went down.

Carlos helped Lafferty limp out of the house while a medic applied a Rescue Wave to an AWOL Army Ranger who had taken a shot to the hip and couldn't move because of the excruciating pain. Special Air Service members bound the two loyalists who survived.

Carlos lowered Lafferty to the ground. After the soldier received treatment for his bleeding foot, he turned on Carlos. "Never pull that shit again. We're a team."

"I don't know what you're talking about," Carlos said.

Lafferty nodded in thanks to the medic and got to his feet. "The fuck you don't. You jumped in front of me like you had some kind of death wish. We're a team, a unit. You hindered my line of sight. I don't know what the hell is going on with you, but you need to stow your shit before going into battle."

Carlos opened his mouth but realized he had no real defense and would have been equally pissed if Lafferty had done the same. He couldn't think straight. He knew he wasn't himself. They were the same rank and had no particular power over each other, except for the fact that Lafferty was absolutely right. "Roger that," Carlos said. Lafferty stared him down a moment more, seemed to relax, nodded, and walked over to his pack and grabbed his water rations.

Carlos found Jack staring at him again from where he stood with Alvaro. A conversation was coming. He was sure of it. His best friend and former commanding officer would never let this one go.

• • •

Hours later, after the mission debrief, the exhausted warriors said their goodbyes and filed out of central command. Just as Carlos suspected, Jack was hanging back for an opportunity to speak with him. "You look like a man in need of a drink," Jack offered.

"I'm a man in need of a few," Carlos said. "But not O'Malley's. No more people today."

Jack smiled. "I know just the place."

• • •

An hour later, the two had cleaned up, and Jack had Carlos meet him behind the *Ares* where they kept a few livestock. His guards, Evelyn and Devante, stood several yards away.

"Behhh," a goat said as Jack approached, as if annoyed that they disrupted its concentration as it gnawed on the carbon fiber picnic table.

"You can't eat that, goofball," Jack said before sitting atop the table. Carlos joined him. Jack handed Carlos a beer.

"Thanks."

"You look positively knackered, mate," Jack said.

"I am."

Jack took a swig of his beer. "The last time I sat here was when my world was collapsing. That very goat watched me drink myself into oblivion. Then Mike O'Malley showed up and knocked the hell out of me."

"You two have a weird relationship," Carlos said.

"Yes, well, we were both throwing a bit of a wobbly."

"Safia left with Bella." It came out in a rush as if the words themselves would hurt if he lingered on them.

Jack nodded.

"You already know," Carlos said.

"Judith was worried about you. She called Harlow and…"

"Yeah."

"Were you trying to get yourself killed this morning?"

Carlos respected that he got right to the point. "No, of course not, but I didn't have my head on straight either. Maybe I was looking for a situation I *could* control." He looked down and noticed there were still traces of the purple paint beneath his fingernails from Safia's painting. "I know better. It won't happen again."

"I'm not here to scold you. Lafferty took care of that, and you know the truth when you hear it. I just want to make sure you're okay."

Carlos took a long drink of his beer. "No, I'm not okay. I'm confused as hell. She didn't tell me she was leaving. I don't even know when I'll get to see Bella again."

"It's muddle, but I don't think she's trying to hurt you. One thing I do know is that when everything was going on with Harlow, I wished I had believed in her longer than my pride allowed. There was so much more to the situation than I understood."

"That situation had only been going on for a few months. Safia and I have been together for four years. I've raised her daughter, and she just leaves and hurts me *and* Bella, like those years meant nothing. It's selfish. I would have never done something like this to her."

"True enough, but you don't come from the same place she does. From what I understand, it was horrible. All I'm saying is, don't give up yet. Have a little faith."

"Not a big fan of false hope. Kinda like that goat, thinking he'll eat this table."

"But you *are* a big fan of hope," Jack said.

"How do you figure that?" Carlos gestured to his sorry state.

Jack slapped him on the back. "You're still here, mate."

Carlos felt the saint's medal he always wore on a chain. St. Jude, the patron saint of lost causes, weighed heavy against his chest.

• • •

The two talked and drank until the shadows became long, and then they went back inside the *Ares.*

Hidden by a small greenhouse nearby, Alvaro sat as the same goat that had been staring at Jack and Carlos rounded the corner and looked at him curiously. Alvaro smiled at the visitor and contemplated all he had heard.

CHAPTER 11

TRAINING DAY

Safia waited with Bella in the old, dusty warehouse where colonists many generations ago had kept supplies. There was even a cracked helmet from an old pressurization suit. A shiver went up her spine at the thought of whoever had been in that suit. She hoped they weren't in it when it cracked. She couldn't imagine a time when people couldn't breathe on Mars or travel from one planet to the other without bone-density issues. Mars had been a hostile, forbidding place for them, but it had become home for her.

Now Alvaro was threatening to take that sense of home—ironically, as he tried to protect it from the grasp of terrorists. Nearly every night since moving in with Judith, Safia had awoke next to Bella in a panicked sweat, dreaming Alvaro had gotten in through the window and attacked her again or taken Bella. She had felt safer lying next to Carlos but was annoyed that she couldn't feel that way on her own and angry that being on the same ship with Alvaro terrified her so. That's why she waited here for Harlow, who was already a few minutes late. That wasn't like her.

Harlow and Selah appeared in front of her, out of thin air. Safia jumped back and screamed while Bella began laughing.

"I'm sorry. Are you okay?" Harlow asked.

"Oh, dear Lord! How?"

"You have to get used to reacting in a split second. Push past being startled or any other damn thing and handle it. Do you know how to spot a chameleon cloak?"

Safia blew out a long breath to calm herself. "No."

"Well, I'll go to the back of the warehouse. Just watch as I put it on and get used to tracing me with your eyes as I walk toward you. The fluctuation is very slight, but you can learn to spot it."

Bella went to play with Selah as Harlow ran to the back of the warehouse to cover herself with the cloak. At first, Safia could only catch the slight fluctuation for a second as Harlow moved toward her, but the more she practiced, the better she got at detecting it. She tracked her friend until her eyes were dry and burning.

"Good. That's enough for now," Harlow said.

Safia rubbed her eyes. "What's next?"

Harlow smiled. "Breaking and entering."

"Well, I'm in it now."

Harlow laughed. "The genetic scanning tech has broken down in over half the homes in the colonies, and people still haven't been able to get them repaired. Lucky for you, this is the case with Maricopa's house." Harlow tilted her hand around in a pattern and then opened her palm. A clear picture of the front door appeared hovering above her hand. She jiggled her hand and an x-ray image of the locking mechanism inside appeared.

"Oh, wow. This is the tech Jack gave you years ago when he was crushing on you but hadn't admitted it yet." Safia winked at her friend. "Nice."

"It's come in handy once or twice. As you can see, this is basically just a crude bar shoved into a hole in the door frame on the other side. I believe they call it a death lock, deadly bolt, dead bolt. It's some archaic name. Pft! I don't know why; there's nothing deadly about it."

Safia leaned in and looked closer at the mechanism. "Does it shoot spikes, lasers, or something? Where does the dead or deathly part come into play? I don't get it."

"Me either," Harlow said. "Old tech and old names baffle me, but no, it doesn't do any of those things. It's just a tiny bar holding the damn door in place." Harlow reached into her back pocket and pulled something out. "And this is all you need to get past it."

Safia held out her hand and Harlow handed her the tiny silver key. "Oh, I've seen something like this before. The Sojourner has a crude storage box in the back room that uses one of these things. Where did you get it, though?"

Harlow twisted her hand in the opposite pattern from when she began, making the image disappear. "Once she told us she was going back to her husband Vince, I snuck into the infirmary while she was sleeping, took the key, made a copy, and replaced it. I had a feeling we'd need it later."

"You think of everything."

"I try. Let's run through some more scenarios, but before we do, let me stress again, never go in alone, or at least without backup waiting just outside. Things can go south quick."

"You know who you're talking to, right?"

"Yeah, you're right. I'm sorry. I don't mean to be insensitive."

"It's fine." Safia smiled to set Harlow at ease and then listened as she ran through some more scenarios. It also baffled her how damned intuitive her friend was. Part of her *did* want to prove she could stand on her own against a predator, *one on one*, with no safety net, just like in that warehouse in Toledo.

CHAPTER 12

KARMIC CIRCLES

Breathe in. Breathe out. Control your breath. Don't let it control you. Safia continued to speak to herself on the way to the house Maricopa shared with her husband, Vince. *Harlow knows where you are. If you don't check in by eleven, she will come get you. He won't be able to hold you here. You know Harlow will go get Carlos, and despite what's happened between the two of you, you know the man will stop at nothing if he believes a maniac is holding you prisoner.* She felt a pang of guilt that she didn't bring Seraph, Evelyn's wife, with her as backup, as Harlow had suggested. She simply let Harlow assume she'd asked her already.

You've trained for years with the best jiujitsu professor in the colony. She remembered training beneath Carlos's intense gaze. *Oh, no. Don't get lost in that memory.*

The houses on the outskirts of town were farther apart than they were in the village proper and tended to be bigger. These were remnants from the first colonists who had come with private funding to help enhance the crude red regolith brick construction with some decorative carbon fiber touches and reinforcements. Some of these houses actually had two stories and porches, whereas the house Safia shared with Judith was more bare bones by comparison.

She took out the scanner to read the heat signatures inside the house. The fewer surprises, the better. She pushed aside the chameleon cloak just enough to get her hands and the scanner out, as the device couldn't read past the camouflaging mechanism in the cape.

"Damn it," she whispered as the cloak slid in front of the scanner for the third time. She hadn't wanted to use the camo, anyway, and a new thought gave her the perfect excuse to ditch it. *It's hindering the mission.* She pressed a button on the neck of the cloak. It retracted back into a package no bigger than the size of her palm. She slipped it into her pocket, noting that she didn't feel exposed or fearful at the idea of going in without it but oddly powerful.

Returning her attention to the scanner, she saw one medium-sized heat signature on the far lefthand side of the home. She'd snuck in earlier that week to look for weapons. She found one broken phaser and several knives. The phase pistol she carried concealed in her vest was not broken. She called for the best backup she knew of.

"Bismillah," she whispered into the Martian night as she took a deep breath, believing the God she called upon would understand the need to defend the innocent. She pressed her back against the wall of the house. *Vince is not Alvaro. Even if he was, you're a strong woman, a powerful woman.* Looking through the small gaps between the wall and curtain, she noted the living room, kitchen, and a couple of side rooms.

Vince emerged from the kitchen and walked into the living room with a sandwich. He looked to be just under six feet and was lean—not enormous, but certainly in shape. Her resolve wavered a little.

She forced herself to remember the pictures Harlow had shown her that documented the abuse Maricopa had suffered. No one had done a damn thing. Mars was supposed to present a chance to do things right, but politics allowed assbags like this to skate here, too.

Now Vince wanted to keep Maricopa's son from her as a punishment for not returning.

Anger flared in Safia's gut, replacing the fear. She pulled the crude "key" from her pocket before rounding the corner. The key slid home almost silently.

When she walked in, he startled. She didn't wonder that he did. She had worn one of the full-face masks the miners wore, black clothing from head to toe, and a breast-binder so he couldn't identify her by shape later, and she'd carefully concealed her hair.

"Who the hell are you?"

"Justice," she said into a simple distortion device around her neck that made her voice sound deeper but oddly comical, like a character in one of Bella's vids.

He threw his head back and laughed.

At first, Safia felt insulted, but it quickly turned to glee as she realized this would work to her advantage. His guard would be down. She felt a sense of power and turned to the door.

He spoke. "Too late to run now, hotshot."

She laughed in reply and engaged the bolt. "Who the hell's running? I'm locking you in with me, big man."

"Maricopa? Our son needs to be with his father so he can learn to be a real man."

"He won't learn that from you. You're a coward. Besides, I'm not your wife," Safia strode closer to him.

He narrowed his eyes at her, finally looking a little concerned but dropping the sandwich and moving in her direction cautiously. "Who are you?"

"I'm your worst fucking nightmare."

Watching him glance toward the kitchen, her first thought was "knife."

She positioned herself between him and the doorway to the kitchen. She thought about just shooting him with the phase weapon and beating him while he was unconscious but that would've been unsatisfying. She wanted him awake for what she was going to do. Needed him awake for it.

"I've had enough of this," he said as he rushed toward her.

"So has your wife."

He'd probably never had a woman strike first. She knew deep in her bones it wasn't just Maricopa he'd victimized. Most likely, they were always just standing there. Trembling. Scared. Turning to run when he grabbed them and then hoping it would be over soon. *Well, fuck him*, she thought as she slammed the brass knuckles into his jaw.

He stumbled backwards. A look of shock took over as he cupped his bloody chin.

"How does it feel?"

Vince wiped the blood on his pant leg and squared his shoulders. "It feels like you broke into my house with no provocation and attacked me. Now I have every right to kill you."

"Even my death won't make a man out of a coward."

He rushed her, blindly attempting to knock her off her feet. He wanted her submissive. Memories of her attack in Toledo five years ago threatened to overwhelm her as they tore through her brain. A wave of panic washed over her. He plowed into her like a human battering ram, and she tumbled to the floor. Her voice screamed in her mind; *I wasn't ready for this. What was I thinking?*

She tried to recall the years of jiujitsu but came up empty. Panic started coiling around her.

Everything seemed to slow down.

Framing, she heard Carlos say in her head. *You can't push me off you. Stop trying! Take control and frame the situation.*

As soon as she hit the ground, and Vince tried to get on top of her, she scooted onto her side, stuck her butt out and slid.

Grab your attacker. That's right. This in itself will surprise him. He'll think you'll be trying to push him away. The word omoplata appeared in her mind, a jiujitsu move. She grabbed his left arm and pulled it down while wrapping her right leg around his neck; her left arm braced into his collarbone. She created a locked triangle with her legs, immobilizing his left arm.

"Fucking bitch!" he screamed as his elbow bent at an unnatural angle.

Images of being attacked in Toledo came racing back to her. Alvaro had called her a bitch as she'd struggled to get free. *He'd* attacked her. Yet *she* was the bitch. That had never made any sense to her.

She held his arm captive and her legs tight as she sat up. She brought her body weight over his far shoulder until something popped, and he screamed in pain. Getting to her feet, she shook with adrenaline. Vince writhed and hollered.

Her hand found the phase weapon in her pocket, and she made sure she set it as a simple stun gun. She trained the weapon on the pathetic mess of a man before her. "Swear you will never threaten her or attempt to take her child from her, or I will kill you where you lie."

"I swear," he ground out between moans of pain. Her finger paused over the switch from stun to kill for a split second. Maricopa could be free forever. *I might actually be saving a life. What if I let him go, and he punishes her for this?* A cold sweat broke out over her entire body. *You can't. You aren't that person.* One quick burst, and his screaming stopped as he passed out.

Safia took a deep breath to steady her nerves. It was all harder than she thought. How did Harlow do this kind of thing for years? Then again, the bulk of what Harlow had done was thievery and stealth with only occasional vigilante justice.

She stepped into the night and disappeared into the deepest shadows. Between her heart pounding in her ears and the thrill of survival still coursing through her veins, she didn't notice she was being followed.

CHAPTER 13

THE LOVE WE DON'T KNOW

Since Safia had left him, Carlos had found it nearly impossible to just sit in his quarters at night reading or relaxing. The place was haunted now. It made his chest hurt. He'd taken to either having beers with some of the others at O'Malley's or patrolling the area around the *Ares*, or village streets. He watched a figure emerge from the shadows near Judith's home, look in every direction, and slip into yet another shadow, and then just when he thought he'd lost them, he caught a shimmer of something, a chameleon cloak. Thanks to his superior night vision and training to see the subtle displacement in the visual field the cloak created, he could follow whoever it was as they continued to the outskirts of the village. This was clearly someone looking to do something on the sly, and that meant trouble.

He couldn't see their face in the darkness. It occurred to him to simply call out, but he worried he'd be passing up a golden opportunity to find out where a terrorist cell might be hidden, a chance to gain info that might save Jack's life someday. That thought alone kept him from making his presence known.

They were getting closer to that jackass Vince's house. Anger flared deep in his gut. Just that morning he'd been discussing with Jack how they might bring that bastard to justice. He'd beaten his wife on more than one occasion, and now he was threatening to take their son from her if she didn't return to let him do more of the same. He was claiming it wasn't him who did it but her lover. She swore she'd not been seeing anyone. Plus, there were old charges filed on Vince for assault. So, he clearly had a history. His father was on the colony council and had made some deals previously to keep his son out of the Bastille.

If this stealthy person was planning on breaking and entering, then Carlos had a moral obligation to call colony security, but he didn't want to. What if this person killed Vince? Did he care? After seeing what he had done to Maricopa and knowing he wanted to get his son back just so he could teach him to do the same, Carlos wasn't sure this man deserved to live.

The shadowed figure paused a good thirty feet from the home and scanned it. They knew what they were doing. They were tagging the man's location within the house. Smart. Oddly, though, they ditched their chameleon cloak. That part made no sense to him, unless they wanted him to know who they were, or they didn't want any advantages. He studied the person as they scanned the house. They were actually fairly small. Maybe 5'6" and, shit, was this a woman?

What if the person going in got killed? How skilled were they? The men and women under his command were very well trained, gender aside. He had confidence in them. The person pulled a mask over their face, though he still couldn't make out who it was in the shadows, took a key from their pocket, and went inside.

Still, he worried. Was it Maricopa going in there to kill him? No, she was shorter than this woman. How did they get a key? He ran low to the window where the vigilante had just stood. Vince walked into the living room with a sandwich. Now he moved out of view. *Damn it!*

Carlos moved to another window, hearing muffled voices from inside, but he couldn't see past the curtain. He searched one window after another and ended up running all the way around the house, looking for a way to see what was happening. By the time he found a window with an unobscured view, Vince had got the woman on the ground. He saw only their legs. Panic flared in Carlos's gut. The man could be about to beat her to death or rape her. Then, to his relief, he saw only one set of legs, Vincent's, and the man had rolled onto his side. Carlos spotted a small ledge of brick jutting from the wall and tucked the toe of his boot in so that he could pull himself up and to the left to see more. The vigilante held a phaser weapon on Vincent, shot him, then turned to leave, he assumed.

He ran around to the front door just in time to hear it opening. When he saw the woman emerge, he ducked back into the shadows and exhaled a deep breath.

He began following her, but she seemed to walk in circles. Whoever she was, she had thought about this, received some training, and prepared for the possibility of being followed. Then she walked to Judith's house, and Carlos knew the silence had to end. He didn't know what business this person had there, but it couldn't be with Safia and... dear Lord, was Harlow at it again? Jack had enough problems without her going rogue.

"Harlow?"

The woman whipped her head around. "Carlos?" she said in a voice thick with distortion and took off running.

She ran into a bank of trees behind Judith's house, but he guessed her mask would end up being a hindrance to her once they entered the uneven, rocky ground of the forest. It wasn't long before she tripped and quickly scrambled to her feet but not before giving him the advantage he needed to tackle her.

As she lay gasping beneath him, he yanked the mask from her face. "Safia! What the hell are you doing?"

She shoved him off her and stood. "I'm doing what no one else will do. We..." She stopped speaking, turned off the distortion necklace, and continued. "We have an entire army, and we can't bring in one wife-beating sonofabitch?"

He exhaled his own frustration over the issue. "You're absolutely right, but I don't want you doing it."

"I didn't ask your permission."

"I don't mean it that way. Why are you so mad at me? I just don't want you to get hurt or killed. I couldn't live with that. I couldn't..." He clamped his mouth shut as he realized he was talking to the woman who left him. He felt suddenly vulnerable and angry. He'd already said too much. Tipped too much of his hand. Now she could see she'd hurt him. Why did it matter? Why was he protecting her? She *did* hurt him.

"I'm not mad at you," she breathed. "I've never been mad at you."

"Vince could've killed you."

He watched as she sighed, took the mask the rest of the way off her head, removed her gloves, shook her hair from its bun, and looked at him. "It's something I had to do."

"Because of what happened to you in Toledo? Vince was a stand-in for whoever that guy was?"

She remained silent.

In the distance, they heard the emergency code repeating from a colony security vehicle headed, likely, to Vince's home.

Carlos turned to look through the tree line and confirmed the security vehicles in the distance. "Jesus. You didn't kill him, did you?"

"Of course not!"

"Well, I wasn't about to turn you in if you did. I just wondered—"

"You wouldn't? I mean, no second thoughts. You wouldn't?"

"Well, no."

He held his breath for a long moment as her eyes locked with his. He watched her take a long, shuddering breath.

"You okay?"

"Yeah. Carlos, I thought about it. You know, I could free Maricopa by killing Vince. I didn't know it was so easy to consider doing something like that."

Carlos watched her struggling to breathe. She reached underneath her shirt and pulled at some sort of undergarment. "It clearly isn't easy for you. It's tearing you up."

"I can't breathe. I've got to get this thing off."

"What thing?"

"I wore a binder to hide my shape." She turned around and removed her shirt. She twisted and struggled to get out of it. "I'm stuck in this damn thing."

"Hold still. I'll help you."

He ran his hands underneath the binder, feeling her warm skin beneath his. She felt so good. She'd only been gone a few weeks, but already he ached every night as he tried to fall asleep without her next to him. He was barely able to get his next words out. "Hold your arms up."

He peeled the garment off her and dropped it to the ground. He moved slowly. Afraid he would scare her off, but she didn't seem to object when he embraced her and backed her against his chest and his arms cradled her breasts. He whispered into her ear. "You're a badass."

"I don't feel like one."

"It never felt like I thought it would either," he said before planting a kiss beneath her ear.

"What? When you joined the service. Went off to war?"

"Yeah. We have a picture of what things will be like, feel like. Reality is different."

"Oh, I thought I was doing it wrong or that I'm just weak."

"Nothing weak about you." He kissed her neck and ran his hands up her stomach, over her breasts, and lingered there, enjoying the weight of them. She moaned softly, and his pants tightened uncomfortably. He was lost in the touch, sight, and smell of her—she smelled of jasmine and vanilla. It mixed beautifully with the pine undertones from the forest. But one intrusive thought made him stop; he realized he might be ruining their chances together. He dropped his hands and took a small step away.

She turned to face him, looking confused. "What's wrong?"

"You're vulnerable. I guess I worry that you'll feel like I'm taking advantage of you in a crisis situation. I don't want to be another bastard, some jackass that—"

She cut him off with a kiss that threatened to bruise his mouth.

Okay then, he thought, as her tongue explored his mouth, demanding. He returned the kiss as hard. He understood what she was going through. There were many times he'd come back from one of the riot calls when the bullets were flying, with hours of nonstop chaos, and God help him, all he'd wanted to do back then was lay his girlfriend down and warp the bed frame. He didn't want to talk about his feelings. That could wait until the next day. Judging from the fact that Safia already had her hand inside his pants, that was all she wanted, too.

He looked back through the branches and noted the lights and sounds of colony security headed in the other direction.

Carlos threw his shirt to the ground, and his pants landed beside them. Safia had gotten rid of her clothes in the time it took him to toss his boots aside. Only the pale illumination of distant house lights gave a faint glow to their bodies. Safia looked like an apparition before him. He grabbed her wrist just to prove to himself she was indeed solid. He grabbed the other and pulled her firm against his bare body. His erection pulsed against her with every heartbeat, begging for release. He leaned his forehead onto hers. "You'll always be safe with me. You know that, right?"

"I need to be safe with me, too."

"Is that why you left? To prove you didn't need me. If so, I think you—"

"No, that's not why."

Don't get needy man. "It's okay we don't have to go there tonight." He threaded his fingers through her thick, dark hair, tilted her head back, and kissed her, ending conversation. He needed to touch her, take her, get lost in her.

She broke the kiss and pulled him to the ground, turned to face away from him, squatted down in front of him, kneeled on the binder, then placed her palms on the ground. If he had to guess, after what had happened at Vince's house, she wanted to forget for a while and didn't really want to be in control either. Yeah, it was exactly how he'd felt after the riots, but now wasn't the time to talk about that or anything else. Oh, no, not now.

He reached down between her legs to stroke her and found her trembling and pushing back into his touch. He pressed two fingers inside her but did not move them. He was curious, wanted to see what she would do if he simply held them in place.

"Please," she gasped and then whimpered when he still didn't move a muscle.

Despite how close he felt to her now, he knew a stronger man might use this as an opportunity to ask her how it felt to want something, someone, and be denied, but he couldn't do it. When it came to her. God, when it came to her... He gave her what she wanted and plunged his fingers deeper still until he could no longer deny himself. He removed his fingers and placed himself inside her, inch by inch, until she shoved back onto him, taking everything.

He growled. "I see how it is. You better hang on," he said to her as she placed a palm on the pine tree in front of her to brace herself. He plunged into her repeatedly with all the longing he'd held pent up over the past weeks of missing her.

• • •

He didn't ask her to come home with him as they both got dressed. They said little. It felt right, for tonight, to just let it go. She still needed him. Still wanted him, and that's what he needed to know above all else. He watched her head into Judith's house. She turned back and looked at him. There was no smile, no blowing a kiss. This time, the look that passed between them felt like one warrior looking to another for understanding, and he did understand.

Now, if he could just figure out every other damn thing about their relationship.

CHAPTER 14

MARCUS IN THE MOURNING

The King had died two weeks prior, and Marcus was to be coronated at Westminster Abbey in three months. There were normally a few months between the death of a monarch and the coronation, anyway, but they needed time for more than mourning. Rioters had vandalized the Abbey in the Gray Death's wake, and the extensive repairs were ongoing. Besides, Marcus yearned to return to Mars to visit his brother. He had wanted to go again before the death of their father but knew the people would interpret it as taking sides.

Since the king's death, he had an excellent reason to travel both politically and personally. Sure, he'd spoken to Jack first thing when their father passed, and Jack didn't require his younger brother to console him, but Marcus felt it might bring them both some sense of closure.

His father's aide, Worthington, had suggested the trip. It was the only bit of warmth he'd gotten from the man who seemed as calculating as the king had been. He'd pointed out that, with the right spin, Marcus could appear as a merciful monarch, reaching out to a grieving, rogue family member who could never be united with his clan but still deserved sympathy. He could also observe the condition of the colony. Even Worthington's suggestion for him to visit family was replete with an opportunistic angle. Nonetheless, he needed the trip.

As Marcus traveled in the EM bubble toward the colony, he let the isolation settle in. He'd brought his guards along for this trip, but they kept to themselves. Still, he laughed to himself at the memory of discovering the rum. He couldn't drink himself properly sloshed and make bold declarations to an empty cabin like he did last time he visited the colonies.

And because he didn't sneak away for this journey, the Special Air Service—SAS—sent a contingent of two dozen guards ahead of him to arrange security with Jack. For now, though, the quiet was an ever-present, almost tangible thing. Initially, he'd feared the solitude. The space between Mars and Earth was a chasm with nowhere to stop and climb out when it became suffocating. The idea of spending that much time alone with himself brought waves of panic, but on the way there, he had the epiphany that he'd been alone since the day Jack left for good.

He thought about what he wanted out of life, if he could make any difference in the colonies after he considered the demands of the old coalition and his people's needs. He realized it would be hard to keep track of what he felt at all because he had to consider his own thoughts and opinions last. For the first time, he had the slightest twinge of sympathy for the position his father had been in.

• • •

When he disembarked in the *Ares* hangar, Jack and Aunt Mary waited for him just as before. Jack wrapped his arms around him. "Are you doing okay?" he asked.

"I am. It's a lot."

"And then some," Jack agreed as Mary embraced Marcus.

As he stood there with his brother, it suddenly occurred to him that Aunt Mary had lost *her* brother. "How are you?"

"Thank you for asking, sweetheart. I've been remembering our childhood lately." She smiled, and he understood that those were her fond memories of his father, the ones she could hold close. They didn't have many from their adult life, he knew. He was thankful he and Jack could remain friends and vowed somewhere in his heart to keep it that way. He looked up at his brother and thought it possible he was thinking the same. Jack gave him a sad smile.

He dismissed his guards to head into their own quarters to unpack. Once he walked into his old guest room and dropped his belongings on the bed, the four years between now and his last visit disappeared. He took a deep breath, exhaled, and marveled at the irony of the closer quarters feeling *less* oppressive.

He looked out the window to find orange regolith broken by a smattering of trees instead of the cityscape thickly layered as far as the eye could see. Yawning, he sat, stared, and thought of the space pioneers hundreds of years ago in their large suits and helmets tethered by an umbilicus to the ship. He saw himself in the same way, as if a cord stretched between the Earth and where he was on the *Ares* by the window. His eyelids drooped as he pictured the spaceman surprising everyone as he removed a knife from his toolkit and cut the cord that bound him to the ship, drifting free. He shook his head. Too much time in the void, he thought.

Later that evening, Marcus's guards argued with him about going to O'Malley's, given the recent terrorist activities. When he insisted he would go with or without them, they toured the bar and looked behind every wall, under every table, and at every inch of the stockroom. They set up scanners that would detect weapons and disarm them as patrons walked through the door, similar to the security on the *Ares.* Even after all their precautions, they still advised against his visiting the bar, but he wouldn't be deterred.

Soon thereafter, Marcus, Harlow, Judith, and Eoghan O'Malley sat at a table in the pub talking. The smell of fermented hops and O'Malley's beef stew hung in the air as the soulful sounds of a violin rose over the melody carried by an acoustic guitar. Marcus felt the same sense of freedom and joy he had when he'd visited four years earlier; it wrapped around him like a caress. *Careful*, he cautioned himself. *This isn't your life. It never will be.*

Jack had gotten delayed with matters onboard the *Ares* and agreed to join as soon as he could.

Eoghan looked at Marcus and asked. "Have you seen my beautiful pub lately, Prince? Pardon me, Your Highness?"

"Drove past it recently. It's still thriving. Do you miss it?" Marcus asked.

"I do, but I have better things here to tend to," he said as he placed an arm around Judith.

Marcus watched her smile and lean in closer. The red-haired woman was the mother-in-law that his brother had been terrified of. She didn't seem so bad when she was with Eoghan. He hoped for Jack's sake they never broke up.

Mike O'Malley walked over with another round of beers and commented. "Well, he'd be more use to me if he'd stop mooning over his little Irish lass here and get to work!"

Eoghan laughed. "Sod off, Mike."

"The thanks I get for taking his sorry arse in!" Mike sat the tray down and joined them at the table. After another hour, Jack walked in and had a beer, but minutes later, he declared it was time to pick Selah up from her babysitter and get her tucked in for the night.

Harlow said, "Oh, come on, you just got here. We could stay another half hour. I bet Selah is already asleep by now, anyway. I'll let Tara know we're going to be late."

"We don't want to wear out our sitter privileges with Tara."

Judith laughed and told Marcus, "Your niece has already worn out their welcome with two different sitters. Selah doesn't know her own strength and accidentally breaks things."

"Like what? She's not even five yet, right?" Marcus said.

Judith nodded. "She was playing with clay the first time, and when she was trying to flatten it out, she flattened out their dinner table as well. The second time, she accidentally gave one of her playmates a concussion when they were playing duck, duck, goose."

Marcus's eyes went wide. "Oh, my God! So, I need to hire her to be one of my guards then."

"Yep," Jack replied. "You'd only need one."

"Poor Selah thought she'd killed the girl!" Harlow said. "Everybody wants a superpower until they realize how often it can get you into trouble."

"Is there some way to monitor the progression of her strength?"

"Yeah, Dr. Nakamura does that. She's over there." Harlow pointed to a woman at the bar, chatting with some other patrons. She was no taller than 5'3" or so, with long black hair pulled back from her face. He realized she was the doctor Safia had told him about on his last trip to Mars. She'd had the son who died of tetanus and the husband with deadly lung disease.

As the pub continued to fill up, Jack and Harlow said their reluctant goodbyes and headed for the door. Friends wanting to chat stopped them every few feet. No wonder the man had no urge to return home. He was beloved despite the loyalist factions that existed in the colonies.

Marcus watched them slowly make their way out and then decided to speak with Dr. Nakamura. If he were going to address parliament on the conditions of the colonies, who better to talk with than one of the doctors, especially one who'd suffered such loss.

"I'll be back in a few minutes," he said to Mike, Eoghan, and Judith. He felt the watchful eyes of his guards on him as he made his way over to Yua.

She looked up, studied him for a moment, then recognition seemed to cross her face.

Before he could speak, the floor shifted beneath his feet, and a great wave slammed into him. Everything went dark, and he remembered nothing more.

CHAPTER 15

A DARK SACRIFICE

Rupert Whitlow kept an eye on the front entrance to O'Malley's Pub from his position across the street. He'd been watching and waiting for just the right time, and when he'd heard that the SAS, the royal guards, had done a sweep of the pub earlier that day, he knew tonight was it. They wouldn't be sweeping it without reason. The King would pay a visit, and as much as Jack loved that pub, his brother visiting it would be the perfect excuse for him to come in and have a few beers as well. He'd bet his own life Jack would show up tonight.

Rupert's partner, Ailish, spoke through their auditory implants, a tech few could afford but the Brotherhood had funded to make their operations in the colonies easier. "Three buggies just left the *Ares*. Guards in front and back. Target in the middle. Gonna give them a head start and then hit the northwest corner of the sidewalk outside the pub."

Rupert turned to face the wall of the building and whispered, "Acknowledged." He took a deep breath of the cold, dry Martian air to clear his head and brace himself for his glorious mission, the end of the monarchy, the restoration of the people's rule.

Ten minutes later, he watched Jack and Harlow enter, escorted by their ever-watchful guards. He lamented for the hundredth time the loss of Harlow Hanson. Killing her tonight brought him no pleasure. He'd watched her grow up to be the people's champion, but her lack of fidelity to the colonists since she fell for that pompous prick was the deepest and most painful loss. She'd been their hero, but now... well, no sense mourning the past.

He heard a buggy stop around the corner and then Ailish's voice was in his ear again. "In position."

He glanced at his partner down the sidewalk and nodded once. The man took the cue and disappeared into the shadows. Rupert did the same.

"Our contact says they're right where we need them. Are you ready?"

Rupert started to answer when another buggy pulled into the lot and members of the Ares Army piled out. He recognized a few of them: Lafferty, McNamara, Naadir. These were people who would fight him to the death if allowed to escape. He wondered how many more fortune might place in the bullseye if he waited longer.

The voice in his ear grew impatient. "Do you copy? Are you ready?"

"No, we wait."

"Why?"

"Look at what's happening, mate. They're all coming to us."

From across the lot, someone called out. "Jack's here. The King, too. I hear he's buying everyone drinks."

"You hear that," Rupert said. "A loyalist wouldn't take a pint from that prick. Let's get them all in one place and blow 'em all to hell."

Another half hour went by with Ailish warning Rupert every ten minutes that Jack or the King could leave at any moment, and Rupert trusting his patience.

The man on the inside spoke to both of them and sounded winded, as if he were running. "Target is leaving! Do you copy?

Target is making his way toward the door. Now or never." Their inside contact was getting out, preparing for Rupert to take it down.

"Right, then. Get out of there." Rupert said.

Evelyn and Devante emerged from the bar and got in their transport to drive Jack and Harlow back to the *Ares.* They were sure to be steps behind.

"Blow it," Ailish yelled into his ear.

Rupert's fingers danced across the panel of the remote detonator as a surge of adrenaline that felt a lot like victory rushed through his body. He braced himself for the shock wave, heat, and debris. He prepared to run away, duck, cover his head, but...

"What's the fucking hold up, man? Blow it!"

"I bloody well did!" Rupert said. He tried again and again to no avail. He slid the detonator into his pocket. "Ailish, I've told you where I keep my farewell box, yes?"

"Yeah, mate."

"It's been an honor," Rupert said as he ran around the pub, pulled his phase weapon, shot the guard at the back door, and ran inside. He knew his weapon was deactivated the moment he crossed the threshold. The SAS would never allow active weapons in the pub with the king visiting. A dishwasher and cook looked at him in both recognition and confusion as he grabbed a bottle of whiskey, stuffed a rag into it, and held it to a burner.

Rupert saw the cook's confusion turn too slowly into a horrified realization for this glass maker and friend they'd known for over two decades.

Rupert threw the flame beneath the bottles before they could react.

A blinding light was his last memory.

CHAPTER 16

FALLING FROM GRACE

Earlier that evening, Safia ran through the darkness toward the home of the bottle maker. A sliver of conversation she'd overheard during the lunch shift had driven her to action: "It's going down. I wouldn't want to be anywhere near that place... He could put anything in those bottles."

The most logical conclusion was O'Malley's. Who used more bottles than Mike's bar? No one she could think of, but why in the world would someone go to so much trouble to cause problems with O'Malley's? Mike was one of the people. Eternally on the side of the colonists. But he did welcome Jack into his bar. Still, wouldn't it make more sense to cause trouble on the *Ares*?

She looked around her and saw no one, but then again, she hadn't the night that Carlos had followed her to Vince's house either. Scanning Rupert Whitlow's house for heat signatures, she found nothing and continued with her operation by using a signal jammer on the cameras under the eaves. No surprises so far. She exhaled in relief. Closing in on the house, she took comfort in knowing his front door scanner had been broken for years. Harlow had it on good authority that Rupert used another crude, deadly bold, deathless bolt, or whatever they called them. She didn't have a key but had a magnetic pinpointing system that should be able to zero in on the bar in a specific spot, grab hold of the bolt, and unlock the door.

As she adjusted the magnetism, a soft whirring sound began, and a pressure started building in her ears. She remembered Carlos and a few of his friends sitting at the Sojourner and talking about a security officer in District Three recently attempting to enter a home when a crude energy pulse fired. The warning sign was pressure on the ears before the pulse released. By the time one noticed the pressure, they were already being knocked off their....

Safia heard nothing and thought nothing for how long she couldn't tell but felt someone removing something from her body before her sight returned. Panic ricocheted through her until she saw Carlos's face leaning over her by the faint glow of the house light. His mouth moved, but she couldn't hear what he was saying. *He's angry, but he would never hurt me.* She wanted to push him away, though. This was her mission. He shouldn't be here. She tried to speak, but her mouth barely moved. Her body was numb.

He removed her miner's mask, weapons, even took her hair out of its ponytail. He ran his fingers along her scalp. "I don't think you have a head injury," she heard him say as her hearing began to return. She watched him stash her various belongings in his cargo pockets.

"It'll be a minute before you're able to move or talk. Just stay still. Don't make it worse." He continued running his hands down her body, looking for injuries, she surmised. "Jesus, your right arm is broken. I have to get you onto the *Ares* for treatment. but damned if I'll let you get arrested. Although it might be the best way to keep you from doing this shit anymore."

His show of concern was making her madder by the minute. He went on, "I see the beginnings of a scowl. You must be getting your feeling back. Sorry, but it's going to hurt like hell when you do. You need to quit this nonsense. I couldn't stand it if—"

Carlos's communicator gave a soft ping, and he looked into the distance. "Yeah, I see you. I've tagged my location. Thanks. I appreciate this."

"You tol some..." Safia struggled to get the words out and slurred as the feeling slowly returned to her mouth.

"I had to tell someone to come get us. You can't walk back like this, and we need to get the hell out of here before you're spotted. Alvaro won't tell anyone."

"No," Safia gasped.

"Don't be so damned stubborn. You need treatment for your arm." He looked back at the house. "Why are you at Whitlow's? Is he beating up on his wife too?"

Before she could reply, Alvaro pulled up beside them. Carlos lifted her, taking care with her broken arm, and held her on the way to the *Ares* as Alvaro drove.

All she wanted to do was run, but as the numbness subsided, the sharp pain in her arm became all-consuming. She held back the sobs that threatened to escape. She'd never broken a bone before. It was excruciating.

After several lies from Carlos on their way through the *Ares*—about a fall from a ladder while stocking shelves after hours at the Sojourner—she lay in sick bay. Carlos said, "I'll go grab Dr. Hagen. I think Dr. Nakamura is at O'Malley's."

"Don't worry," Alvaro said. "I'll keep an eye on her."

Safia felt a surge of anger toward Carlos. She knew she shouldn't blame him for leaving her alone with Alvaro if she were unwilling to be honest with him. It wasn't fair. Yet some illogical part of her was mad at him for not seeing the evil behind his mask.

The moment Carlos left the room, Alvaro leaned over and whispered in her ear, "You look breathtaking right now. You know that, right? Like a helpless little kitten." He swept her hair back from her forehead.

"Don't touch me," she ground out between clenched teeth. She raised her good arm to try to shove him away, but her strength was still slow to return. Luckily, Carlos entered with Dr. Hagen. Carlos nodded his thanks to Alvaro, who left the room. The tightness in Safia's chest loosened a notch.

Doc said, "I heard you took a fall. Whoa, you've got a level nine grimace going too." He grabbed the Rescue Wave, glided his fingers across the panel, and then placed it against her head. She almost cried with relief. "Any chance you might have hit your head?"

"No," Safia said.

"It's possible," Carlos said almost simultaneously.

"Well, we can put the cap on you while we look at the arm. No one likes the way the thing looks, but it can tell us what's going on in there." Doc placed the device on her skull and a hologram of her brain started building in front of them while Doc examined Safia's arm. "Looks like a compound fracture."

He placed the Med Wave around her arm and in a few minutes, the arm was fine again. "Head looks good. Serotonin is low. You doin' okay?" He placed a hand on her shoulder. His Irish accent became more pronounced when he was being sincere. The brogue was coming in thick right now.

"Yeah, I'm fine," she blurted. She could tell from the look on Doc's face she'd answered a little too quickly but doubted he would say anything more in front of Carlos. There were various bruises she didn't bother telling Doc about. She wanted to keep them, to remember not to take anything else for granted.

Carlos offered to drive her home. Safia sucked in her breath as she got into the buggy.

He paused before sliding into the driver's side. "You're still hurt."

She eased into the seat as every major muscle group protested. "It's nothing. I'm fine."

"Why didn't you just let Doc use the Wave?"

"I want to remember. Don't want to get sloppy again."

He started the buggy and headed toward Judith's. "I get it. I just don't know that, uh..."

She glanced over at Carlos as he scratched at the stubble along his jawline. Damn handsome jawline. She thought about what they had done in the woods behind Judith's house and might have suggested they do it again if she could be sure her ribs wouldn't break the rest of the way. But he was getting at something. She suspected it was something she didn't want to hear. "What?"

"I don't think you should be doing this kind of thing anymore."

"And why not? I never asked you to stop doing what you've been doing all these years."

"I don't do it all alone. I have an entire squad, a whole army of people who have my back. You disappear into the night, and no one knows what the hell you're doing. You have no backup."

"I don't need it."

"*Everyone* needs it. Tonight is proof of that. I'm scared for you."

"I can take care of myself."

"What would have happened if I wasn't there and someone else had found you? You had evidence all over you, Safia. Think about Bella."

"Excuse me?"

"It's not meant as an insult. I simply mean that if you get put in jail, and you clearly don't want me to raise her, who will raise our child?"

"I *do* want you to raise her. I just..."

"What? Jesus Christ. What? Why can't you just talk to me?" he said, frustration charging every word. She couldn't blame him. They rode on in silence for a few more minutes until they arrived in front of Judith's flat.

He turned the engine off before he spoke again. "I love you, but I cannot play this game with you anymore. Do you have any idea what you do to me? Every time I see you? Every time I'm near you? Whenever I see families together, it rips my heart out. If you loved me, you wouldn't hurt me like this."

"I love you more than anything," she said, the words catching on the lump in her throat, unable to hide the tears in her voice.

"You wouldn't do this to someone you loved." He reached into his pockets and began removing all the things he'd taken off her to hide the fact that she'd been trying to break into Whitlow's residence earlier.

She took them from him with trembling hands and stepped, carefully, from the buggy without responding.

After looking at her for another moment, clearly giving her a last chance to open up to him, he muttered, "I've had enough." She watched his buggy disappear around the corner.

As bad as her body hurt, her heart ached so much more.

She stood in the doorway knowing she needed to get inside. Bella was in there with the sitter since Harlow and Judith had been at O'Malley's. Just before she turned to go inside a massive wave of energy nearly knocked her from her feet and the flash of light from O'Malley's drove home the point that she had failed in her mission that night.

CHAPTER 17

AFTERMATH

Jack and Harlow rode home through the cold night air. Harlow turned to look at her husband and noticed a peaceful smile illuminated by the faint starlight.

Harlow's warm hand touched the side of his face. "Now, to what do we owe that satisfied look on your face? We're nowhere near our bed," she laughed.

"Ah, I guess it's just pride, hopefulness. My brother isn't the same man who came here four years ago, stumbling off the transport reeking of rum and trying to hide it. This man is, well, a man. I hate to say it, but I don't know if he could have ever come to this if father hadn't passed. He's come a long way."

"He has. He—" A flash caused Jack and Harlow to turn around. The buggy jerked, and Evelyn struggled to hold the wheel steady.

What Jack and Harlow saw made them both gasp. A fireball rose over O'Malley's.

"Stop the buggy!" Jack demanded.

"Your Highness, this is dangerous. We should get you back to the *Ares*."

"Stop calling me that and stop the damn buggy!"

Evelyn stopped. Jack got out and began trying to reach Marcus on his comm unit. There was no answer. "What the hell was I thinking? I shouldn't have let him go in there."

Devante spun the buggy he was driving around such that the headlights shone on Evelyn, Jack, and Harlow, then he got out. McNamara, Allan, and Naadir got out of their buggies as well. Devante began questioning Evelyn. "Why the hell did you stop? We've got to get him back to the *Ares*. Now!"

"It was a direct order," she defended.

"Yes, well, I've got another direct order. Sir, get back in your vehicle. They may be coming to finish you off *right now*!" Devante pointed at him. Harlow had seen no one be so direct with Jack before. Not only was Jack, until a few years ago, their sovereign and Marshal, but he was also larger than any of them, but she'd never seen this look on any of his guards before. It was a look that chilled her to her core. They were *scared*.

"Sir, you know what this is," he said to Jack. Then lowered his voice looked around and spoke softly, deadly. "You know what the fuck this is. They're going to roll up on us while we're out here in the middle of nowhere, between here and there, sitting damn ducks with a few phasers, and no chance in hell to outrun them in a couple of shit buggies. They didn't get you in the bar. They're going to get you now. Let's. Go."

"I've got to get to my brother. Evelyn, drive me to O'Malley's. Now!"

Devante took two steps toward Jack. "You can court martial my ass tomorrow, but she's not driving you anywhere." He pointed at Evelyn. "You know I'm right."

She nodded. "Sir. He's right."

Harlow spoke softly. "Please, Jack. Believe me. I know how hard this is. Go back to the *Ares*."

Jack looked at her, chest heaving, sweat pouring down his face despite the cold Martian night. Grief lined his features as he turned back to the burning pub. "I'm going to help my brother and your mother," he said quietly to Harlow, and then turned and attempted to push past Evelyn. Movement behind him caught Harlow's attention. McNamara raced past Evelyn.

McNamara turned his phaser on Jack and said, "It's set to stun. I've checked four times while they've been arguing with you. *I* won't argue with you. Get in the buggy now, or I'll render you unconscious and get you to the *Ares* that way. Don't make me do it, sir."

Jack got in the buggy without another word, and they drove the rest of the way to the *Ares* in silence as O'Malley's burned in the distance behind them.

Harlow wept with relief for Jack and boundless grief for those trapped in the rubble of O'Malley's.

CHAPTER 18

IN DARKNESS I RISE

Marcus woke in darkness, confused. Somewhere in the distance, he heard muffled screams and moans. He lay on his back. With every breath, he felt a weight rise and fall on top of him. He reached down to decipher what it was. *Chair?* He pushed it to the side and slowly sat up. He carefully reached out a hand to touch rough edges, jagged stone, and a floor littered with the now-crumbled Martian clay used to make bricks. Warm, thick liquid was running down the back of his head. He swiped at it and rubbed it on his shirt. "Hello?" he called into the dark.

He heard a woman coughing a couple of feet away. "Over here. I'm Yua Nakamura."

"Yua." His brain raced to catch up. "I'm Marcus Windsor. Anyone else in here?" he called.

No answer came back.

"Are you hurt, Marcus?" Yua asked.

"I don't think so. The back of my head stings, but I think I'm fine. What about you?"

"I'm okay."

"We were in the bar, right?" Marcus asked, still feeling a little disoriented. The cold pouring in through every crack and seam of the destroyed building was helping to clear some of the brain fog.

"Yes. Maybe there was a quake or another attack."

The sounds of moaning continued through the rubble.

Yua said, "I should be out there helping those people. Not stuck in here."

Marcus could hear the frustration in her voice. He admired her for having purpose in her life. *You're a king and you admire someone else for having purpose? That's rubbish, mate.*

"There's got to be a way out of here," Yua said.

He heard her scooting across the small space. "Don't move!" Marcus warned. "If you hit the rubble, it might come falling down on your head."

Marcus retrieved his comm unit out of his utility pocket. Yua did the same, and they started looking at their surroundings. A chunk of the ceiling had fallen against the wall, creating a triangular space that contained them with rubble on either side. No light crept in anywhere. Marcus spoke Jack's name into his comm unit. The voice recognition contacted his brother.

"Where are you?" Jack said before Marcus spoke a word to him.

"In a pocket of rubble with Yua Nakamura. She's fine. I don't see any way out. I'm not sure it's safe to push or pull on any of this from in here."

"Don't!" Jack said. "Help is on the way. As soon as I can tell you more, I will check back. I'm glad you're safe. I was worried for you, brother."

"Same. Glad you're not trapped. Was it a bomb?"

"Yeah, we think so. I've got your location marked on the comm now. Just stay put. I've got the both of you pinpointed."

Marcus worried about how many of his guards had died. There were a dozen in and around O'Malley's. It seemed impossible that they all could've survived a blast that had caved the building in to this degree. They had families. He'd heard some of them talking about their children. He'd been adamant about going to O'Malley's despite their objections...

He looked over at Yua and noticed that she hadn't called anyone but was still simply using the comm to look around her surroundings. "Is your comm broken? Would you like to borrow mine to contact someone?"

"No, as long as Marshal knows my whereabouts, he can inform the crew. There's no one else I need to call."

Marcus couldn't imagine her not wanting to call her husband. "You sure? You don't need to talk to family or..."

"No, the crew's my family. Anyone I might need to call is on the ship, and they already know to dig me out." She glanced at him. "My husband died of lung disease two years ago."

Marcus felt sick as he thought of his conversation with Safia about Yua's family in the bar four years prior. He'd not forgotten it because it was the first time he'd been confronted so directly. After relaying the details to his father, the King had said they were finding excuses to be angry with the Crown and coalition to drive up prices. *Always something to complain about, he'd said.*

The groaning on the other side of the wall of debris got louder. "Damn it!" Yua said. "They're so close."

Marcus was worried about the way she was examining the dusty orange rubble. "Someone will be here soon," he said.

"I'm a doctor. I can't just sit here and listen to people in pain and do nothing."

She braced herself and pulled at a piece of the ceiling as dust and debris immediately rained down on them.

He grabbed her around the waist and began dragging her away. "Stop it! You're going to get us killed!"

She pivoted in his arms and hit him wherever she could. "People are hurting and dying. I can't just ignore it, like your family did!"

Her words pierced him like a phaser weapon. He immediately released her and watched as she went right back to the piece of ceiling she'd been pulling at earlier.

"I hear you. I'm coming," she called through the rubble.

Moments later, a grinding noise sounded over their heads, and everything went dark again for Marcus.

CHAPTER 19

HIPPOCRATES IN THE REGOLITH

A blinding light gave Marcus an immediate headache. As the light moved off to the side, back again, then to the side once more, he saw the outline of a woman bathed in a soft glow.

A halo? Shite. Am I dead?

"Do you know where you are?" Yua asked.

Marcus's first thought was that he was back home in London before he remembered that he was on Mars, stuck under the rubble of the bar. "O'Malley's."

"What are you feeling?"

"My head hurts in two places now."

"Any nausea?"

"No."

"Good." She snugged a soft cloth around the top and back of his head. A moment later, he noticed she was missing a shirt sleeve. He realized she'd found a patient to tend to after all.

"Lights." He looked up and gestured at the radiance piercing a jagged seam torn along the ceiling, what little of the ceiling was still intact, and the wall of rubble to the right of it.

"Yeah, they've set up some auxiliary lighting and heaters as well."

"How long was I out?"

"Not too long." She pressed two fingers onto the artery on the side of his neck.

He tried pushing through his muddled thoughts. Her time estimate didn't sound quite right. "If they've had time to set up—" Marcus began.

"You're okay for now, but we need to get you back on the ship so I can make sure you don't have any internal damage. I'm truly sorry. I could have gotten you killed. The Hippocratic Oath I swore means everything to me, but I was taking my heartbreaks out on you. I don't know you. You haven't had the chance to prove who you are. When I lost my son, it was unthinkable. When my husband got sick and it became obvious he would not recover, I just..."

He didn't feel as if he were going to die, unless the ceiling fell in the rest of the way, and yet, her devotion to her family made his own life flash before him. Even the good he recalled seemed to have been in order to gain recognition, chasing a sense of pride he believed he ought to possess in his position, but he felt fraudulent when he came close to achieving it. "I'm sorry for all you've been through. I really am. If I could trade my own existence for either of them, I would." In a world of half-truths, feelings barely realized, and an exhausting amount of inauthenticity, he'd lost touch with what his emotions were in any moment, but he meant what he said to her, and somehow, she seemed to realize it, too. She wiped her remaining shirt sleeve across her cheek.

Marcus coughed. "Oh!" He reached for his right side. "Damn it. That's sharp."

She placed her hand over his ribs. "Any trouble breathing?"

"Only if I try to breathe deep."

"Feels like there's some damage here." Marcus heard her exhale. "C'mon. C'mon," she whispered. "It sounds like they're making progress out there."

He didn't know if she was reassuring him or herself, but muffled conversation from the other side of the ruins was starting to sound clearer and the tumbling rubble and machines were sounding closer.

"We were lucky," Marcus said.

"Very."

They sat in silence for a while, listening to the sounds of the colonists slowly digging them out as Yua checked his pulse periodically. More light was seeping into their tiny chamber as additional layers of debris were being cleared. Marcus spotted a little alcove beneath the base of the door frame heading to the basement. The ceiling beyond appeared to be collapsed, but the frame looked sturdy. "Yua, look," he said, gesturing to the area he'd been studying. "You could fit under there when they clear out the rubble. If it survived the first blast, it would probably hold while they're being careful with the excavation."

"Hmm, maybe."

He didn't care for the way she answered. *Stubborn.*

"All my injuries happened during the first collapse," he said.

"No, I don't think so. Your ribs weren't hurt then. You were sitting up just fine. It wasn't until I was reckless enough to pull at the rubble and all that debris fell on top of you that your right side was injured."

"No, it was only a little red dust that fell. That's all I'll be telling anyone, and I think you should do the same, *doctor.*"

"You don't have to lie for me. I'll own what I did. Your injuries are my fault."

"And I'll deny it."

Jack's voice came through Marcus's comm unit. "Are you two still okay in there?"

"Yeah, we're both hunky-dory."

Yua snatched the communicator from Marcus's hand. "Marcus has a possible broken rib or two and sustained some head injuries. We'll need use of the Rescue Wave before we can move him."

Jack paused. "All right. I'm going to need you to get somewhere and cover your heads as best as possible, but injured ribs make that a little tougher. There's a chunk of ceiling leaning over where you are, and we don't know what may be between you and it and what we may knock loose when we move it." Marcus knew if they were in London they would have access to high-tech rubble removal, but here in the colonies, it was just old-school grab a bucketful and pray.

"Understood. I'll make sure his head is covered," she said.

Marcus watched Yua use the light on her comm to look around for something to shield them, but the biggest piece of ceiling was what she had been pulling at, causing the second cave-in.

"We're about to lift the lid off this thing. Are you two ready?" Jack asked.

Marcus and Yua looked at each other. She sighed, tilted her head, and answered, "Yeah, let's do it."

"Okay, take cover."

Yua leaned over the top half of Marcus as best she could.

He felt the warmth of her breasts settle over his face and despite his weakened state, God help him, he was glad she couldn't see what she was doing to him. Still, she couldn't sacrifice herself for him. As bad as he hated for her to move her warm body… "No," he said beneath her. "Go over there." He tried shoving her off him and toward the area that he thought might hold up better when things started moving, but the effort sent excruciating waves of pain through his ribs, and he had to stifle a cry. As the scraping and tumbling of falling bricks and carbon fiber began, there was nothing left to do but find her hand and hold on tight.

Her hand was already there when he reached for it.

CHAPTER 20

FRANKENSTITCH

Searing light again pierced his eyes once the rumbling stopped, and Yua sat up. He attempted to join her and failed. He looked up to find that dawn was almost at hand. A smattering of stars still sprinkled the sky. His body had no feeling or sensation, no pain, just a humming in his ears as he gazed at Yua. He watched the chilly breeze pick up her hair and blow it back from her face as her eyes seemed to glitter with the reflection of the stars. The angular moon, Phobos, stood guard behind her in the night sky. The moment felt surreal, and she suddenly looked like a goddess to him. Perhaps the concussion he surely had was getting to him. His brother rushed over with Aunt Mary close behind and knelt beside him, but his voice sounded as if it came from far away. "Jesus, bro. You look like hell."

"Buzzing to see you, too, mate." Marcus coughed from the orange dust hanging in the air. The effort brought feeling back to his body in the worst way possible. The shockwaves of pain made him try to suppress it, but to no avail. Both kept happening in a sickening loop. He gasped, wheezed, and gritted his teeth against the agony. Jack placed a hand on his shoulder.

"I need a Rescue Wave over here!" Yua called.

Dr. Seamus Hagen ran over with the requested item, and a nurse followed at his heels. They both had dirt and blood smeared on their medical-issue uniforms. Yua quickly programmed the device, held it to Marcus's side, and he experienced relief in moments.

"Thank you," he gasped and then sat up slowly, testing his aching body for signs of protest. Aunt Mary smoothed the makeshift bandage on his head and offered him a drink of water.

"We'll get you back to the ship for the rest," Yua said. "You really need a brain scan. It's beyond the scope of what can be done out here."

"Yua," Marcus gestured to blood running down her arm.

She turned her body as if trying to hide her own injuries, but Dr. Hagen intervened.

"He's right," Dr. Hagen said. He nodded at the nurse, who tended to Yua's wound and began checking her vitals.

Marcus noted five of his guards standing by, their uniforms now torn and covered in orange-red dust. Jack's guards looked to be patrolling the perimeter along with half the Ares Army. It appeared no one was taking a chance on another attack, especially with Jack and his brother on scene. God help them if they got hit again on the heels of this thing. "Where are the rest of my people?" he asked with a deep sense of foreboding.

Jack and Aunt Mary exchanged a glance. She looked to Jack to deliver the news. "Two of them, Ellis and Nguyen, didn't make it. The rest have been helping us."

Guilt swept over Marcus. He'd insisted on going to the bar. He didn't want to look back up at the grieving members of the SAS, but he forced himself to. "I'm sorry."

They nodded.

"Wait. How is it almost dawn? It's only been, what, an hour since the bomb went off? Two hours?" Marcus noticed Jack's look of concern. "Okay, none of that dodgy rubbish. What am I missing here?"

Jack spoke. "You were unconscious for five hours. The entire structure was so unstable that we've been working through the night just to get enough braces in place to move anything without it burying you all even deeper."

"They already know what I did to you," Yua said.

Marcus felt sick. He'd only wanted to protect her so Jack wouldn't be angry, but not only did Jack already know, she'd had to sit there with him while he was unconscious the whole time, with none of them knowing whether he was going to wake up. Marcus studied Jack to try and determine if he were upset with Yua, but there seemed to be a thousand things going on behind his brother's eyes. He somehow doubted holding a grudge against her was a top priority.

Marcus noted Yua turning to see the wounded who were still being rescued from the debris. He knew she wanted to jump in and help. "Thank you. I'll be all right now. You go assist the others," he said.

Dr. Hagen said, "It's fine. These three are the last of those we've managed to retrieve," he said.

Aunt Mary added, "The others can't be helped." She traced a cross on her chest.

Farther from what remained of the building, a dozen bodies lay covered with blankets. He felt sick and was sure it wasn't just the head injury and dehydration. Marcus guessed that even more fatalities had already been removed from the scene.

He had a thought that made his chest heavy and his palms suddenly cold. "Are Ellis and Nguyen under—"

"No," Jack interrupted. "They've already been removed and taken to the *Ares*."

Marcus nodded, suddenly unable to make eye contact with his brother as a fresh wave of guilt swept over him.

Aunt Mary placed her hand on his arm. "Get back to the ship to see to your head injuries. We'll be fine wrapping up here."

Dr. Hagen nodded in agreement.

They loaded Marcus with three of his guards in tow and a few other wounded onto transports.

As they pulled away, Marcus looked back toward the gutted O'Malley's just in time to see his brother place a hard hat on his head, walk back into the fray, and be swallowed up by the swirl of red dust and debris.

• • •

"I feel utterly daft with this thing on my skull," Marcus said.

Yua smiled. "Yes, well, daft or not, we need a good look inside your brain, and that silly hat lets me do just that." She looked at the hologram projected from the cap and turned the image with her fingers, tilting it this way and that, looking at it from every angle for damage or bleeding as the AI spoke, "... hematoma between the temporal lobe and Wernicke's area. Areas 12, 13, 14, clear." Yua listened to the rest of the AI's report, shut off the program, and removed the cap.

"It looks as if there was a small bleed and swelling early on, but we were lucky it wasn't worse. We need to keep checking on it for sure, but I believe you're going to be just fine."

She exhaled like air being released from a balloon and threw a couple of instruments into a drawer so hard they made a loud clatter, then she slammed it shut.

"I'm sorry. Did I say something wrong?"

"You're sorry? I almost got you killed! Don't apologize to me." She reached up to the bridge of her nose and pinched.

He knew a little something of what she was feeling after Ellis and Nguyen's deaths. He sat up. "Come here," he breathed. "Did they check you well enough? Did you get hit on *your* head at any point?"

"No. It's just a stress headache."

"Then use the Rescue Wave on it."

She hesitated. "No, it's fine."

Marcus knit his eyebrows together. "How does the saying go? 'Physician, heal thyself?'"

"If I deserved it."

Marcus reached out and placed both palms on the sides of her head and ran his thumbs in small circles over her temples. He realized what he was doing would have been presumptuous under other circumstances, but after their brush with death it felt oddly right. She closed her eyes for a few moments. "I'm sorry. I can't believe I let this happen."

"Let it go," Marcus said softly.

He noted her eyes go shiny with tears, and she abruptly moved away, wiped her eyes, and focused on the injury. "We need to close that scalp wound before it scabs. Lie back," she said, gently pushing his shoulder. She picked up a bottle from the side table and poured saline into the wound.

Marcus winced.

"Sorry. This is deep. Hold this against your head, please." She handed him the gauze and then went to the cabinet to gather supplies and placed them onto a tray that she wheeled over to him. "I'll get this stitched up quick."

Marcus's eyes grew wide as he watched her thread an actual curved suture needle. "What are you *doing*?"

"I'm going to close up that wound. Don't worry. I'm very skilled with stitches. Can you believe some medical schools even stopped teaching it once everyone started using the nanobots to mend lacerations? Utter foolishness. What will those doctors do in a situation like this? Lucky for you, some of us still know how."

Though her confidence was reassuring, Marcus held up a hand. He couldn't fathom walking around with stitches in his skin. "Go get the medbots. This is a sickbay. You must have them here."

"Once upon a time we did. Your Highness, or is it Majesty?"

"I'm not coronated yet. It's still Highness, but please, call me Marcus."

"Well, Highness, Marcus this—"

"That's weird. Pick one."

"As I was saying, this is Mars. When things break or get stolen, that's it. I've requisitioned replacements, but other things take priority." She sighed and walked over to the cabinet once more and retrieved a GloNumb. She came back to him, removed the cap, adjusted the setting, and held the blue light over the wound for several seconds. When she looked at him, he became conscious of their eye contact and quickly looked away. "It ought to be nice and numb now. You shouldn't feel the needle *too* much."

Her sentiment sounded sincere, though the tone was a bit wry. "Thank you," Marcus said.

"Maybe close your eyes."

He did as she said but began shaking a little. *Jesus, I know I'm not laying here shaking over a few stitches, but it is barbaric.* Images of the rubble and bodies lying outside O'Malley's played through his mind, and he blurted out, "There were more bodies than I thought there would be." He felt her fingers stop moving over his head. "I'm sorry. That was a crude thing to say. I just never..."

"It's okay," she said as she laid a gloved hand on his arm. He opened his eyes to find her looking at him. "Just a couple more stitches, and we'll be done."

His arm warmed where she touched him.

For the first time in years, he felt calm.

CHAPTER 21

WARRIOR UNDONE

Safia knew where she'd find Carlos. No force on Earth would have kept him from driving to O'Malley's after the explosion. At least he hadn't been in the attack; she saw the pub go up moments after he'd dropped her off, but she worried about him. Harlow said he'd been working nonstop since the explosion. She knew he would be grieving. So many of the dead were members of the Ares Army, men he'd worked with for years. She'd known them, too. Their faces had kept her awake for hours the night before. Would he even want to see her? She didn't know.

She remembered what Harlow had said about feeling the need to be there for her people, but being a mother meant having to stay with your child when everything inside urged you to run toward the danger and help. It was frustrating. She didn't think Judith would be back anytime soon. She'd made it out of the rubble alive, but Eoghan had not. They were still trying to dig him out, couldn't make contact, and feared the worst.

Finally, Safia got in touch with Tara, one of the women she'd known from the compound whose son was also genetically gifted—none of them cared for the word "modified," as it made their children sound like crops. Tara agreed to bring her son and come stay with Bella while Safia went to check on Carlos. She'd already been watching Selah while Harlow and Jack were at the site.

As soon as Tara entered Judith's house, Gabriel levitated a toy car from the bag his mother carried, and Bella jumped up and down as he moved it through the air to stick against the wall, where it rolled all over as Bella laughed. His mother forbade him to show off his abilities in public, as all the mothers from the compound did, at least to some extent, to keep others from gawking and possibly shunning their kids.

"Thanks for helping me out," Safia said.

"I get it. I'm sure it would do him a world of good to see you right now. He's really been having a tough time," Tara said.

Safia didn't miss the slight edge to Tara's voice—she'd been alone since she was pregnant with Gabriel. The colonies weren't overflowing with choices. Now that there were more visitors, that was changing, but the women from the compound had to be extra careful who they let into their lives. The threat of someone connected to the genetic experimenting showing up and getting close to them to gain information about their children was always a worry. It wasn't the first time Tara had expressed envy. Now she was looking at Safia as if she were a complete fool for leaving a man as remarkable as Carlos. Tara wasn't wrong; she just didn't understand the situation. Safia couldn't help but wonder if Tara would make a move on him now. She couldn't blame her if she did. If she were in her shoes, she might feel the same way.

She thanked her again before heading out the door. Smoke rose from O'Malley's, and she felt sick, but that wasn't the only reason. She knew she might well run into Alvaro at the scene. *To hell with him. He's not going to keep me from Carlos this time.*

When she arrived, the immediately recovered bodies and wounded were being taken to the *Ares*, and the hard work of digging out survivors and the buried dead was ongoing. The work was all so much harder because the top-of-the-line tech Mars had once boasted for levitating boulders and equipment, which would have served wonderfully in this situation, was in need of repair. Replacement parts were difficult to obtain on Earth, since the Gray Death, and impossible on Mars.

She didn't see Carlos around front. She stopped to ask if he'd gone through the makeshift tunnel they'd created to get deeper into the rubble but was informed he wasn't in there. Someone mentioned seeing him go around back, where the worst of the explosion had occurred.

The sight of him stopped her cold. He leaned over, took the hard hat from his head, and shook the soot from his hair. He was covered in ash, red dirt, and blood—the whites of his eyes the only clear thing recognizable. She watched him take a deep, shuddering breath. She'd seen the hopeless expression on his face only once before: when his sister had contacted him from Earth a year ago to tell him his mother had a stroke. Getting an unscheduled transport to Earth wasn't easy in the best of times, but now that he'd gone AWOL, it was impossible to see her. Luckily, she'd survived. He looked like he was barely surviving this.

When he looked up and locked eyes with her, his shaking got worse. For a moment, she feared he would send her away. But instead, he said, voice cracking, "You were right. We should have stayed with the old coalition."

She closed the distance between them and shook her head. "Just because this happened doesn't make me right." They stood only a foot apart. His body seemed to quake from the inside. She took his hand, led him inside a nearby storage shed that had somehow survived the blast, and shut the door. Dim light seeped through the cracks of the old structure. The smell of hops and mold around them competed with the char coming off Carlos's hair and clothing. She put her hands on either side of his face. "Have you stopped to take a break at all? I know you haven't slept since you dropped me off at the house last night."

He shook his head in answer.

She pulled him close, and he lay his cheek on her shoulder, and wrapped his arms around her tightly. His fingers gathered the fabric of her jacket as if grasping a lifeline. “You’re exhausted, Carlos.” She reached her arms under his thick jacket and rubbed his back slowly.

The sounds outside the shed seemed to shift. The voices were louder. Something was happening.

Carlos spoke, “Baby, I really—”

“She’s alive!” someone called.

“All hands!” another yelled.

“I have to go,” Carlos said.

“Get some sleep soon,” she called to him as he ran out the door, grabbed his hard hat, and raced toward the smoldering ruins of O’Malley’s.

She looked down at the filth he’d left on her clothes, but she didn’t mind. It was evidence that he didn’t hate her for breaking his heart.

CHAPTER 22

JUDITH OF THE LOST

Harlow watched her mother sitting on the ground beside the body of Eoghan O'Malley. Judith had slipped the sheet free of his face and her trembling, pale hand caressed his bloodied and soot covered cheek. As the wind shifted, smoke and red dust wrapped around her as completely as the shroud of grief she wore. Judith had been that way since they'd brought him out and laid him there twenty minutes ago. She had stood in the cold all night long waiting for word. Harlow remembered seeing them in the bar, side by side. She did not know how one made it out and the other didn't. Devastation felt cruelly random.

The woman had staggered from the death of Harlow's father to drag her weary, embittered body through this life alone. Light had just began to seep into the recesses of her heart, dark and shut down for so long, too long, and now... Harlow very much feared this might end her mother. She dug deep for the ache she wanted to feel for her. She couldn't grab hold of the emotion; it was all too cruel to fathom. Too raw.

Five feet away, Mike O'Malley sat on a corner of what used to be the front wall of his bar. He had a bottle of booze in one hand and a cigarette in the other. He swayed a little as he stared at his brother's body. Harlow wondered how long it would be before he fell over altogether. She intended to stay until he passed out and had no intention of trying to take the bottle from him. He could deal with his brother's death and decimated bar and home another day. If he chose to forget on this day, she couldn't blame him.

After Jack sent his brother to the *Ares*, he'd gone back into the rubble along with several others, to make sure there were no unreported survivors—or more deceased. Mike O'Malley's girlfriend Janet, an engineer on the *Ares*, accompanied them. Mike was drinking himself into oblivion, shrugging off comfort from Janet and everyone else, so she helped in the only way she knew how: by getting her hands dirty.

A guttural, disturbing sound rose from Judith. She rocked back and forth, wailing until her voice cracked. Shocking for a woman so stoic.

From across the rubble, an exhausted Carlos looked up at Harlow, his eyes the only thing recognizable through the thick layer of dust and soot coating his face and neck beneath the hard hat he wore. He'd skipped beers with them the night before, keeping to himself since Safia left. He looked toward Judith; though ever kind and caring, he appeared to possess the same sense of shock and futility Harlow felt. He went back to removing the rubble piece by piece in the off chance someone might still be alive under it all.

Harlow knew her mother's keening was about much more than Eoghan O'Malley. Judith had never grieved Harlow's father, not really. After he'd been gone for twenty years, she finally opened her heart to Eoghan, and they'd enjoyed four years together, before some soulless thug intent on terror took him out. Had she and Jack not left moments earlier, would they lie where Eoghan did now? Could Jack have been the target, or was it random violence in order to scare the colonists back into submission?

Mike looked up at the sound of Judith's broken soul and wobbled a little but went right back to making sure he placed as much distance as he could between himself and the level of grief Judith was experiencing.

Aunt Mary, Judith's friend since Harlow was a little girl, walked over and sat down beside Judith, offering presence but understanding the emptiness of words, or even touch. She understood Judith well. Even Harlow knew better than to touch her mother right now.

A few moments later, Jack emerged from the makeshift entrance to the rubble they'd stabilized. When their eyes met, a dozen emotions passed between them. It surprised Harlow to find that it was parallel to talking with the *Ares*; neither required direct speech. Without words, they grounded each other as the chaos swirled around them. They kept their own turmoil from caving in on them as they struggled to hold the world up for those they loved. It reminded her of the day she was on trial for treason and the courtroom had been bombed. They'd tried desperately to make their way to each other through the dust, debris, and pandemonium before Aldric and the Brotherhood took her away.

The sound of a crashing bottle broke the spell as it slipped from Mike O'Malley's hands. He swayed one last time. Jack caught him before he hit the ground.

"Janet!" Jack called.

Janet emerged and removed her hard hat. "Jesus," she said as she looked at Mike's unconscious frame, a dead weight against Jack. "He can sleep it off in my quarters on the *Ares*. His apartment is gone."

Harlow noted the front half of O'Malley's still stood. It was the back half of the building that was blown away. It would be a serious hazard until the rebuild.

Jack hefted Mike over his shoulder, carefully placed him in the buggy, and strapped him in for the ride back. His head lolled to one side, but Jack placed his hand between Mike's skull and the door frame so he wouldn't hurt himself further, grabbed a jacket he found in the back seat, and tucked it in as a pillow against the metal. It was hard to believe those two had beaten the hell out of each other on more than one occasion. Then again, maybe it wasn't hard to believe. Jack might have been a rebel prince by blood, but Mike O'Malley had held court in that bar and looked out for what could be considered his kingdom for as long as she could remember. Maybe they actually understood each other quite well. She wondered if either knew it. If they did, would they ever admit it?

"Thank you, Jack," Janet said, as she slid into the driver's seat.

"Sure. Let me know if he needs anything."

"Will do," she said.

Harlow placed her hand on Janet's arm. "Please tell him I'm here if he needs me."

"Of course."

Janet gave them both one last sad smile before turning to look at the rubble that had been O'Malley's. She sighed, then started the ancient, sputtering buggy and headed home to the *Ares*.

Jack surprised Harlow by pulling her in for a hug so quickly that she almost lost her balance.

Hot tears stung her eyes and made trails down the dirt that had swirled through the burning rubble all night and coated the faces of those searching for survivors and aiding those who grieved. *Damn it.* She'd been able to avoid emotion throughout the night. When they'd arrived at the scene, even when the sheets were pulled up over one, two, three, and more—even Eoghan—she kept her mourning in check, but the contact, the hug… it was her undoing. This was why her mother avoided touch and talking about her father all those years. It was just too damn much. Jack shuddered against her body. Was it tears, shock, grief? She didn't know. Words failed. She searched for a way to drag him to shore through the waves of horror that had broken over them through the night.

She found no words but held on tight.

CHAPTER 23

BREAKING POINT

Harlow watched Jack hard at work at his desk—the same place he was every night, building a profitable new coalition that would give them more than mere slave wages, and now it was getting half the colony killed. His hair was still wet from the shower that had washed the grime away from days at the bombed-out O'Malley's, but it couldn't wash the exhaustion and grief away: dark circles ringed his bloodshot eyes. Harlow couldn't remember the last time he'd slept for more than a couple of hours at a time. "How's Selah?"

"Asleep," Harlow said as she sat down on the bed and began unlacing her boots. She was oscillating between feeling absolutely numb inside and teetering on the verge of an emotional explosion that she feared, once freed, would not be easily reigned in. The boot dropped to the floor with a thud. Harlow stared at it. Orange dust, soot, remnants of the pub, circled the area where her boot landed. She kept seeing the gutted O'Malley's. The bodies. She reached down to unlace the other boot and blurted it out before thinking: "Disband the new coalition. It's not worth it anymore."

"We can't do that," he said, his voice sounding defeated in exhaustion.

"People are dying, Jack."

"Jesus, Harlow! You don't think I know that? I thought my brother was dead." He scrubbed a hand across his face as if to clear the memories. "We can't go back now. We will starve to death without the new coalition. The Nexus is necessary. Spain, India, PIUS, the African countries that buy from us, they are all getting decent offers from the old coalition to buy from *them*. If we disband now, they will start bidding against each other again, prices will go up, our old 'friends' will move in, and goods will sit here."

"Couldn't we find more private corporations to buy from us?"

"Could we find them before we starve? We're too skint to wait anyone out. Over half the countries of the world will charge their corporations with treason, shut them down if they buy from us. We still don't have enough soil diversity or water to grow most crops in large enough quantities. You know that."

"This has to stop. How?"

"We have experts to help us deal with the attacks now. Hopefully, we will see some more arrests soon."

She watched Jack's jaw work back and forth as he gazed out the window at the deepening night sky. "I'm sorry," she said. "I'm not used to feeling helpless. At least when I was stealing, I was bringing comfort. It may sound silly, but I had a plan I could execute and see results."

"No, I get it." He looked at her. Just a blank look. She'd never seen him do that before. There was usually a plan brewing behind those eyes, an answer. This time only a hollow exhaustion stared back at her. She wanted to tell him to stop doing that and just *be the answer* again, but it wasn't fair to expect that of this exhausted, overwhelmed man. Had it ever been fair? She watched him inhale, place his hands on the desk, and stand. *Off to solve someone else's problems while half the planet tried to kill him.*

She walked over and wrapped her arms around him. Wherever he'd been about to go, he wasn't now. He pressed her body against him, hard, and took her mouth hungrily. His touch was insistent and demanding. She realized that while some people avoided touch when they were devastated—the way she sometimes did, her mother certainly did, and Mike O'Malley seemed to as well, judging by the way he had drank himself into oblivion earlier—Jack ran to it. At least he did with her.

She thought about her longing to gain control in her life, but somehow it didn't matter tonight. Jack desperately needed a lifeline. She wanted to give him whatever he needed.

• • •

When they lay in bed entwined and spent, he gazed at her and spoke. "Every time I've cried out to the heavens for mercy, the answer has always been you."

She found no words to reply but pulled him to her chest, and he fell asleep in her arms. She didn't know about being heaven's answer to anything, but for him, she knew she would try.

Unfortunately, sleep eluded her. She lay staring up at the ceiling. O'Malley's had been part of the colony as long as she could remember. It was inconceivable that she would walk out there and find a pile of rubble where it once was. It could be rebuilt, sure, but it would take time and the grief would be ever present for anyone who entered the bar from now on. She gave up on sleep and headed to the observation deck.

She was glad to find it empty. Memories of the night she had visited the deck after Aldric and Doc had given her the serum to help her interface with the *Ares*, which had a terrible effect on her, came flooding back. She remembered dissolving into tears and feeling helpless, a foreign and much-despised feeling, but most of all, she recalled how Jack had looked out for her and how furious he'd been with the two experimenters. He had been there for her when she couldn't look out for herself. Now she wanted to help him but didn't know how.

She placed her hand on the wall, thankfully no serum was needed now, and let the energy from the ship run up her arm. She walked very slowly, feeling the skin of the *Ares*. No wonder they named ships throughout history. *Living, breathing things.*

When someone entered the room, her eyes popped open.

"I'm sorry. I didn't mean to disturb you," Marcus said.

"You aren't, but I suppose I must look pretty strange to you right now."

"Well, I hear you have a special connection to the ship. Besides, you can't possibly look any more barmy than me right now." He pointed to the five stitches above his right eyebrow.

"I'm guessing Dr. Nakamura had fun with those."

Marcus winced. "She was properly chuffed about it. Yes."

Harlow smiled and looked at her splayed fingers against the wall and nodded. "Sometimes, I think my dad might have transferred a bit of his consciousness into this ship. There are times when I almost feel like I can… I don't know. It might sound silly to you."

"Please tell me," Marcus said.

"Sometimes it's like I think I'm going to turn around and see him when I'm connected to the ship. It's as if I've got my dad back in some small way." Harlow realized her mistake the moment the words were out. "I'm sorry. I'm being insensitive. You just lost your father. That's a fresh wound for you."

"No. It's fine. I'm glad you can have that experience. My father and I weren't close."

"And I barely remember mine, but here, I believe the ship *knew* him and likes to share that with me, or it puts the two languages together, so to speak. It has the genetic code of everyone who's ever been on board, so perhaps when I touch the ship, it remembers him, and I feel it."

Marcus remained silent.

"I haven't been drinking. I swear it."

"For the record, I didn't think you had. I'm sure you're spot on." Marcus smiled, gave a slight bow, and spoke formally. "Your logic is sound, m'lady."

Harlow laughed, took her hand off the wall, and walked behind the unmanned bar and retrieved two glasses. "What'll ya have?" She set several bottles on top of the counter. "We've got Carlos's terrifying home brew, the Russian botanists' attempt at vodka, and—" Harlow paused and swallowed past the lump in her throat before she could speak again. "—Mike O'Malley's Irish whiskey."

"Oh, I think it has to be the whiskey. We drink to O'Malley's," Marcus said.

Harlow nodded and poured a little in each glass.

They held their tumblers up and looked at each other as if they might think of something to say, until an unspoken agreement seemed to take over and they clinked their glasses together and said softly, "O'Malley's," before turning them up.

"How are you feeling?" Harlow asked as she poured a little more for each of them.

Marcus puckered his lips, exhaled, and blinked over the sting of the whiskey before answering. "Horrible, but I can't sleep."

"Same." She couldn't help but notice that with the stubble grown in on his face, something she'd never seen on him before, he looked more like his older brother, though his bone structure was a bit narrower, his hair just a shade lighter. She almost laughed when she saw his jaw working just like Jack's did and knew he must be building up to a very serious question.

He was silent for a few more moments before speaking again. "Do you think the bomb was meant for me or Jack?"

There it was. Harlow slid the glass toward him.

"Jack. The attacks were happening before you got here. Why would they switch targets now?"

Marcus nodded but still looked thoughtful. He turned the tumbler this way and that. "Might be advantageous to have me out of the way though."

Harlow nodded. "I'm glad you're thinking like that. I'm sure it'll help keep you alive."

Marcus went in for another sip before speaking again. "You know, with Father gone, there's no reason you, Jack, and Selah couldn't come back. I know this is your home, but if you ever get too worried about Jack—"

"I'm too worried about Jack everyday now, but your government is more than just you. To them, he's a traitor who stole the most powerful piece of technology in the solar system. I don't know that he could go back."

"Much of politics is in framing. If I frame it the right way, he could become a freedom fighter, protecting an innocent, ignored colony."

Harlow looked at him over the top of her glass. "That doesn't require *framing*. It's true."

Marcus sat his glass down. "Yeah, it is true."

"Anyway, Jack would never leave."

Marcus downed the last of his whiskey. "Then I fear for him."

Harlow nodded. "Every day." She looked into her glass and wondered how much to tell Marcus. He clearly loved his brother, but that didn't mean she could trust him with everything. Knowledge was power.

"You know, it's not as simple as disbanding the new coalition Jack's formed. Sometimes I get angry and blurt that out, but there's more to it than that. No one will give us a fair price for our goods, and we don't yet have enough here to be completely self-sufficient."

"Right, but when does the bombing end?" Marcus asked. "How long does Jack's luck hold out?"

"Suppose we did everything the old Earth coalition wants: return the *Ares* to their control, make Mars a coalition-controlled colony again. Who's to say we would get a fair deal?" The hurt on Marcus's face startled Harlow.

"Do you really think so little of me? Father had no faith in me, and you don't either?"

"Marcus, no. That's not what I'm saying. You and I both know that yours is *one* country, and the Earth coalition is huge. Just how much sway can you even hold with everyone waiting for you to show bias with Jack as your brother? For the record, I believe you have what it takes to make a fine king, but politics can get away from the best leaders. Situations unravel beyond the reach of one person, even a king."

Harlow watched Marcus reach up and touch the stitches on his forehead and look at the bar as if lost in thought for a moment. "You are right, but I've come to love the people here," he said.

"Even so, if the *Ares* is gone—and you know the coalition will want to 'secure' it after all that's happened—how long will it be before the Brotherhood or the Chinese show up? I'm sure everyone in the coalition will say 'We won't abandon the colony,' but how much damage will be done before the *Ares* comes back to help?" As she spoke, Harlow felt a tightness in her chest at the idea of losing the *Ares*.

She continued in hopes that Marcus would understand exactly how the colonists felt. "Might Mars be bargained away if the Chinese have some weapon the coalition is unaware of, and they hold Earth hostage? We're far away and might be easily sacrificed in order to secure Earth's safety. Throughout history, promises have been made by one country about defending another, but when the threat came, those promises were broken. They always had a really good reason. Right?"

"I would never abandon you all. You're my family."

Harlow smiled and hoped it was true. "And you are ours." She reached across the bar and squeezed his hand before grabbing the whiskey again and pouring them each another shot. "So, your government will vote against our sovereignty in an effort to keep Jack safe?"

"You get right to the point, huh?"

"We don't have the luxury not to."

"I doubt it will ever be simple and straightforward like that. I'll always vote in favor of what keeps you safe and as prosperous as possible. The bombings are happening because many here believe the old coalition can still be convinced to give the colonists a fair deal. The vote only makes it difficult for allied nations and businesses within those nations to trade with Mars. Harlow, Jack refused to return the *Ares,* the *HMS Ares,* to the very country that funded it and built it. The coalition played no small part in its building as well."

"We don't see it that way. The very reason the *Ares* was built was to defend Mars. Now the coalition says, 'return it.' Has anyone bothered to explain to Parliament that without that ship, Mars becomes a sitting duck for any terrorist group to swoop in at any moment?" Harlow's frustration rose. How could he possibly understand when he wasn't raised in the colonies? After seeing the bodies lined up outside O'Malley's, did she even understand anymore? She'd just asked Jack to disband the new coalition. Now she was going to try and defend it to Marcus? Why, out of habit? When did things get so muddy? Even Safia's daughter, Bella, couldn't see through this much murk and darkness.

They both turned at the sound of gentle knocking. Yua walked onto the observation deck. "I went to check on my patient, only to find he'd disappeared. Naturally, I'm alarmed that a head injury case is roaming the ship alone. Now he's drinking," she said as she picked up the glass.

"I apologize for corrupting him. Sleep seems to allude us tonight," Harlow said.

"Yes, well, as you can see, I'm awake, too," Yua said.

Harlow looked from one to the other and, despite the horror of the last day, she detected something that almost made her smile. The way Marcus and Yua looked at each other seemed for all the galaxy like they were falling in love. Maybe she didn't have to worry about Marcus's intentions after all. She knew Yua was devoted to

Mars without question. If Marcus became devoted to Yua, well, that was good, very good.

Harlow summoned a yawn in order to stage an exit and give the two of them some privacy. The yawn wasn't altogether fake. She'd drunk a fair amount of whiskey and Jack had pleased her properly not long before that. Her eyes were getting heavy and her thoughts a little fuzzy. "I'm going to leave this bottle with you two and go give sleep another go. It was nice getting to know you, brother." She held out a hand, but Marcus ignored it and hugged her.

"Good night, sis. Well, there's still day left, but get some sleep."

Harlow smiled. "G'night."

Yua hugged her as well. She couldn't ever recall seeing Yua hug anyone. It had been a terrifying couple of days. Perhaps everyone realized they needed each other now more than ever.

Harlow started out the door but turned to look behind her when she heard soft talking. Marcus was pouring Yua a drink with what little was left of the bottle of whiskey. Yua might have found companionship at long last after losing her son and husband. Maybe things could work out.

Then again, she remembered her mother wailing over the body of Eoghan O'Malley, and the whiskey in her gut no longer had a pleasant burn.

When she got back to her room, she took her boots off, then her cargo pants, and slid into bed beside Jack. She wrapped her arms around him and held on tight, grateful for every moment.

CHAPTER 24

ALL THE PAINT IN THE WORLD

Safia knocked on the door of Eoghan's home. Judith had been holed up in it since he'd died a week ago. Harlow was deeply worried about her mother but respected her privacy. Safia tried to do the same, but here she stood, waiting on her to come to the door. She knew her motivation was selfish, but she reasoned that sometimes knowing someone else needed you was the best way to get out of one's own head.

Judith opened the door and motioned for her to come in. Safia said, "I brought some of the leftover pot pie from the diner. It's a good batch."

"I'm not very hungry."

As she turned to walk back inside, Safia couldn't help but notice how Judith's clothes were hanging on her. For her to have gotten this gaunt in only a week, she must not have eaten a bite the whole time.

"Judith, eat something. Please."

"Fine."

They walked into the kitchen, and Safia started going through the cabinets while Judith poured them each a little beer. At least it looked like beer, but it was oddly cloudy. With O'Malley's out of commission, people were getting their booze from some pretty questionable sources.

Safia spooned generous portions of pot pie onto their plates. It was still warm from the lunch service.

Judith took a bite. "You're right. It is a good batch."

"Has anyone else been by, or rather, have you let them in?"

Judith gave a wry laugh. "Mary came by and yes, I let her in. She brought me the beer. In a booze drought, Mary will always be able to make it rain."

Safia laughed. "She's good company. I like her."

"Me too. How are things with you and Carlos?"

"Umm, mostly the same. I still love him. I can't live with him, can't tell him why. It's frustrating. Everyone thinks I'm an asshole."

"I don't."

"Thank you. I miss him." Her voice cracked as she spoke. She blinked quickly to keep her eyes from pooling up. "I went to see him at the site last week. He doesn't hate me. He let me hug him."

"Then don't let go," she said with tears in her own eyes. She took one more bite, then shoved her plate away. Safia did the same. Judith rose from her chair with her beer in hand. "Come on. I've got something to show you."

Safia grabbed her own drink, stood up, and followed her down the stairs.

Judith switched on a light, and in the room stood several easels. There were paintings of an O'Malley's pub, but it wasn't Mike's. "This is Eoghan's pub in London. He missed it, but never wanted anyone to know how much. I mean, he loved being here with his brother, and I honestly think he wouldn't have changed that, but he would get wistful about his pub."

There was another painting of cliffs with an ocean below. Safia didn't think she'd ever seen such a place in person. "This is the Cliffs of Moher. It's in Ireland, in County Clare, where the O'Malleys are from."

"They're gorgeous. I had no idea he was a painter."

"Yeah, he asked me about your mural. He didn't talk about his own work much. I guess it was just something he did to relax."

Safia moved from one painting to the other, feeling as if she were getting a glimpse into this man, she would never get the chance to know now. The beautiful painting before her of a turbulent ocean became blurry as she thought of the bombing and Judith's loss. "I'm sorry," she whispered through a voice thick with unexpressed grief. The feelings of selfishness for coming here, wanting comfort of her own, returned.

"The only thing he liked more than painting was making paint. He has jars and jars of it." Judith pointed to a corner of the room. It was more paint than Safia had ever seen, in a spectrum of colors.

"Paint with me, Safia." Judith turned up her beer, sat the glass down, walked over to the corner, and grabbed random hues of paint. "Just look at that big empty wall." She gave Safia a feral smile as a shock of wayward red hair fell across her face.

"Okay, do you have an easel?"

"Yes. That wall." Judith pointed to the blank terra cotta-colored wall before her and opened the lid of the bright blue paint. The scents of linseed oil and hyacinth filled the basement. She dipped a hand into the jar and flung the paint onto the wall with a splat.

Safia grabbed a bright orange, opened it, and detected daylilies. Like her, he'd not been able to order manufactured paint and had learned to make it from nature. Soon the two women were flinging paint at the wall with all their might. Safia didn't know for how long. They just kept going until exhaustion set in. Safia cried with an occasional laugh, punctuating the madness of the moment. She felt something loosen and break free deep inside her heart.

Judith walked forward and smeared her hands in a circular pattern in the paint in one corner, as if creating a moon in a lighter blue portion of the wall canvas. She stepped back to admire their work but rubbed a shirt sleeve across her eyes first.

Safia felt suddenly spent and eased herself onto the cold brick floor. Judith sat down next to her. "Thanks for that," Safia said.

Judith nodded and sat in silence for a moment before speaking. "I like it."

"Might be the most worthwhile thing I've ever created." Safia offered Judith a paint-splattered hand. They clasped briefly and then admired their handy work some more.

Judith said, "Harlow's going to faint when I tell her this, but I think I'm going to ask Jack to put in a good word for me with Dr. Hagen and Nakamura so I can finish my nursing training on board the *Ares*. There's no reason but stubborn bullshit that I haven't done it already. I was so close to completing my degree. I could do it."

"Of course you could."

Safia looked at the woman as she nodded her head. If the fog could lift for someone grieving as deeply as Judith, then there was a way out for her, too. She just had to find it.

CHAPTER 25

A WOMAN WITH A PLAN

Harlow sat in the kitchen of her mother's old flat with Safia. Even though it was barely noon, Harlow had brought over a few beers that she'd purchased from district four. Word had traveled about O'Malley's destruction, and brewers in neighboring districts cashed in. She couldn't blame them. Lance from hydraulics said the brewer was his cousin and promised the drink wouldn't kill anyone. She suspected Safia would need it. After giving it a good sniff, she took a tentative sip and was pleasantly surprised.

She watched Judith playing with Bella and Selah on the worn living room rug. No one questioned what had finally made Judith leave Eoghan's. Apparently Safia had been by to see Judith but hadn't said much about the visit. It had been two weeks since the bombing and other than the funeral, Judith had not emerged from his house. Harlow had sent several messages inviting her to dinner or asking to come over and sit with her, all to no avail, but she'd messaged that she was bringing Selah over to play with Bella that morning, and when she arrived, Judith was there.

The girls and Judith were throwing popcorn into each other's mouths, and, of course, also eating what missed. No one wasted food on Mars. Bella had popped it herself, literally. She'd held her hands over the kernels and laughed as each one began to slowly pop beneath her touch. Harlow was always amazed that the girl could use heat in that way without burning herself. Yet Selah could freeze without freezing herself. She supposed the heat and cold transfer had more to do with manipulating the atoms around them than it did with generating something inside them and pushing it outward, or it likely would've burned or frozen them.

Harlow watched Safia take a drink of the beer and nod in appreciation. "Not bad." Then she looked at Harlow and sighed.

"He's a wreck, if you must know," Harlow said. She tried not to be defensive toward her, but Carlos was her friend, too, and he was hurting.

"You're angry at me. I get it. There's more to this than you know."

Harlow remembered her own situation when she couldn't tell anyone about Aldric blackmailing her for fear he would drop viruses on the unvaccinated colonists. "Who's blackmailing *you*?"

"It's not that simple, but I hope when things get better around here, we'll be able to find our way back to each other. I love him. I really do."

Harlow didn't miss the quiver in Safia's voice or the tears that she held suspended at the corners of her eyes.

"Good Lord! Whatever it is, just tell him about it already. You two can work it out."

"Do you believe it was that simple for you and Jack?" Safia asked.

"I guess not." Harlow took another swig of her beer and thought it was best to move on to a subject they could have some sense of control over. Keeping her voice low, she said, "Listen, I've been considering something for a while. Jack says that it's technically 'unethical.'" Harlow held up finger quotes and rolled her eyes. "But since I saw bodies lying in front of a gutted O'Malley's, I don't give a shit about ethics. I want to bug the restaurant."

Safia's eyebrows shot up. Harlow laughed and glanced into the living room to make sure her mother wasn't listening, then leaned in and spoke softer. "Think about it. Now that O'Malley's is gone, it's the only place in this district where people settle in to stay awhile and talk. Not all planning happens in secret. At some point, one of them is bound to slip up and say something. This way, we'll know who it is and maybe prevent the next bombing."

Safia lowered her beer and looked at Harlow before looking at the floor. "I tried to stop it. Someone *did* talk in the restaurant. There was chatter about Rupert, the man that made the bottles for O'Malley's. I went to his house the night of the bombing, and his door was rigged. I got blown off my ass. It was too late, anyway. I went the very night I heard it. Even if I'd told security, they'd have had to wait on a warrant. It would have been the next day before they could have gotten in."

Harlow leaned in and spoke to Safia in a venomous whisper. "Who was with you?"

"No one."

"Damn it, you and I need to have a very long talk later about you not going in alone. I didn't teach you that! You aren't being smart about this. You're making me wish I'd never suggested any of it."

The look on Safia's face made Harlow regret scolding her but only partly. She'd feel even worse if she'd gotten killed or gone to jail. Harlow took a deep breath. "We can talk more about this later. I love you. I don't want to lose anyone else." Harlow leaned back. "Anyway, I think we need to start listening in on the Sojourner on the daily."

Judith walked over, picked up Harlow's beer, and took a drink before speaking, "I want in."

"Jesus, Mom, you've got ears like a bat!"

"Yeah, I know. I've spent every day since Eoghan died searching for a way to find out who bombed O'Malley's and who was behind the person who did it, supplying them, informing them, encouraging them. No way it was just one person."

"She's right," Safia said. "This was an everyday thing when I was growing up in Spain during the war. For every bombing like this, there's usually an entire network. You can't stop at the guy who lit the fuse."

Judith spoke with fire in her eyes. "Then we don't stop."

• • •

It had been a week since Safia and Judith had set the listening devices. So far, they hadn't recovered much of anything. But they had listened with a mix of horror and humor as they heard one paranoid theory after another about Safia and Harlow's children and the others who'd survived Aldric's compound. Because Bella, Selah, Tara's son, Gabriel, and Tamar's daughter, Behar, had special abilities, some people in their district had strange theories that the children were either alien-human hybrids or full-on aliens themselves, perhaps even planted among their own children to infiltrate humanity. Though that kind of conspiracy mongering might be something they'd need to keep their eyes on, it wasn't exactly what they were looking for.

Bella sat in the corner booth coloring and singing a soothing tune. She drew a Martian sunset with a blending of colors that was hard to look away from. Safia knew the artistry came from her, but the beautiful singing voice, well, she couldn't carry a tune if her life depended on it. She wondered, not for the first time, if this were some sort of genetic quirk from the tampering or if Bella would have had this ability, regardless. Or did it come from her father? She banished the thought. Though she had to admit, since seeing Alvaro, she wondered about him more and what Bella might have inherited from him. If only there was a way to get that information from him without him knowing she was his child. But there wasn't.

It was almost closing time. She wiped down the last of the tables and grabbed the trash cans as she usually did. She put her jacket on and stepped into the frigid Martian night. They placed the composters just over a small hill in order to control the smell. Composting was mandatory on Mars. There were no landfills. Each business was responsible for either breaking down its own biological waste or repurposing or recycling what couldn't be composted. Safia walked over the hill and immediately experienced the smells of composting debris: what little food got thrown out, mold, and rancid oils. Her path was lit by the soft glow of a solar-powered light that would stay illuminated for half the night, and down the few steps leading to the platform she would stand on to drop the material in. She emptied the can, hit the button for the solar-powered arms that would mix the compost and soil, then turned to head back in.

"How's our daughter doing?" Alvaro stood at the base of the hill.

Safia's heart began slamming against her chest. She thought about Bella in the restaurant with Judith and hoped the cook hadn't left yet. His lungs weren't in the best shape, but he was handy with a knife.

"What are you talking about?" she hissed.

"I know that girl belongs to me."

"She belongs to Carlos!"

"Then why isn't she *with* Carlos?"

Safia was wondering that herself as she stood looking at her nightmare in the flesh. She was also wondering why she hadn't remembered to put the stun gun back into her jacket pocket that morning before work. "That's none of your business." She tried to sound brave, but terror was washing over her in waves. He could just kill her, dump her into the compost heap, race in and grab Bella, and be gone before anyone knew what happened. What was wrong with her? Harlow had been training with her. She knew jiujitsu better than many of the men on board the ship; she'd even beaten the hell out of Maricopa's husband. Yet the man before her had her terrified. Flashes of that night in the alley played out in her mind.

He came up the steps and stood right in front of her. If she backed up, she would tumble onto the compost and dirt below. It was dark, and she was unsure of her footing if she stepped down. The last thing she wanted was to end up sprawled on the ground where he could get on top of her again. If she shoved past him, he would react by grabbing her. She knew it clear to her bones. So, she held still, hoping he would become bored by the conversation and leave. How many women had done the same? She'd tried running past him long ago and could never forget how that had ended.

She said, "I don't know what you hope to gain."

"I just want to know my daughter. I have a right."

Safia scoffed. "She isn't yours, and even if she was, you wouldn't 'have a right.' A rapist doesn't have a right to a child they sire. That's nonsense."

Rage flashed behind his eyes. He slapped her so hard her ears rang for a second.

She couldn't believe it could all be happening again. A feeling of absolute defeat washed over her to know that there was nowhere in the solar system she could go to be free of this monster. *Think, think. Despair won't help you now.*

She remembered the night Judith had dropped the trash can behind the restaurant. It had been loud enough that she ran out to check on her. She tossed the trash can over the hill, and it gave the satisfying crash that she intended.

"This isn't over," he said through clenched teeth that was quickly replaced by a wicked grin as he leaned in as if to kiss her. Rage swept through her, and she shoved his chest with both hands. Wild eyes looked at her as his arms pinwheeled, and he stumbled backwards off the platform and tumbled into the regolith and decaying compost. He thrashed around before he got his footing and fled into the area obscured by the hillside.

It baffled her that he had given up so easily. The smell of burning cotton reached her nose above the stench of the composting bin beside them. Something clung to her fingertips. She strained to see what it was in the dim light. Bits of his charred shirt clung to her trembling fingers. "What the hell?" she whispered.

She heard the backdoor to the restaurant open. "Safia?" Judith called into the night. "Are you okay?"

Safia took a deep breath to calm her racing heart. How did she explain all this? Judith could be a hothead. If she told her the truth, she would stomp onto the *Ares* before sunrise, drag Jack out of bed, and force him to activate the entire Ares Army to hunt down Alvaro. Hell, she'd likely demand his head, or take it herself. Safia would like to see that, but he was actually doing a good job rooting out the Brotherhood, despite the pub bombing. They needed him now more than ever, from a tactical standpoint. *No, he's after Bella. I have to do something.*

"Safia? What are you doing?"

"I'm sorry. There was a rat in the can. I threw it without even thinking."

Judith looked over her head and into the night, as if sensing the danger. "Well, come on inside. It's fucking creepy out here."

You have no idea, she thought, as she looked down at her palms.

CHAPTER 26

WE NEED TO TALK

Harlow sat on the bed with a digital slate, designing a small garden for Selah's class, while Jack sat at his desk dealing with colony business. She didn't envy him that job; she'd much rather be working on the garden. With all the chaos going on after the explosion, it felt good to do something she could control. The diagram before her represented the order life here was lacking. It made her wonder if her father had similar feelings as he designed components of the *Ares.*

A hologram popped up in front of her, breaking her concentration. Next to an image of Carlos's face was a message that read, "We need to talk. Observation deck? Now?"

Her eyebrows scrunched together. It wasn't like Carlos to be so demanding or to want to talk this late at night. She powered down the slate and shoved her feet back into her boots. "Jack, Carlos wants to talk to me about something."

"Hmm, let me guess."

"Probably. Yeah. I'm meeting him on the observation deck."

Jack looked up from his work. "It's awfully late."

"I know. So, it must be pretty important." Harlow leaned over and gave Jack a kiss on the cheek before leaving, but he grabbed the back of her head and pulled her in for a deeper kiss. Since the explosion, every moment had become precious. When he drew back, she saw the longing in his eyes. It would be a late night again. He needed her. She needed him, too.

When Harlow reached the observation deck, she found it deserted except for Carlos. Whether it was that way when he arrived or his storm-cloud countenance had made it so, she didn't know. She couldn't recall ever seeing him this brooding before. He stood with his arms crossed over his chest and met her eye the second she entered the room.

"Carlos, what's going on? You all right?"

"No. I'm not. Safia's been going full-on vigilante lately. I wanted to talk to you about it before the explosion, but things have been complete chaos since, and I'm afraid all of this shit is just going to make it worse until she ends up getting herself killed. Would you know anything about that?"

"She mentioned a couple of days ago that she'd tried to get into Rupert's house and got knocked on her ass. I told her how stupid it was to go in alone."

He looked at her just a beat long enough to let her know he believed she was the instigator. While she'd trained Safia, the attempt to break into Rupert's was Safia's idea alone. Except for debriefing her about meting out justice to Vincent and their exchange at Judith's about bugging the Sojourner, Safia had scarcely spoken to her. They'd all been too busy.

He said, "Safia almost got herself killed the night O'Malley's went up." He walked closer to Harlow and lowered his voice. "She broke her arm and cracked her ribs. It could've been even worse. Don't tell me you didn't know about all this."

"I had no idea until she told me about taking a tumble."

"But you knew about the other thing?"

"The situation with Maricopa? Yes, but she had backup," Harlow said.

"No, she didn't."

"What? Are you sure?" Harlow felt sick.

"Very. That's the first night I caught her. She was definitely alone."

"Damn it. I told her to always bring backup. Did she get caught? Did anyone get evidence of her doing it?"

"No, when she got injured at Rupert's, I told Hagen she fell while working overtime at the Sojourner."

Harlow nodded. "I'll talk to her. Carlos, this was never my intention. I really thought that if she could get a little of her power back, it would help the two of you find your way to each other again. God, I never thought she would go in alone. I told her to always bring backup. I guess I underestimated just how dark her state of mind is. I swear I could just kill the son of a bitch that did this to her. All this shit started five years ago."

Carlos nodded. "If I knew who that bastard was, I'd beat you to it." He exhaled and dropped his shoulders. "Sorry, I'm not looking to tear into you, mi hermana pequeña."

"I know," she said and then leaned in and gave him a hug. "I'll talk to her."

"Please do. I don't think she'll listen to me right now."

Harlow released the hug so she could see his face. "Why not? She still loves and respects you."

"I might have just made things worse. I got after her about being reckless with the incident at Rupert's house, and that led to a discussion about our relationship that didn't go too well either. I don't know what's changed lately. I mean, she never wanted to marry me, but we didn't fight either. We were happy," Carlos said with a sad smile. "Maybe it's because, you know, she's never been with anyone other than me. Bella's father," he said as if the word were stabbing him, "certainly doesn't count."

"No, he does not," Harlow said through a well of barely contained rage. "But I don't think a lack of partners is the problem. She's just dealing with some serious stuff."

She watched him walk over to the large observation windows, lean against the window frame, and look out into the night. "We loved each other so much. You know."

"I know. It's like she has a death wish now," Harlow said. "Or..."

"Or what?"

"Maybe somewhere inside she's trying to prove she can be okay if it's just her alone, facing another situation like what happened in Spain. I don't know. Whatever it is, it has to stop. I'll talk to her."

"Please do."

"Carlos, just don't give up."

When he turned to face her, Harlow could see the pain etched across his face. "I don't want to, but I'm beginning to think that holding on is what's hurting me."

CHAPTER 27

WHAT IT'S LIKE

Safia's comm started going off before her eyes opened. She mumbled the command to activate the mic and speaker—no way would she let anyone see a hologram of her. It was still an hour before she had to wake up to go get breakfast service started at the Sojourner with Judith. "Yes?" she said in a scratchy voice.

Her eyes went wide as Dr. Hagen's nurse explained the situation. A scaffolding had fallen during the rebuild of O'Malley's, and she was listed as Carlos's emergency contact. It did not surprise her to hear that he'd gotten hurt by shoving someone out of harm's way.

"There's a serious shoulder injury, but we're more worried about internal damage. He's conscious. That's a good sign. You might want to come over, though."

Safia got dressed in a hurry and called Judith at Eoghan's asking if she could drop Bella off there before heading to the *Ares.*

When she arrived in the hallway outside the infirmary, Jack, McNamara and his younger brother, Lennon, and Mike O'Malley—whom Safia hadn't seen in over two weeks—waited. O'Malley had always had wild auburn hair, as if he'd taken the worst of a Martian sandstorm every morning when he woke up. Only now, he had the haunted, manic look in his eyes to match the hair.

Safia wanted to ask one of them what had happened. So, she quickly tallied up the odds who would be the least hostile towards her. Carlos was very well-liked and from their point of view, she was hurting him for no reason.

She approached Jack first. He said, “Doc just came out and said there was a rupture in his spleen, but they got it patched up. He’s going to be okay.”

“It was horrible,” Lennon McNamara said. “He was bleeding everywhere.”

Safia realized O’Malley wasn’t the only one with haunted eyes. She nodded and tried her best at a reassuring look.

McNamara said, “He’s dealing with a little survivor’s guilt. Carlos shoved Lennon out of the way of the collapsing scaffolding.”

“That definitely sounds like Carlos.”

Jack and the two McNamaras nodded and gave various versions of agreement, but Mike O’Malley remained silent and glared at her. It was beyond unsettling. She’d never known him to be anything but kind, friendly, and generous of spirit.

Jack turned and addressed Safia, “Well, I’m sure it will be a while, and it sounds as if he’s right brill now. I’m going to go take care of a couple things and come back.” He placed a hand on her shoulder. “He’ll be happy you are here.”

She replied softly. “Do I look that unsure?”

“Aye, well. A little. Yes.”

Across from them Mike O’Malley snorted.

Jack patted Safia’s arm reassuringly before walking over and speaking quietly to Mike. She couldn’t hear what they said, but from the look on Mike’s face as he whisper-argued with Jack, she wasn’t sure she wanted to.

• • •

When Dr. Hagen finished treating his shoulder, Carlos moved it in circles, testing his range of motion.

“Feels better?” Doc asked.

“Much, thank you.”

"All right then, hero. I'll let you get dressed." Dr. Hagen headed toward the door.

As Carlos slipped into his ripped and bloodied shirt, Safia came into the room. His heart picked up its pace to a thundering rhythm. There it was, that post-action adrenaline that made him want to take her to bed but *not* to sleep. He stopped buttoning his shirt, knowing how Safia loved to run her hands over his chest, but he wouldn't allow it if she tried. *Are you really that strong? She's got that look in her eye. Button your shirt up, fool. Unless you want it...*

They stood facing each other for what felt like minutes but was only seconds. "I was scared I would never see you again," she said.

"It shouldn't take a near-death experience to make you want me," Carlos said.

"It doesn't. I want you all day, every day."

He walked over to her and kept walking until he had her pressed against the wall. He couldn't allow her to touch him. It would be too much. He would fall and keep falling with no hope of catching himself. Logic was dismissed as he grabbed her forearms, pinning her to the wall, and kissed her hungrily. He moved his mouth down to her neck, raking his teeth against skin. He felt himself get hard instantly and pressed it against her. He heard her breath catch in her throat. He knew what she craved, didn't like, couldn't resist. He slid a hand beneath her shirt and touched her the way she liked.

She moaned in response. He looked around the room for somewhere to take her. He could bend her over the exam table and... *No, damn it!* With a Herculean effort, he tore himself away from her, putting distance between their bodies but gripping her forearms in his hands.

"Please, Carlos. Don't let go."

"Don't let go? And keep holding on while you ignore me, play games with me?" He started to say "hurt me" but wouldn't give her that much, to let her see him that vulnerable. "How does it feel to be denied?" He knew what he was doing was cruel on some level, but it was cruel to ask the woman he loved to marry him and be denied over and over, for her to leave him and take their daughter with no warning, to destroy his favorite painting, to never tell him why.

He let go of her and stepped away. Looking down at his cargo pants, he realized he couldn't go anywhere just yet. He opened the door and motioned for her to leave, refusing to look at her again.

CHAPTER 28

HOMEWARD BOUND

Marcus knew it was time to return home. His guards stood a few feet away as he sat on the hood of the buggy and watched Mike O'Malley, a few villagers, and people he recognized from the ship—Carlos, Evelyn, her wife Seraph, McNamara, and others—raise the frame of the south wall. Within a week or two, the bar would receive customers again. He marveled at their resilience. His heart ached as he thought of heading to his cavernous home. It was one thing to live in the palace with a father he couldn't please but quite another to have no one there at all anymore.

He'd received Mikhail's messages and knew the man had his own utopian, dictator agenda. Getting the *Ares* back into the hands of the original coalition might put that dream one small step closer to reality for him, but it wouldn't change things that much. Mikhail just didn't like seeing Jack aboard the *Ares*. It smacked of a monarchy-controlled Mars, which Mikhail viewed as a shackle upon people everywhere. Hell, he wasn't entirely wrong either. There had been some real bastards through the ages, and his family was no exception, but Jack wasn't looking to be king of Mars. The thought was ridiculous to Jack. No, Marcus decided, he'd tell Mikhail to get a damn hobby, and he'd go back to London where he belonged, although he had to admit he'd miss Yua, perhaps more than Jack.

As he motioned to his guards that it was time to go and they got in the buggy to head back to the *Ares* where his transport was docked, he saw Harlow and Safia racing toward him in their own sputtering ride. His guards jumped back out and started to go for their weapons. The bombing had them understandably jumpy.

"Whoa! It's Harlow." They relaxed, and he got out to meet them as they stopped a few feet away and parked.

Harlow slammed her door and jogged to meet Marcus. "We need to talk."

Marcus watched Harlow cut her eyes at the guards who were sticking closer than ever, given the recent bombings, and he realized she didn't want them within earshot. He held out a hand for them to stay put while he walked farther away from them, and Harlow and Safia began telling their story about the listening devices in the Sojourner. The more they talked, the sicker he felt. "You've been doing what? That's an invasion of privacy, you know," Marcus said.

"Yeah," Harlow said, "we get it. Just listen. They know where Jack is every second of the day. They know everything! We need more than a couple of anti-terrorist specialists. We need you to go back to Earth and send actual help. Jesus Christ, Marcus. They're going to kill him." She looked away quickly, but not before he saw the glassy look of tears threatening to spill over.

Marcus had never seen Harlow rattled. On his visits to Mars, he'd come to respect her strong, calm, intelligent personality, but this time... she had him scared, though he tried not to show it for her sake.

"Parliament won't help Jack unless he disbands the new coalition and turns over the *Ares* to the Crown and the countries that helped built it."

Safia looked sick. "If he does that, Carlos and all the others who've been declared traitors will be punished—maybe even executed. They've given up everything to support Jack. If you don't stand behind them..."

"Yes. I know. I'll do all I can to have that overturned. Listen, framing is everything." He recalled what he'd discussed with Worthington about visiting the colony and how to frame it. "I can meet with the President and explain to him how Carlos and the others are heroes for not abandoning these families who had nowhere else to go. How they stayed here to keep order and defend Mars from falling into lawlessness. I can tell him how the colony would have ended up in the hands of terrorists without the likes of Carlos. I really believe we can work this out." He didn't know what had gone on between Safia and Carlos, but clearly, she loved him despite their breakup. Everyone knowing everyone else's business was one thing he wouldn't miss when he went back to London, but he supposed it came with the territory.

"I promise I will do what I can. There are contractors who would come here and help root out the terrorists. They are very good at what they do. I can put Jack in touch with the right people, off the record, but I can't do anything in any official capacity unless he is willing to let go of everything. If he doesn't, he'll be tried for treason."

"They can't do that," Harlow said.

"They can, Harlow. They have declared him to have abdicated by virtue of desertion, so, now he can be tried for treason. Parliament tried Charles the First for treason and executed him. Of course, I would do everything I could, and I doubt it would come to that. He hasn't fired on London or anything of the sort, but it could get extremely ugly." Marcus exhaled and scrubbed his hands across his face. "None of that matters if we can't keep him alive. Let me hear these conversations that *don't exist*," he said, looking at them both to make sure they knew not to tell anyone else about them, "but also go against the charter of the colonies." He motioned for them to return to their ride as he muttered curses under his breath.

The guards drove Marcus to Judith's flat, then waited outside while he went in.

The good news was, Safia, Harlow, and Judith had gotten solid information, enough to help Jack avoid certain places, and they even knew of at least two people who needed arresting immediately, but the man and woman they'd recorded spoke of a web of not only loyalist but Brotherhood terrorists on Mars as well. He knew it deep in his bones: if Jack didn't leave this place, he would die.

Marcus sat in silence after he finished listening. The silence was a presence unto itself, just as it was when his father lay dead beside him at the palace.

"Okay, I know what must be done," Marcus said as he rose from his chair.

"What?" Harlow asked.

"I need time to straighten it out. Just give me a day, and I'll let you know."

Marcus nodded at Judith on the way out, and Selah smiled up at him as he left. He wasn't just doing this for Jack anymore. All these people had become his family, and he'd do what he had to, to protect them.

He thought of Harlow and her connection to the *Ares*. He remembered her running her hand along the wall of the ship and telling him about how she believed her father's consciousness was somewhere inside it. It almost made him cry, but a king had to make hard choices, even if it meant the only family he'd ever loved would hate him.

Marcus got back in the buggy and his guards drove him to the ship.

He mourned what he needed to do.

CHAPTER 29

JOSEF

Josef walked into the compound garden with seven-year-old Rory on his shoulders. He reached up to the child and spun him down and around, as he had many times. Together, they gathered the last of the tomatoes from the vines and placed them in the bag.

Josef heard stones cracking against each other on the other side of the yard as Goliath, the largest of the children, started in on the stacks of rock that Evangeline had pulled from the ground for him after he'd smashed all the rocks he could find nearby. All the children had boiling fast metabolisms, and Goliath needed the physical release.

Kailani and Cordelia disappeared for hours at a time in the large pool they'd built near the compound; they could hold their breath for nearly 45 minutes, even longer if need be. The golden-eyed twins, due to a natural Mars mutation, Sabre and Favor, could channel light through their bodies, due to the genomic tampering, and they were just beginning to understand what that meant, other than being able to light up the darkness. Jung was a telekinetic as was Evangeline, who also bore the burden of extreme empathy. Martin and Levi each had an incredible head for math. At six, they devoured equations but had no physical manifestation of power. Rory, who had a gift for healing, seldom ventured out on his own. He stayed close to Josef and watched, always. He watched Josef, the others, animals, always looking for an opportunity to relieve suffering. His gift *could* work in reverse. Mikhail pointed that out many times. Josef had refused to allow him to be used in that way at such a young age; perhaps once he was older and needed to defend himself.

"Tell me about my name again, Father Josef," the little, red-headed boy said to his caregiver.

Josef smiled every time he or the other children called him Father Josef. He was certainly no priest. One of them wanted to call him father, but he wasn't their father, though he'd been raising many of them since birth—they'd even taken on a slight Russian accent from being in his care. The children heard others call him Josef, a name he liked because he so admired Josef of the Holy Family who had raised the Blessed Messiah so selflessly.

At some point, one child had combined the two. It had caught on with the ten children, and it felt right to him. These children were small messiahs, not yet aware of their glorious potential. They thought their abilities were normal. The miraculous strength, budding telekinesis, imperviousness to heat or cold, being able to breathe underwater, read auras, and who knew what was yet to emerge. The children had various incarnations of these gifts, all fascinating.

He, Aldric, and Mikhail had found that altering one gene often enhanced others and brought surprising results. He saw it with all the children there and was sure the ones that had escaped them: Harlow, Safia, Tara, and Tamar's children would be the same.

"Well, when you were born, you had fiery red hair, and when you cried, it was no ordinary wail but sounded like a battle cry. That's when I knew your name should be Rory. It means red-haired chief. Your hair is red, this land is red." Josef gestured beyond the patch of green where he and the boy stood to the red-orange Mars regolith beyond. "You are a chief, born to rule. Never forget. That is your birthright. And it is my calling to lead you, guide you." He placed his hand over his heart.

"Just like Josef from the picture of the Holy Family that you put in my room."

Josef nodded. "Just so." He could feel Rory staring at him and met his gaze. "Yes?"

"How did you get the mark across your eye?"

Josef thought about the day that changed his life forever. When the memories flooded in, he felt as if the scar were burning. "Father Josef doesn't like to talk about it," he said. He leaned over and began moving leaves back from the underside of the tomato plant. It was easy to miss the smaller cherry tomatoes when the foliage was thick. Out of his periphery, Rory's small hand came into view, reaching toward his old injury. Josef jerked away quickly as his pulse quickened. For the first time, he feared the child before him. Rory looked startled by his reaction.

"I'm sorry," Rory said.

"It's okay. You are only trying to help."

"You don't want to be healed?" Rory asked.

"No, I do not."

"But everyone should want to be healed."

"Not if it reminds them of something important. Something they should never forget."

Rory tilted his head and looked at him. Josef knew that despite how advanced Rory's genetics were, the absolute *miracle* that they were, there were still things that only time and experience could teach him. "Someday you'll understand."

The little boy picked a couple more tomatoes and placed them in the bag. Josef felt eyes on him again. "You have more questions?"

"Where is my mother?" Rory asked.

Josef's mouth went dry, and his palms sweated despite the crisp fall day. His hand instinctively made its way toward the scar until he noticed the motion and stopped himself. "She has passed to the other realm, just like the Holy Family, and she looks over you now like they do."

"Oh," the little boy said while looking away from Josef. They continued their gardening in silence. Josef tried to mask his feelings. It wasn't easy as images of Rory's mother pressed down on him, oppressive, beautiful, painful, conflicting... gone. He suspected that in addition to being a healer, Rory was also a budding empath. It made sense that the two gifts might go hand in hand. He hoped the empathy never grew too strong. It would only hurt the child.

A few minutes later, Evangeline came over and began using telekinesis to pick the rest of the tomatoes. She made them bounce gently against the top of Rory's head by delicately wiggling her fingers in his direction. Evangeline was also an empath. Josef was sure she'd sensed Rory's sorrow from across the yard and couldn't help but respond.

Sometimes he worried that empathy would be her downfall. The gift had been a byproduct of trying to create a human capable of mind reading to detect threats or take secrets for the righteous cause. Instead, it had produced a gentle soul who read emotions and auras, someone more likely to empathize with an enemy and get herself killed, perhaps along with the rest of them as well. Josef didn't know whether to teach Rory to protect her or be willing to let her go the moment she sold them out someday to protect an enemy she felt too much compassion for. Deep down, he knew he feared the same fate for Rory.

Rory giggled as he reached up to catch the tomatoes and looked back at Josef.

"We've got all the vegetables for today. Go tell the others it's time for training."

He watched disappointment cloud Rory's face for the briefest of moments before he carefully concealed his feelings once more. Ten minutes later, they met in the training building where he had walled off individual cell blocks to mimic the Bastille. He knew it so well because of the time he'd spent there. It gave him a shudder to know he had to go back into that place, but he'd do it for the cause. He'd do it to create a better world for the flock he led.

"Kailani, pretend to be a prisoner coming at me with a weapon."

Kailani picked up a stick and ran toward Josef, but Evangeline hesitated.

"Evangeline! Wake up!" Jung, the other telekinetic, yelled at her. He yanked the stick from Kailani's grasp and levitated her, pressing her back against the wall. She gave a slight grunt as she hit the Martian bricks.

Rory ran to the wall and looked up at Kailani. "You okay?"

"She's fine. I didn't hurt her." Jung rolled his eyes at the ever-sensitive Rory and lowered Kailani back to the ground.

Josef patted Rory on the shoulder. "She's fine. Jung wouldn't hurt his sister. That's exactly my point, children. You only need to separate them from their weapons. Pull the weapon from their grasp, pin it to the wall out of their reach. Don't just throw it across the room where someone else could pick it up and shoot a member of your family. Yes?"

"Yes, Father," they replied.

"Let's try this again. This time, in the dark. Sabre and Favor will channel light for us." Josef turned and looked at the sensitive little empath. "Evangeline, we need you." He watched her take a deep breath and wipe her palms across her pant legs.

• • •

Later, Josef sat in his chair in the garden contemplating the awesome responsibility he'd been given. No, had been destined for, a fate established with the foundation of the universe. He'd read many scriptures about predestination. This was the first generation of humans born with capabilities this advanced. Sure, past scientists had learned to weed out common ailments from the human genome like diabetes, certain cancers and diseases, but tapping the brain's potential, pushing the lungs beyond what they were created to do,

Rory's ability to rearrange at a cellular level and heal... He was the overseer of these young gods, the father, the one chosen, The Chosen One...

"Josef!"

Mikhail's sharp voice startled him from his reverie. He looked up to find Mikhail holding the two antique cut crystal glasses he'd carried with him from Earth to his exile on Enceladus, now here to Mars, and an unlabeled bottle of honey-colored liquor of some sort. The man had a wild look in his eye. Joseph had seen it before. The look frightened and exhilarated him. On the heels of that look, that madness, often came genius. Other times... he didn't like to think of the other times. He just tried his best to stand clear.

Mikhail sat the two glasses down on the old carbon fiber table, pulled the glass stopper from the bottle and poured both glasses a quarter full of the liquid. Josef noticed he did not sit down with him in the opposite chair.

Mikhail spoke. "This is a momentous occasion. From here, the wheels turn quickly. For this, you stand."

Josef stood and picked up the glass.

Mikhail lifted his drink and proclaimed, "The *Ares* is ours." He nodded to Josef, and they both drank. "The king requests a meeting."

Josef enjoyed the burn of the alcohol and the licorice-like aftertaste. "As long as Harlow is on board, the *Ares* will obey her."

"Who says she'll be on board?"

CHAPTER 30

DEALS WITH A DEVIL

Marcus slipped the watchful gaze of the guards when he went into the washroom. His quarters were a suite, and he'd noted that the door on the opposite side opened into another hallway after it turned at a ninety-degree angle.

He dressed down, way down, wearing the comfortable cargos and t-shirt he'd worn on the transport ride to the colonies. Pulling his hat low over his head, he hoped no one would notice him until he reached the buggy he and his personnel had been using. He lifted his hat to show the posted *Ares* guard it was indeed his ride. The man on duty was originally from London and had been star-struck whenever in Marcus's presence. Now, he seemed so overwhelmed that Marcus simply gave him a wink and a smile and drove away. In time, the guard might come to his senses and tell Jack, but Marcus figured he'd be back before anyone got properly panicked.

He rode away into the outback. The coordinates arrived via an unmonitored channel. Bile made a searing path up his throat as he drove across the regolith to meet the dragon but was certain that if it were the right thing, then it was sure to be hard.

Mikhail arrived with another man in the buggy beside him. The man looked to be in his forties, with Asian features. This time, Marcus had activated a shield around himself, just in case. He contemplated the stupidity of driving out here alone. Mikhail got out of the vehicle, but the other man stayed inside.

As before, Mikhail lit a cigar before speaking. He took a deep puff and smoke rose around him, making him appear as the dragon Marcus had thought him to be all these years. "Now you know what's happening on Mars," he said.

"Yes."

"You can make it stop. You take that ship, give them the same deals they're getting now with their newly formed coalition, but with the old one instead, and let them keep their colony intact. Your brother can even save all the face he wants. Once the Earth coalition is back in control of Mars, it won't be hard to convince them he was just acting in the best interest of the colonists and that you and the others should be merciful. Your parents are gone; let the world know just enough about the raw deal your father was giving these people in order to spite Jack but not so much that it looks like you are siding with him.

Marcus thought about what Mikhail was saying. He didn't trust the man, that was true, but he had a point. The old coalition didn't hate the people of Mars, they just couldn't afford to supply them anymore. Well, some of them were taking advantage. His father had been one of them, but getting supplies to Mars was a major undertaking. Things were tough all over. He reached up and felt the stitches on his forehead. No one at the palace would have had to endure anything as barbaric, or a heart attack for that matter, yet colonists on Mars still received sutures and died of cardiac arrest because Earth wouldn't part with their medical equipment or the parts to rebuild broken med tech on Mars. The colonists lived or rather died, on scraps.

"It won't end until they kill your brother. Probably Harlow, too, and your aunt Mary, of course."

Marcus felt panic race through his body at the thought. They'd survived what happened at O'Malley's, but their luck couldn't hold forever. He would be a fool to believe the bombings would simply stop. "I couldn't take that ship if I tried. I simply don't know how."

"I do."

"See, that's what troubles me."

Mikhail held up a hand and motioned for the man in the buggy to come forward.

"This is Jianyu. He can get past any encryption."

"Nice to meet you, but this is the *Ares.* What makes you think you can get past the encryption on the most powerful piece of tech in the solar system?"

"Because I've gotten past it before."

Marcus cringed. Jack had almost gotten killed on Enceladus when the *Ares* had been disabled. He asked Jianyu, "You were on Enceladus?"

The man said nothing, but his cold gaze spoke volumes.

"No, I'm out," Marcus said, and began walking away. Voices came from behind him that belonged to neither Mikhail nor Jianyu. It was a recording. "He goes out unprotected half the time. You'd think with all the bombings, he would keep a shield up constantly. Those two guards that are with him can't protect him from a sniper aiming at his head. An opportunity to take that arrogant bastard out is a guarantee." The recording ended. Apparently, Safia and Harlow weren't the only ones eavesdropping.

"They won't go after him once you take the ship back. There won't be any reason to."

"He will never forgive me."

"If he's dead, it won't matter."

"As long as Harlow's on the ship, she can regain control," Marcus countered.

"She won't be on the ship. Leave that to me."

"No killing."

"You have my word."

Marcus considered what that man's word was worth.

. . .

The quartz monitor plates above the command consoles on the bridge had been upgraded. The new holograms provided greater clarity and more data. Marcus saw the old ones stacked up and ready for recycling when he had an idea. He'd spent hours of his teen years etching art into quartz panels as hologram technology slowly replaced them. It had been tearing at his guts that he would soon take the *Ares* from Harlow, knowing it was her connection to her father.

He took one of the panels to engineering and borrowed some tools. He worked through the night with the laser, etching the quartz into a work of art the size of his palm that held a picture of the starship with the words "*HMS Ares*" etched across the top. On the other side was her father's name. *It won't matter what you give her. After you take this ship from them, they will never forgive you.* He knew he couldn't live with himself if he lost his brother and did nothing to prevent it. The piece he was giving her actually contained the *Ares*, much as every cell of the body contained its DNA. Quartz held onto information like silicon chips of old but could hold it forever. Perhaps she would still be able to feel a connection to her father through it when the ship was long gone.

He stepped back from his work and admired it, feeling certain she would treasure this piece of her father's legacy, even if she ended up hating him for what he was about to do. He wrapped it in a cloth and walked outside the *Ares* to watch the sunrise over the ridge. His heart ached knowing that the only family he had would be lost to him after he did this. But, ironically, Jack had taught him that being king meant making hard choices, ones that you didn't want to make. He hated this one. It would render him utterly alone in two worlds.

He thought about who he could leave it with. Once he took the *Ares,* it might be a while before he could get their belongings back to them. He worried his niece would have a favorite toy he'd be taking from her. A lump formed in his throat at the thought. *How can you do this? It isn't just a ship. It's their home.*

In his mind's eye, though, he saw the bodies outside O'Malley's again and pictured himself pulling the sheet back from one of them and finding his brother there, and he knew his course of action was correct.

He walked into the Sojourner trailed by his guards, minutes after Judith had opened the doors for the breakfast crowd. He was glad to see her back among the living. She hadn't been back to work since Eoghan died weeks before.

"Good morning, Highness. Will you and your people be dining with us?" she said.

"Good morning. Well, I was hoping you could hold on to something for me and give it to Harlow after I'm gone. It's really important that she receive it then."

He watched Judith knit her brows and study him. "Okay. Sure." She held out her hand.

He gave her the package wrapped in a linen cloth, tied with ribbon, with a note tucked beneath the ribbon. She looked at the gift and back at him. "Are you okay?" She touched his arm briefly.

Damn, the woman was perceptive. "These are just daft times. I think we're all trying desperately to do the right thing, make the right choices for the people we love, even if they are unimaginably difficult ones."

She held his eyes a moment longer. "Huh, do I ever understand that one."

Maybe when the Earth coalition's relationship with Mars was restored and things calmed down in the colony, Judith could find happiness again. "I have a feeling things will start looking up soon."

"Let's hope so," she said.

He made a quick exit. He feared that one more moment beneath the shrewd woman's gaze would expose all his plans.

CHAPTER 31

LOSING *ARES*

Harlow ran through the ship, frantic. "Where is Selah?" She tore through the kitchen, the classrooms, everywhere she could think. Jack came running down the hallway with Aunt Mary. Harlow ran to him. "I can't find her anywhere. I don't know where else to look. What if the Brotherhood took her?"

"Jesus, Harlow! Don't say things like that. She's on this ship somewhere. We just have to find her."

Jack got on his comm device and began talking, but it was lost on Harlow. She tried to calm herself in order to think clearly, but panic was clouding her thoughts.

Carlos ran down the hallway next. "I'm here, boss."

Jack slapped him on the back and asked. "Can you go look around the goat pen and garden area?"

"Of course," Carlos said and looked at Harlow before leaving. "We're *going* to find her."

Aunt Mary put her arm around Harlow. "Why don't I go check in my quarters? She likes to come see me."

Harlow nodded. Daniel caught up with them in the hallway. Have you asked the *Ares* to run a facial image scan? See if it can find her anywhere aboard right now. It won't cover private quarters, but it will at least cover common areas. "Of course. What's wrong with me?"

Daniel gave a gentle smile. "Nothing. You're just worried."

Harlow placed her hands on the wall and thought her commands to the *Ares.* She felt it looking everywhere but found nothing. The implications of that made her feel even worse. If she was on the ship, she was in someone's private quarters.

Jack read another message on his device. "Someone saw her by the lake. See, it's all right. She's fine, Harlow. Let's go get her."

Before leaving with Harlow, he looked at Daniel. "Go ahead and have the *Ares* make a ship wide announcement about this please."

Her stomach ached at his words. He wasn't even certain Selah *was* at the lake.

• • •

Jack, his guards, Harlow, and Marcus, along with Marcus's guards, who'd also joined in the search, looked around the lake in utter confusion. Selah was nowhere to be found. Jack called the colony patrol, alarming Harlow further. If he believed it was time to call the patrol, then Selah was officially in danger.

"Evelyn, call Safia again," Jack said. "Maybe Selah was here and left to be with Bella."

Evelyn opened her comm and conversed with Safia while looking at Jack. She shook her head as she listened to Safia. "I'm sorry. She's still not there."

"Jack, what do we do?" Harlow asked.

He scrubbed his hands across his face and walked a few steps in one direction as if he had an idea, then stopped.

"Jack?" Harlow felt waves of panic washing over her.

"I don't know. I'm trying to think," he said.

Harlow saw the water on the lake begin to vibrate. A familiar feeling pulsed through her body, different from the adrenaline making her sick over Selah's disappearance. She didn't want to turn her head to confirm what she already knew in her heart. The ground shook beneath their feet. Only then did she turn to look at Jack as fresh tears streamed down her face. He was already looking at her, and they both knew. They'd been lured off the ship. Tricked.

She started running toward the *Ares*. She knew it was too far—there was no chance she would get there in time to make contact with it and keep it grounded. Dust swirled in all directions as it lifted from the ground, higher and higher, in a matter of heartbeats escape velocity took it from their atmosphere and out of her sight.

"Harlow!" Jack shouted. She could hear the grief and futility tearing through him just as it ripped through her own heart.

"What the hell's happening?" Evelyn said.

Harlow crumpled to the ground, feeling as if a piece of her soul was leaving the planet along with the ship. Behind her, she heard Jack, Evelyn, and Devante attempt to call different people on the *Ares*: Aunt Mary, Janet from engineering, Marcus, Doc, to no avail. All communication had been cut.

Harlow's thoughts were scattered, fragmented, every piece a grieving dark chasm that she could get lost in. She saw Jack in front of her with his mouth moving but couldn't process what he was saying. Slowly, her brain began to track the words coming from his mouth. "Harlow! You're scaring me. C'mon." Jack pulled her to her feet. She walked mechanically in the direction they took her.

"It's been hijacked," Jack said.

"Communication wouldn't be cut off otherwise," Evelyn concurred.

Harlow hadn't realized where they were going until they were already standing in Judith's front room, in the house where she'd grown up. It made sense; there was really nowhere else to go. Their home was the *Ares*. They were technically homeless now. All their belongings. *Oh, God!* "What if Selah was just lost on the ship somewhere, and she's not even on the planet anymore?" Harlow said, her words beginning to slur as the stress brought to the surface the remnants of her childhood speech and language disorder.

Harlow realized Evelyn was by her side with her hand on her back. It barely registered. "We'll find her. I promise," she said. "Maybe I should call your mother," she offered.

"No, she's still grieving Eoghan. She can't deal with this." Though she didn't want to say it but couldn't help thinking it, *She'll blame Jack again. She'll start saying that damn ship is destroying everyone's life again.* "We'll be seeing her soon enough. By now, everyone knows it took off."

There was a hard knock at the door. "It's Mike O'Malley," Devante reported.

Jack nodded to let him in.

"Bloody hell, man. Where's the fucking *Ares* going without you?"

Harlow looked at him.

The color drained from his face as he spoke. "Jesus, Mary, and Joseph, the Brotherhood took it."

"We don't know who, but we've lost contact with the ship. It's clearly a hostile act," Jack said.

"Who else is on the ship?" Mike asked.

"Everyone, maybe even Selah. They used her disappearance to lure Harlow off the ship. Both of us." Harlow watched Jack make a fist as if he were about to punch the wall before taking a deep breath and raking a hand across his face.

A wave of nausea swept over her. She raced to the bathroom and vomited. A headache came rushing in behind it. It reminded her of the devastating pain she experienced when the ship first started talking to her. Jack walked in and wet a washcloth and placed it on the back of her neck. She turned to him and spoke, "I can't do this."

He pulled her to his chest, but it wasn't enough to keep her from falling through one level of grief after another. "Do you have a headache?"

"Yes. It's an *Ares* headache. What if it hurts because the *Ares* is disconnecting from me?"

"Maybe it will disconnect entirely and go offline without you like it did before," Jack said.

"When we were on Enceladus, they bypassed my connection and messed with the ship. They already know how. It's them again." She squeezed her eyes shut. The slightest movement was starting to send jarring pain through her skull. The irony of the situation wasn't lost on her. When the *Ares* first started talking to her years ago, it gave her blinding headaches. Now the absence of the ship hurt her.

Jack walked out into the common room and asked, "Devante, can you see if anyone from colony five or seven can spare a Rescue Wave for Harlow?"

All of Colony Six had their hospital on the *Ares*. The best medical care on Mars was now gone. If anyone got sick, they would have to be taken to one of the smaller farming, mining, or science colonies. Even for them, all the serious procedures were taken care of with a trip to the *Ares*. Taking the ship from them wasn't just a matter of losing weapons and cargo hauling. It was a tremendous resource to Mars even when grounded.

"Someone's on the way with it, Marshal," Devante said.

"Evelyn, where was Safia when you spoke with her about Selah's whereabouts?" Jack inquired.

"She was on the *Ares* with Bella. She said she was picking her up from one of her classes."

"Yeah, they are in the same class. God, are Safia and Bella stuck on there too?" Harlow asked as she watched Evelyn and Jack exchange a look. Evelyn tried to contact Safia on her comm again, but this time got no answer. The loneliness dug deeper into Harlow's chest.

"Any word from Carlos?" Jack asked.

"No, I've been trying him over and over," Devante said. "Nothing."

"Me too," Jack said. "He's on the ship." Jack raked a hand through his hair then looked at Harlow, Evelyn, Devante, and Mike O'Malley who oddly, blended right in with the SAS members that were Jack's highly trained personal guards, simply because he seemed to see no reason he wouldn't. "I think we need our allies in on this. It may be time to test our new coalition. We're going to call the *Vijayee.* The Indian ship is the next best thing to the *Ares.* It has the blueprints for her, and if anyone can help us get us back onboard, it's them. I'll contact Marshal Chaturvedi."

Harlow nodded. It didn't ease any of the grief about where Selah might be, but at least the rescue crew would be more than a handful of grounded individuals sitting around in her mother's living room.

Word had traveled fast, and soon Judith came over from the Sojourner and brought food for them. Harlow picked at her sandwich but couldn't get anything down. The Rescue Wave only dulled her headache but failed to eradicate it, which it should have had no problem with. This had to do with the ship. She very much feared it would get worse the farther away and longer time apart she spent from the *Ares,* but she said nothing to Jack. She didn't want to give him more to worry about when they had to *think* their way out of this.

Judith spoke. "I know no one wants to hear this, but Marcus is on that ship. Surely, we could get help from Parliament."

Jack looked at Evelyn and Devante as if this were something they had already discussed and were hesitant to even talk about. "We've thought of that, but we must consider that if we allow them to help, then the old coalition might intercept the ship and take it back to Earth with them—or their crew will die trying. The *Ares* is a massive resource for the colonies. We can't let our adversaries on Earth have it either."

Judith leaned over and looked directly at Jack. "If it saves Selah from getting killed, then I don't give a fuck who ends up with the ship."

Harlow didn't miss the anger and hurt that passed over Jack's features like a storm cloud, but to his credit, she watched him take a deep breath before answering. "There is no ship worth more than my child's life. Surely you know that, Judith, but if we can do this with *our* allies, we should."

"Okay. I didn't mean..." Judith's eyes misted over in a rare show of vulnerability, and Harlow could see the stress taking its toll. First Eoghan's death. Now this.

"I know," Jack said softly as he looked at Judith.

Judith's eyes suddenly went wide, and she jumped up. "I saw Marcus this morning just after the restaurant opened. He looked like he had been up all night. I was worried about him. He seemed... depressed." She got up and walked over to the tote bag she'd came in with and retrieved a small package.

"He brought this and said that I was to give it to you after he left. I thought he meant after he returned to London. You know, when his visit was over. But he must've meant now." She handed the package to Harlow.

Harlow pulled a folded paper from underneath the ribbon and opened it, as Jack began reading it over her shoulder.

"Shite," Jack said as he leaned over and put his head into his hands. "Marcus, no."

Silence permeated the room as Harlow sat the letter down and opened the package with trembling hands.

CHAPTER 32
MUTINY

Carlos had looked around the goat pen, the garden, and inside the shed with no luck. He'd gotten a message on his comm that someone spotted Selah by the lake. Turning to head that way, he heard a buggy approaching a seldom-used cargo entrance. He crept around to see who it was and knew immediately something was terribly wrong. These weren't *Ares* crew—worse, he knew them from somewhere else—when he'd visited the base on Enceladus, and they'd nearly lost the ship and Jack almost lost his life. They killed only the people who came outside the Enceladus base to take the *Ares,* and their lives, on the icy planet before they'd left. The crew left inside the base were spared because Jack knew entire families lived there. Jack's mercy was coming back to bite him in the ass.

Carlos knew he was no match for the buggy full of men. He would undoubtedly be killed before he could take out all six of them, but he could get back on board and find out what they were up to. He needed to tell Jack but wanted to wait until he was out of range of the intruders. He crept back onboard the *Ares* and then attempted to call Jack, but there was only silence. He looked at the comm device that had never malfunctioned. Beneath his feet, the giant discs inside the core of the ship began to rotate.

He felt sick. The *Ares* was being hijacked. Selah going missing had been the impetus to get Harlow off the ship. She'd thwarted their plans to take it last time. They knew it was best to have her out of the way.

He slipped into a storage room and checked his weapon. His worst fears were realized when he saw that, like his comm unit, his phase weapon had been taken offline as well. "Fuck," he whispered. That's where Jack had it right with the old pistol he liked to keep. Projectile weapons might have been barbaric and grotesque, creating huge, bloody holes in people, but they couldn't be taken offline, which was why Jack liked them. Case in point.

An alarm sounded, and he heard an announcement in the *Ares* AI voice for everyone to remain in their quarters for their own safety. He guessed right about now the ship's residents discovered that this pronouncement was not a suggestion when they went to try to get out of their rooms, only to find themselves locked in. When living in a dictatorship, beware the statement of "for your own safety."

The good news was that Selah was likely safe, unless the people hijacking the ship were in league with the ones messing with the children's genomes. Then perhaps they'd decided to take the ship and at least one of their experiments at once. Well, that was one good thing about Safia leaving him: if they were trying to take the children and the ship, Bella was not where they expected, since she no longer lived on the ship. Then a fresh wave of worry hit him when he remembered Bella took a couple of her classes on board the *Ares*. He broke out in a cold sweat at the thought. As the ship rose into the air, he took comfort in at least knowing he could defend them if they were there.

A new thought hit him hard. Harlow couldn't retake the ship like last time. Worse, the one person who he went to for advice, Jack, wasn't on the ship either.

Well, he thought, you can sit here and whine about it or be the ass-kicking Marine you signed up to be in the first place. He took his knife out of its boot sheath and headed toward the armory.

Let's dance, motherfuckers.

CHAPTER 33

MARCUS AND THE MACHINE

Marcus looked around at all the strangers on the bridge of the *Ares*, Mikhail in the captain's chair, and felt as if he might vomit as the ship rose from the Martian soil. *Be strong. This is for the best.* The crew had been ushered from their stations and confined to their quarters after a few had attempted to fight back against the Chinese commandos from Enceladus, only to find that their weapons had been disabled and the invaders' weapons were operational, thanks to Jianyu's hacking, no doubt. One hijacker shot the navigator in the knee to drive home this point.

"You're doing the right thing," Mikhail said.

He didn't want the man talking to him. Even though he'd been cleared of wrongdoing in the murder of Jack's wife and child, something about him was off. He was enjoying this. There was no smile, but Marcus felt it.

"Don't get weak now. We discussed this. You knew some of them would fight back."

Marcus nodded.

"We'll be in London in no time. These people will be happy to be back on Earth," Mikhail said.

"I'm going for a walk."

Marcus felt Mikhail's poisonous glare on him as he left. *You're doing this for Jack. Once you're in London, you can deal with this bastard.*

He walked down the hall alone. When Selah had gone missing, he'd immediately sent his guards off to aid in the search. A couple of them had protested that he shouldn't be left unprotected. They'd argued it might all be leading to some larger scheme and until they were sure, neither he nor Jack should be left exposed. Had Mikhail staged a kidnapping to get Harlow off the *Ares*? He'd said he would handle it without killing. Marcus could only hope the man had some sense of honor, however warped it was.

A second wave of nausea washed over him. The coincidences were adding up just a little too perfectly. Not only would Jack hate him for taking the *Ares* back, he'd also be hated for making them sick with worry. It was doubtful Jack and Harlow would believe him if he said he knew nothing about Selah's staged disappearance. His mind went to an even darker place. What if it weren't staged? He saw how Mikhail handled the bridge crew. What if he'd just inadvertently handed his niece over to the hijackers as a means of control—*stop!* He cut into his own line of thought. *That way lies madness.* There was no hope for it now.

No one approached him as he wandered the halls. The commandos were on the bridge, stationed at the reactor core, and walking the decks in pairs around those areas, but there weren't enough personnel to patrol the entire ship. The *Ares* was massive, and Mikhail couldn't sneak in that many hijackers unnoticed. Everyone who'd been aboard when they took over was locked in their quarters. Their doors were sealed, but only if a presence was detected inside. This was a Code Blue emergency feature that kept people from venturing out if there were a sudden depressurization, while anyone in a hallway could get into an empty room. The commandos had initiated the Code Blue when they took over.

He knew where he wanted to go. His own room scared the hell out of him; he didn't need to be alone with his thoughts in there. He would go to Jack and Harlow's room. Being in their quarters would help remind him of why he was doing this. Who he was fighting to protect—the ultimate case of the ends justifying the means.

He tried to get into his brother's room, which should have opened for him right away, but it didn't. He knew Jack and Harlow weren't in there. Then who was? Anger swept through him at the idea that one of the hijackers would use this opportunity to go through his brother's personal items. Betraying him was one thing, allowing these people to pilfer his and Harlow's things was quite another. He was angry at himself for what he had to do. At least he could control this much.

He didn't have Jack or Harlow's genetic code to get him through the door, but he knew he could pull back the panel and type in a code. He thought perhaps trying to guess it would take his mind off losing his family for good. To his surprise, he got it on the first try. It was the name of the mutt dog they'd begged their dad to let them bring in off the streets. In public, they called him Pumpernickel. In private, they referred to him as Sir Badassington due to his left ear looking as if another dog had bitten half of it off, and most of his tail was missing.

The minute he walked in, his eyes burned with unexpected tears as he looked around. *You took their home from them.*

To make sure the door didn't slide closed and seal him in, he reached for the scarred chunk of wood from O'Malley's that Jack had salvaged from the rubble and placed it between the door and the wall. Mike O'Malley had won the right to bring that bar over in a weight lottery when he first moved to Mars and opened his pub. Jack confided in Marcus that he kept it by the door, so he'd see it the moment he walked in and every time he left—to remember what he fought for, why he stayed.

From the direction of Selah's bedroom, he heard muffled screams. He palmed the door, and a new wave of fear hit him when he saw his niece lying on the floor of her room wrapped in a restraining cloak that went all the way over her mouth. It could easily be removed by someone else. They just had to locate the seam in the back, but it was very traumatic for the person wearing it. It fit like a second skin.

Selah's eyes grew wide and filled with tears when she saw him. Marcus knelt down and rolled her over to locate the release mechanism on the back. "Selah! My God! What happened to you?" Marcus said.

"I was having lunch in the mess hall with some other kids from my science class. When I ran to the pantry to get more cookies, someone grabbed me. When they pressed something against my head, everything went dark. I'm super strong. I don't know why I can't get away."

Marcus saw a blinking, bendable rectangle the size of his thumb attached to a piece of the rope he'd cut off her. He picked it up and showed it to Selah. "Do you feel different when I hold this next to you?"

"It buzzes. Just a little bit," she replied.

"Hmm." Marcus held it to his ear but heard nothing and realized that was likely because it did nothing to him.

Clarity and guilt washed over him as his worst fears were confirmed. Kidnapping Selah was exactly how they'd gotten Jack and Harlow off the ship. He would have never approved of that. "I'm sorry, sweetie. You stay with me until we can get you back to your parents. Okay?"

"Okay. Are they all right? Where are they?"

"They're back on Mars. We're in space, In an EM bubble."

"Why aren't they on the ship with me?" Tears filled her eyes.

He wasn't ready to answer that question at all. He settled on honesty. "The bombs that have been going off are because some people on Earth want this ship. I'm afraid if we don't give it to them, the colonists are going to just keep getting hurt. So, there are people taking the ship back to Earth."

"I don't want to go to Earth. I want to stay with Mommy and Daddy on Mars," she sobbed.

Marcus cursed Mikhail in his head for putting him in this position. "You will be reunited with them. I promise. You weren't supposed to get separated. I'm very sorry."

She looked at him strangely, and despite the fact that she was just five years old, he knew she felt something was off about the whole thing. Thanks to her genetic enhancements, she had talked within a few months, walked by six months, and read by two years. *She will hate me someday, too.*

"The lady might be coming back."

"What lady?"

"After the man with all the gray hair on his face put me in here, a lady came by to check on me. She may come back. It doesn't matter. I can break her arm or freeze her or something, but you know, she might scream and make too much noise."

"Jesus, Selah."

"What?"

Marcus took her hand, and they headed through her parents' room. Before he left, he remembered Jack's affinity for old projectile weapons. It was just what he needed at the moment. He tapped the same password into the safe under Jack's desk and found it did indeed contain an old-school pistol, fully loaded.

He remembered going to the range and shooting it with Jack long ago. At the time, he'd not cared anything about learning how to fire it, he just wanted to spend time with Jack. He felt his chest tighten at the thought and wondered all over again if forgiveness would be possible. He tucked it into his belt, put the extra ammo in his pocket, and went out the door with Selah.

"Mom always does this when she's upset." Selah closed her eyes and ran a hand down the wall of the ship as she walked.

Selah stopped, and her eyes flew open.

"Selah? Are you okay?"

"No," she said in a frightened voice. "I don't want to go to Enceladus. I heard my mother talking about how Daddy almost died there."

"We aren't going to Enceladus. We're going to London. You'll love it there. Your daddy is from there. You get to stay in a big palace."

"No, we're not going to London," she insisted.

"How do you know that?" he asked.

"The ship just told me."

Marcus felt his world tilt and shatter. They had played him for a fool. He watched Selah place her hands on the wall again and close her eyes.

"Tell it to go to London," Marcus said. It was worth a shot. If her mother could do it, maybe she could, too.

She opened one eye and looked at him. "I can't. I've never been able to make it do anything. It won't even make me cake when I ask it to. My brain can't speak new codes. The *Ares* can only tell me what it already knows. Mom says maybe it speaks to the part of me that looks like my grandfather." Selah pointed at the nameplate on the wall in front of her parents' room. *Colonel Michael Hanson.*

Marcus felt guilty all over again and a little spooked, as if he were in the presence of a ghost. Despite the *HMS* in front of the name *Ares*, ownership wasn't so simple. He couldn't help but wonder, since Colonel Hanson designed much of the *Ares*, whether the ship spoke to Harlow and Selah because it recognized them as hailing from its creator. *Is it okay to separate them without any consent? Exactly who is the owner?*

"Then what are you doing, sweetie?"

"Talking to the ship. Asking it to find my mom."

"Oh? I thought it wouldn't take new commands from you?"

"It won't. Mom isn't a new command. *Ares* says finding mom has always been its mission."

"Any luck?"

"It says it's trying."

"But she isn't on the ship," Marcus said.

Selah gave him a small smile. "I don't think it matters."

CHAPTER 34

THE GIFT THAT KEEPS ON GIVING

The room got quiet as Harlow read the note Marcus had left with his gift. The paper shook in her hand: "Jack once told me that being a king meant making hard choices. This is the hardest. If I do nothing, I fear—I know—my brother will die. It's only a fluke of timing they didn't get him at O'Malley's. I hope someday you and Jack can forgive me. You told me how much the *Ares* means to you. I know this gift is little consolation. I'm sorry, Marcus."

Harlow's heart thundered in her chest. She hadn't believed Marcus capable of such a thing. Nearby, Jack stood stock still. She handed the note to him without looking him in the eye. It was a cowardly act, she knew, but she was so terrified for Selah—on the *Ares* and headed God knew where—that she couldn't bear the idea of looking at him and falling into the sea of betrayal she knew he felt for his brother. She heard him pass the note to Evelyn, who must have been worried sick about her wife, Seraph, who was on the *Ares.*

Harlow untied the ribbon from the package and the cloth fell away. In her lap lay a chunk of crystal with the words *HMS ARES* and a likeness of the ship etched beautifully into the surface. She picked it up in a rage and started to throw it across the room when energy shot up her arm and made her gasp. The headache that had been plaguing her for hours suddenly relented, and ones and zeros scrolled across her field of vision. She slowly lowered her arm. "Oh, God, Jack!"

He moved in front of her. "What's wrong?" he asked.

"The *Ares*. It's in this chunk of quartz."

"In it?"

"Yes! It's talking to me. How?"

Harlow held it out for him to study closer but didn't dare release her contact with it.

Jack looked at it in wonder, the old tech with a new purpose. "We just removed the original glass display panels. We originally built the ship with them because of the holo bugs that everyone was worried about, but crystals hold on to information. Every square inch can hold 360 terabytes of data."

"But how can it be talking to me? It's not connected."

"Quantum entanglement?" Devante offered. "You're not just linked with the ship. Perhaps it's become part of your DNA. Maybe the crystal is just the antennae you needed to pick up the signal."

"You might be right." She held onto the crystal with both hands, took a deep breath, and asked the *Ares* where it was headed. The answer made her feel ill. "The ship is going to Enceladus." She concentrated harder, trying to command it to return. "It can give me information, but I can't override its programming this time. It's showing me a hard drive hooked up in the core that's derailing me. Unless someone can get to it and—" Harlow jumped as the scene in her head shifted to the hallway outside her family's quarters. There were optics built into the very skin of the vessel that could allow passengers to be observed in any public area. "It's Selah! I see Marcus, too. They're together." Harlow felt relieved that someone whom she knew would never hurt Selah was looking out for her, but Jack became furious.

"What the hell is he doing with her? Did he use our daughter to lure us from the ship? I'll kill him for this!"

Harlow put her hand on Jack's arm. "No, I don't think so. They're running down the hallway now and hiding as if they're being pursued. Why would they be if Marcus was the one who took the *Ares*?"

"Maybe he thought he was doing the right thing but ended up being used?" Evelyn offered.

That rang true for Harlow. She looked at Jack.

"That's likely the case," he said. "And here we sit, thousands of miles away. I hope to God someone on that ship can help them."

CHAPTER 35

AMONG THIEVES

I need allies, a plan, and weapons, Carlos thought. He knew there were many more of the crew still onboard than there were of the group from Enceladus. Somewhere in his head, he decided he might as well refer to them all as the Brotherhood. Was there really even a separate Chinese agenda? They both wanted the Brotherhood to take over Mars so they could get the countries of the Earth to do as they pleased under the threat of the formidable starship.

Every room he tried was on lockdown. Safia and Bella kept circling back around in his head, and he thought about going to the classrooms to see if they were there, but if they were, given Safia's newfound vigilante mindset, he'd likely just be releasing a loose cannon. He knew she might hate him if he confessed to the thought later, but maybe it was best to leave her in the safety of a locked-down room.

If he could get Daniel from engineering out of his room, then maybe he could help him free more of the other technical and military staff to help. He went to his friend's quarters and tried the door. Nothing. Of course. He knocked three times. Daniel returned the knock. They both knew Morse code, a requirement in case technology went down. The Great Solar Flares of the 24th century had revived the practice, with telegraphs being used from time to time. He informed Daniel who he was and what he needed, having to stop twice to hide in a nearby supply room when people came on or off the bridge. Daniel told him what his passcode was.

When the door slid back, the engineer thanked Carlos and retreated with him to the supply room so they both wouldn't get sealed inside the living quarters.

"Of course, the armory is on lockdown," Carlos said.

"Naturally. Though they probably disabled all our weapons, anyway."

"If we can get to engineering, I can make us stun guns. No problem. But I suspect that's heavily guarded. Too bad that Gabriel's just a kid; otherwise, we could have him levitate these bastards and toss them out of our way. We can't involve them in this shit though."

"Who's next then?"

"That's easy. AVM Miller," Carlos replied.

"Not Alvaro?"

"We can get him after. Miller knows the ship better than anyone. That's what we need right now." What Carlos didn't say was that he feared Alvaro might steamroll Miller before she was able to get her suggestions out.

In only a couple of minutes, they had Miller in the supply room discussing options. She wore a knife sheathed in her belt over each hip and held a shock wave in her hand.

"Nice," Carlos said with appreciation. "You keep one in your room?"

"Damn right. Under my pillow. You never know when these bastards are going to show up. I was here the first two times it happened," she said. There had been an attempted hijacking before Harlow's father had died when the Brotherhood swarmed the ship and nearly a dozen crewmembers were killed in a twelve-hour standoff. And Carlos remembered the trip to Enceladus all too well, when one of the guards was shot and Jack nearly lost his life. "They've never managed to get this far."

"Suggestions?" Carlos said. "I'm willing to blaze a trail of destruction. Just point me in the right direction."

"We need enough personnel to take out the bridge crew, but we shouldn't assume I can just command this ship to turn around. So, we can't kill everyone. We have to find out who the mastermind is. Let's get as many able-bodied warriors in play as possible. Is Alvaro onboard?" she asked.

"I think so," Carlos said. "I don't believe there's a lot of enemy personnel on this ship. They couldn't have snuck that many on board without detection. We have that much on our side." He listened by the door for patrols, then turned toward the others. "I saw a team of six split up and head toward the lower decks. I say we go now. My guess is those are the only teams patrolling." He led the way to Alvaro's quarters, far from the bridge, and Daniel freed him. They set the door to stay open and listened for patrols as they talked.

"What the hell is going on?" Alvaro asked.

They quickly explained the situation.

"We need to free someone that speaks Chinese," Daniel said.

"Grab a damn handheld translator," Alvaro said.

"Already thought of that. They're all connected to the *Ares* and as shut down as our weapons. They want us completely at their mercy."

"Okay. We'll find someone. We can't just head onto the bridge and start firing. We need to know what their plan is first, get as much intel as possible. My guess is that they would have already gone down to the core and interfaced with the ship before taking over the bridge. There's likely a patch that allowed them to get into the system and disable all our weapons or they would have never been able to take the bridge."

A few minutes later, they had freed Jared Chang, a hydraulics engineer who spoke fluent Mandarin and could at least understand Cantonese.

After finding engineering guarded as suspected, they made their way to the student science labs one hallway over.

Daniel tore through supply closets and dumped drawers out on a table, finding what he needed in minutes. "Never tell the students how easy it is to make stun guns with the materials they already have on hand," he said, as he quickly assembled and distributed the crude shock weapons. They weren't the sophisticated phaser weapons capable of multiple settings, but they would deliver an electrical discharge that Daniel assured them would render the intruders unconscious.

They made their way down to the core with little interference—they only had to duck into a supply room once—confirming their theory that the Chinese were working with a skeleton crew.

When they reached the core, Allan and Naadir, the two usual *Ares* guards stationed there were nowhere to be found, and they saw no bodies. However, he did see scorch marks on the wall. Carlos felt sick knowing they likely had no idea their weapons were inoperable until it was too late.

After confirming there were only two guards in the core, AVM Miller ran in with her hands up, feigning tears and panic and trying to pull the two with her as if she needed their help. During the confusion, Carlos, Alvaro, and Daniel shocked the guards, bound them, took their weapons, and waited for them to wake up.

When they came around, Jared began his questioning, interpreting what they were saying for the others.

"Liu says that he is the senior official of the two," Jared said.

"Tell him if he cooperates, we will not kill him," Alvaro said.

Jared relayed the message, and Liu responded.

Jared hesitated before speaking. "He says you may go ahead and kill him. He will not tell you anything."

"The hell he won't." Alvaro shot him in the leg with Liu's own weapon. The wound immediately cauterized. Sweat popped out along Liu's brow. He looked up and yelled something only Jared understood.

"It's an expletive," Jared said.

"We don't have time for this!" Alvaro roared and shot the man in the other leg. "Talk!"

The man said nothing but looked straight ahead and began shaking intensely.

"Talk!" he shot him in the shoulder. "Talk! Talk! Talk!" He punctuated every word with a shot in another part of the man's body.

AVM Miller moved toward Alvaro with her hand out. "Weapon. Now."

Jared's eyes went wide, and he backed away. The other hijacker cowered as best he could in his bindings.

"Fine," Alvaro said to Miller as he set his weapon to stun only and showed it to Miller. He was compliant but the resentment in his voice rang through.

"Alvaro. This isn't working," Carlos said.

"Yes, it will. Everybody has a limit." He stunned the man, who fell unconscious immediately.

Carlos looked at AVM Miller, and she looked back at him with eyes that clearly shared his concerns. Carlos wasn't naïve. He knew sometimes a person had to be driven to the absolute brink before talking; still, the way Alvaro executed the whole thing was unhinged. The difference between what was necessary in an interrogation and what was sadistic torture often had to do with recognizing one thing: pleasure. Alvaro was enjoying this, and it was disturbing.

Blood began to seep from the tortured man's lips. Though his wounds had cauterized, he was bleeding from the inside. His companion spoke to Jared.

"He says he will talk if you spare his life."

"Don't play with us, or I'll kill you, too," Alvaro said.

Carlos leaned over, felt the man's pulse. "He's gone," Carlos reported.

"He says he will go disable the external drive hooked up to the *Ares*." He nodded toward the unfamiliar unit they'd all seen when they entered the room.

"No," Alvaro said. "You will tell Daniel what to do and he will disable it. You could be giving it any command."

The man took another look at his companion and nodded.

He led Daniel through a series of commands to provide via Jared's careful interpretation.

Daniel said, "This only disables the ability to lock out others trying to command the *Ares*, like Harlow could. I'm sure they had her in mind when they made this. Unless we make it to the bridge, overpower the hijackers, and change the destination, we are still headed to Enceladus."

CHAPTER 36

ON THE MOVE

Safia stood by the door panel of the classroom, three levels below the bridge, positioning the gadget Harlow had given her in front of it so that Bella could see the mechanisms inside. This was all very different from the crude door locks she'd been dealing with in the village; it was purely electronic. Still, Harlow had joked that a child with a soldering iron could cause the doors to open if they could get into the panel and apply heat to the right wire. Safia had decided that between Harlow's advice, pocket spyware gift, and Bella's hot hand ability, they ought to be able to get the damn door open, but it was taking a while.

Finally, they located the right wire, applied the right amount of heat, and the wire insulation bubbled and sizzled. The door slid aside. Safia held her breath and waited for an alarm to go off. If the doors locked in the event of a hull breach or some emergency protocol like that, then alarms might well sound, but she heard nothing. That didn't mean a silent alarm hadn't been tripped, in which case she should get moving.

"I'm going to go bring back help," Safia said, trying to sound more confident than she felt. "Stay with Ms. Levy and help protect the others. Can you do that for me?" She gave Bella a big hug.

"I want to go with you."

"I know, but I think the other kids and Ms. Levy need your abilities."

Bella stood up a little straighter and tried to force a smile, but Safia could see the fear in her eyes. She knew it wasn't just about whoever had taken the *Ares* either. It was about all the changes that had occurred in the last few weeks: the move, missing Carlos, living with Judith, O'Malley's bombing. It was too much for one little person. Hell, it was too much for one big person. Safia felt ready to buckle beneath the weight of it herself. She could only imagine what it was doing to Bella.

"I'll be back. I promise."

Bella grabbed her once more and gave her another hug. This time when she pulled away there were tears in her eyes. Safia wiped them away. "Mama is going to fix this for you, okay?"

Ms. Levy wrapped an arm around Bella as Safia left. She looked both ways, listened, then patted the shiv in her pocket that she'd made out of a broken paint stirrer. She tried to pull the door shut before heading down the hallway so that the hijackers wouldn't realize she'd broken out, but it was stuck in the open position. If they noticed, Ms. Levy promised to tell them the door malfunctioned every couple of weeks.

Safia made her way down the hall, moving without a sound as Harlow had taught her, and stopping every few yards to listen for patrols. She knew she might even be watched at that very moment. The walls themselves were lined with optics. She hoped they didn't have enough personnel on board to monitor movement all over the ship.

She headed in the direction of the room she'd shared with Carlos, wondering whether he had already found a way out or was still on Mars. She knew he'd been looking for Selah—maybe he'd been fooled by the same ruse that got Harlow off the *Ares*.

She made her way to the stairs undetected; the elevators were too risky. She jogged up two flights, feeling thankful with every step that she'd kept up with her training, but just as she opened the door to the floor where Carlos's quarters were, she was confronted by a commando shouting something at her she couldn't decipher before he fired.

Safia ducked while simultaneously sidestepping forward and grabbing the arm holding the weapon. She drove the shiv into his neck and yanked down and back toward her as hard as she could. Hating the way the way it felt, she didn't know if she was taking a life or not. He started to scream before it turned into a gurgle. His weapon hit the floor followed by his body a moment later. She watched blood pour from his neck and out his mouth. Tears sprang to her eyes, and a metallic smell filled her nose. She wanted to run, breathe, escape. *These are hijackers. He tried to kill you. Get your shit together.*

When it came to men confronting women, she never ceased to be amazed at how quickly and thoroughly they let their guard down and expected surrender from her. She was finding that if she acted quickly and decisively, she could usually get the upper hand. That didn't mean her heart wasn't about to crack her ribs it was beating so damn hard from fear. Anyone who said they weren't afraid was a liar. She wiped the shiv off on his pant leg, put it in her cargo pocket, and took his weapon from the floor with shaking hands.

No other guards came running to the man's rescue. They obviously didn't have enough coverage for the enormous ship.

The man still bled profusely from the wound in his neck, eyes closed, body twitching. She wasn't sure whether he would bleed out but didn't want him suffering anymore. She looked at the weapon and guessed that the settings were like the phaser Carlos carried, despite the symbols being different. After setting it to stun him, she delivered a quick shot to the man. He went still immediately. She found a pulse in his wrist to confirm she'd rendered him unconscious.

Safia resumed her search for Carlos. He was going to get her help retaking the ship whether he wanted it or not.

CHAPTER 37

ABSOLUTION

A glimmer of hope lit the cavern of guilt Marcus had been sinking into since they'd left the atmosphere. An idea began to form that might just save them. If the ship was talking with Selah, then maybe it wasn't completely under Mikhail's control. If he could get her to Daniel in engineering, or Miller, Jack said she knew everything about the *Ares*; maybe there was something they could do.

He found Daniel's quarters empty. He didn't respond to Morse when he knocked, and it looked as if the panel might have been tampered with and replaced. This was likely good news. *What now?* He clung to a ray of hope that perhaps Daniel was communicating with the ship from engineering or some remote workstation.

"Selah, find out if anything has changed with the ship."

She nodded and placed her palms on the wall. "Mom?"

"What?" Marcus looked at her.

"The *Ares* found Mom. It knows she isn't on the ship. I don't know how it's talking to her, but it is."

Marcus felt guilty that his first thought wasn't for anyone's safety or that perhaps Harlow would sense Selah and know that she was okay. Rather, his first thought was that Harlow and Jack might already know the hijacking was his fault, and now that everything had gone pear-shaped, and he'd placed their daughter in peril, he could never be redeemed in their eyes.

"She isn't locked out anymore. It says something has changed. It shows me Daniel in the core, giving commands to the ship."

"He's free." Hope flooded Marcus's chest. "I just need to find him. Ask the *Ares* if it can unlock a room for you."

"It says, 'Yes.'"

Minutes later, they stood inside Aunt Mary's room. She looked at Marcus as he quickly explained. He told her the facts, even the part where he'd made the biggest mistake of his life in trusting Mikhail.

"Oh, sweetheart."

Marcus cringed at her sympathy.

"What the hell were you thinking?"

Now he felt a little defensive, but it was better than the guilt of her being completely understanding. The smart woman likely knew that, too.

"I thought I could save him."

She nodded and pulled him to her. "Okay, go fix this. I'll watch over Selah." She drew the sign of the cross on his forehead.

"I'm sorry," he said to them both.

"I know," Mary said. Selah said nothing but ran forward and gave Marcus an unexpected—and from his point of view, unearned—hug.

"Thank you, Selah," he said, talking past the lump in his throat. "Hopefully, I'll have Daniel with me when I return, and you can help him talk to the ship and maybe your mother as well."

Selah nodded.

"Before I go, ask the ship to look down this hallway and the ones nearby to make sure no one is approaching."

"No one there."

"Thank you." He looked at them one last time before slipping out.

• • •

He didn't encounter anyone between Mary's quarters and the core. Mikhail had only brought a skeleton crew then, but Marcus was no fighter like his brother, despite having Jack's pistol, and he knew it.

Just outside the core, he rounded a corner and felt like a battering ram slammed into him. Alvaro hit him three times, and he was on the floor before he could form a coherent thought. He looked up at Alvaro and found wild eyes staring back as the man prepared to strike again.

CHAPTER 38

MESSING WITH THE MATRIARCHS

"Stand down! You're out of control," Carlos said to Alvaro as he and AVM Miller pulled Alvaro off Marcus.

"This son of a bitch is going to get us all killed. How could you be so fucking stupid?" Alvaro pointed at a bound and battered man in a Chinese military uniform. "*He* told us who gave them access. It was you. I don't give a shit if you're a fucking king. I ought to kill you right now."

"Calm down," Carlos said to him.

Alvaro turned on him. "Don't you tell me to calm down." He shoved Carlos against the wall and placed a forearm against his throat.

"Back the fuck up, maniac!" Safia had slipped into the core silently and pointed her weapon at Alvaro's head. On the one hand, Carlos felt a sense of smug satisfaction that Safia held a weapon on Alvaro. He instinctively knew it would irk the man to no end that it was a woman besting him. How did he know that? There was something about Alvaro; the man didn't like women. On the other hand, he had to admit, as backward as it was, he didn't like the idea that she had to rescue him. He was supposed to protect her, but he'd be keeping *that* to himself.

Miller quickly took Alvaro's weapons from each side pocket, along with a phaser with Mandarin characters on it. She said in a steady voice, "Stand down. You don't turn on a member of this crew, especially not now, and he's right. You are out of control. Get a hold of yourself this second."

Safia took a step back once he was disarmed but didn't trust him enough yet to lower her weapon.

Alvaro dropped his arm, looked at Carlos, and pointed at both women. "You need to get these women in line."

Safia said, "You need to remember who's holding a weapon in your face, you arrogant bastard."

Carlos started to speak, but Miller beat him to it. Her voice was cool, strong, and contained just the right amount of don't-fuck-with-me as she spoke, "*This woman*," she pointed to herself, "is the senior officer on the entire ship, and you are a liability at the moment. You'll get your weapons back when you gain some self-control."

Carlos looked at Safia as she lowered her weapon. He had so many questions running through his mind. Where the hell did she come from? How did she escape? What was she doing with one of the hijacker's weapons, and did she know she had blood splattered on her arm and the side of her face? It didn't appear to be hers, which both relieved him and chilled him to the bone all at the same time. He placed his hand on her arm as he wondered what she'd been through on her way to find them.

"Where's Bella?" he whispered.

She looked at him with haunted eyes. "Safe with her teacher."

Marcus had gotten to his feet and held his shirt sleeve to his bloody nose. "You're right. I've made a horrible mistake. I thought I could save Jack if I took the *Ares* back to London. When I was trapped beneath the rubble of O'Malley's, it all made sense to me. I had no idea Mikhail was taking the *Ares* to Enceladus until it was too late. I fucked up. It's true, but I've come to tell you that Selah can communicate with the ship and with Harlow to some extent. I don't know how Harlow is doing it. I... I gave her a piece of the ship. The quartz. That's got to be it."

Daniel said, "If Harlow can communicate with the ship now, then maybe she can help us get the *Ares* turned around."

"Maybe. I can take you to Selah, but I don't want that hothead—" Marcus pointed to Alvaro "—around my niece."

"Fuck you, traitor. You can't keep me from anybody," Alvaro spat.

Carlos squared up to Alvaro. "Oh, you will be staying the hell away from her. You're not beating anyone to death in front of a child." In a quiet voice, he added, "I don't know what your malfunction is with me, but button it up until the crisis is over. We'll deal with it then."

Alvaro looked around the room as if deciding his next move, then smiled and looked at Carlos. "Yeah, we'll deal with it then."

When the group arrived at Aunt Mary's door, it was immediately clear something was wrong. The door was open, and Carlos's heart pounded against his ribcage as he feared what he might find inside. Mary lay sprawled on the floor.

"Oh, God," Marcus ran to her and got down on his knees, patted her face, and called her name as he tried to coax her back into consciousness.

Her eyes fluttered open, and she looked around as awareness slowly took hold. Marcus helped her sit up.

A trickle of blood ran down from Mary's hairline and over her temple. "I'm sorry," she said, as tears filled her eyes. "He took her."

CHAPTER 39

DEMONS OF DECISION

"Who took her?" Carlos asked.

"Mikhail. I heard others in the hallway though."

"She might have a brain bleed or something," Marcus said. "Can we get her to someone in medical? Who's closest?"

Safia returned from the washroom with a cold cloth, sat down beside Mary, and placed it on the wound.

"Yua's quarters would be quickest to access. They're on the front side of medical. Doc Hagen is on the back side closest to the bridge, and we aren't quite ready for a grand entrance just yet."

Marcus's heart sank. He didn't want to see Yua. He hoped to put off her finding out about his colossal screw up as long as possible, but he had to place his aunt before his ego.

"Honey, I'm fine, really. Just go get Selah and throw that maniac out the airlock."

"No," Carlos said. "We're going to get Yua. Besides, it couldn't hurt to have another ally loose on this ship."

After Daniel opened Yua's door, she saw Mary's bleeding head and went to work as Carlos gave her a quick rundown of events.

Yua cleaned the wound, then set some newly acquired nanobots loose on the laceration. She looked up at Marcus and warmth filled his body. Quickly on its heels came guilt. He didn't deserve the look he was getting from her, the look that his gut told him was more than friendship and mutual respect, despite his mind telling him even a king couldn't hope for such beauty to rest its gaze on him.

The spell was broken when she asked, "How in the world did Mikhail get access to the ship? I thought we had this place sealed up tight after the last two times this happened."

Carlos simply shook his head, unwilling to rat out Marcus but Alvaro said, "This son of a bitch right here—"

Marcus held up a hand. "I can tell her myself. Yua, this is my fault. I thought if I returned the *Ares* to the Earth coalition, the bombings would stop, and my brother wouldn't be in danger anymore. I was stupid to trust Mikhail. Well, I didn't trust him. I just thought he had the same goals as me but for a different reason, but it turns out, he's been planning on taking the ship to Enceladus the entire time. I may have doomed every one of us."

Yua just looked at him with an unreadable expression. In the short time they'd spent together, they'd shared tragedy, heartache, whiskey, and he'd thought maybe more someday, but now, he was sure he'd bollixed it. He sensed a gulf between them that he feared he would never be able to cross.

Mary looked up at him and gave him an encouraging half-smile. He knew, even without his aunt saying so, that she was proud of him for speaking up. He also knew she'd put in a good word for him with Yua, but could one ever recover from being the git blighter that he'd become in her eyes? He dared another glance at Yua, and she looked away.

Marcus decided not to dwell on it any longer. He couldn't add to his list of sins by pining away for this woman while his niece was missing, and the ship's crew was in danger. *Lick your wounds later, mate. You've got a major fuckup to mend.*

After confirming that Mary was okay and could provide no more information, Marcus decided not to join them when they headed to the core in hopes that Daniel could somehow create an interface with Harlow. If they could, it might also be able to tell them where Selah was. It would be more efficient than searching the enormous ship for her.

"I'm going to check Jack and Harlow's room again. Maybe they left something that will help."

"I don't like you going alone," Carlos said.

Alvaro said, "Hell, I don't *trust* him to go alone."

"Hmpf. Mikhail's gotten all he wanted out of me, mates. I may as well go try and find my niece. Besides, if you uncover something, you might get to her quicker than me and with more firepower and expertise."

"Damn right," Alvaro said.

Marcus said nothing but watched a look of annoyance pass across Carlos's face when Alvaro spoke again. A reckoning was coming between those two. Sure, he himself disliked Alvaro because the bastard had damn near broken his jaw, but *that* he could understand. This was something else. He pushed it from his mind, knowing it was best to leave the man to Carlos and the others, anyway.

"Watch your back. Keep your stun at the ready," Carlos said before Marcus turned to leave.

"Yeah, watch your back," Alvaro muttered.

Marcus didn't turn to look. It didn't matter.

• • •

Marcus walked back into Jack and Harlow's room. He knew he couldn't feel any lower. He thought about what the hijackers might do with them once they reached Enceladus. He'd heard Jack tell the story about the crew's trip to the icy hellhole four years ago and how General Zhou's plan had been to have Jack clear the ship and kill him afterwards. Now, he thought it likely everyone on board would either be killed or held as ransom pieces for when the Brotherhood had various demands.

This could be a nightmare that wouldn't end for years, and it all began with him believing he was saving his brother. *Father was right. I'm no king. No. Now's definitely not the time to wallow in self-pity. Don't be a wanker.* He had another thought he couldn't ignore. Yua was on the ship. He started back out into the hallway before the intercom came on in Jack and Harlow's quarters. The unmistakable Russian accent sent waves of fury through his body.

"I see you, Your Highness. Meet me in cargo bay eighteen. I've got your niece."

Marcus froze. When the hell had Mikhail placed cameras in his brother's room? He was beyond disconcerted at the idea that he was being watched. Taking a deep breath, he said a prayer and resisted touching Jack's ancient, barbaric pistol in his back waistband, hidden under his shirt.

He steadied his nerves and went to find the cargo bay eighteen.

CHAPTER 40

THE ENEMY OF MY ENEMY

Safia stood in front of Yua's bathroom mirror and felt a tremor run through her at the image that stared back at her. Dried blood was on the side of her neck, cheek, and right arm. She'd had no idea how she looked. She supposed the adrenaline kept her from a certain amount of awareness. No wonder Carlos had looked at her strangely. The way he'd placed his big, warm hand on her arm as they stood in the hallway and gazed at her face and neck had stayed with her, comforting and solid in the chaos around them. In hindsight, he had seemed even more concerned for her than usual. It might have been funny, with her looking at him in utter confusion as she stood there slick with the hijacker's blood, if they weren't all fighting for their lives.

She wiped the blood away, held the cloth under the facet and watched the pale red water run down the drain. She thought about very normal things like dinner in the mess hall with her friends—*family*—from the *Ares*, beers at O'Malley's, as the metallic smell of the man's blood filled her nostrils again. How had life spiraled so quickly? She swore when this was all over, she would tell Carlos everything. *He* was everything that was good and beautiful to her. Like Bella: kind, warm, beautiful, sacred.

She walked back into the room with Yua and Mary and tried to tamp down her growing adrenaline and anxiety. Alvaro had gone out to do some recon around the bridge, while Daniel, the interpreter, and their prisoner had gone to try to create an interface with Harlow. Daniel brought Lafferty along to stand guard as he tried to find a way to divert command from the bridge. No one wanted to have to storm the bridge and end up in a firefight if they didn't have to.

Safia had wanted to go with them. They'd refused to let her, with Lafferty claiming she wasn't a warrior—blood splatter on her face from their common enemy notwithstanding.

If she'd gone with Daniel and the others, at least she could have felt useful. Being stuck here was almost more than she could bear. She paced back and forth, listening to Mary and Yua talk about their current situation.

"I still can't believe he let this happen," Yua said. "He doesn't even live in the colonies. Now he's going to assume he knows what's right for our people and take our ship, our life support, for God's sake? Does he even realize this is where most of Mars comes for medical treatment? Does he understand people will die without the *Ares*?"

Safia cringed a little. After all, Yua was talking about Mary's nephew. Mary looked at the doctor with compassion and understanding despite the frustration Yua was directing at Marcus.

"Honey, all he could see was that people were dying because of the *Ares*. His heart was in the right place. His brain was just some damn-where else."

Yua and Mary's conversation, along with Safia's pacing, stopped when the door opened, and two men led Alvaro inside at gunpoint. Safia quickly concealed her weapon.

The men were slowly forcing Alvaro into a corner away from the women. One motioned for him to kneel.

Shit, Safia thought. They're about to execute him.

"No," Mary said. "Tell them I'm the King's aunt, and I'll vouch for them by name if they let you live." She started walking toward the group.

Alvaro said, "Mother. No. Stay away. I've already tried talking to them. They don't have translators."

The two hijackers shouted at him in their language and raised their weapons at the back of his head. He began speaking fast. "Safia, go to Toledo, and contact a man named Alejandro Balsuto. He will make sure Bella gets half my estate." Terror shot through Safia. If this hothead was saying this in front of everyone, then they were definitely about to kill him, and he knew it.

Some instinct kicked in, and she went for her phaser weapon without another thought. Clarity washed over her as she fired, a truth she'd hidden even from herself. Earlier, when she'd turned her phaser on Alvaro, it wasn't programmed to stun him. She'd not thought twice about it until this moment. She'd absolutely intended to kill him if he didn't let Carlos go.

Worse, as the first guard hit the floor, followed by the second—both shot dead by her—she was confused as hell over the fact that she had now killed the men who were about to deliver her from this menace of a man, the cause of her nightmares for the last five years. She could've been rid of the monster who plagued her relationship with Carlos and had warped her sense of security, perhaps forever. This was different than sparing Vince; Alvaro had taken everything from her. Why was she rescuing this bastard when she could have let the guards pull their triggers first before she shot them?

To make matters worse, Alvaro made eye contact with her and smiled, just shy of smug. God help her, she wanted to finish what she'd prevented the hijackers from doing.

Grief flooded her soul. She'd been so close to freedom. Why had she acted so quickly? She turned to Mary to find the shrewd woman already looking at her with a mixture of sympathy, wisdom, and perhaps a few questions. Mary stepped forward, took the phaser from Safia, and led her as far away from the bodies and Alvaro as the room would allow. Safia allowed Mary to lead her but couldn't take her eyes off the scene.

Yua stepped forward and leaned down to check the pulse of the two hijackers.

"They're dead," Alvaro said.

She proceeded to check despite Alvaro's attempts to wave her away. Yua stood and walked away.

"Told you." Alvaro wasted no time confiscating the dead men's phasers and going through their pockets for anything that might prove useful in their fight to take the ship back.

Mary sat Safia down on a couch next to her. "He intended to give Bella half his estate. He's her father?" she asked quietly.

"Yes."

"Full disclosure, Harlow told me long ago that Bella's father forced himself on you."

"He did. I don't know why I saved him just now. I lost everything because of him. It's why I left the *Ares*. I've kept my mouth shut because he's a genius at what he does, and I thought he could help keep Jack alive, help save the colony. He's out of hand, though. I could have been free just now. Why? Why would I save the man? Mother… this is really… I can't understand why I would pass up the opportunity to be free. It wouldn't have been by my hand either. Had I just waited another second or two."

Mary took Safia's hands in hers. "It doesn't mean you like or even respect him for that matter. Have you ever heard the saying, 'the enemy of my enemy is my friend?' This situation turned everything on its ear in a weird way. At that moment, he was an ally, on a very basic, primal level. You made a quick decision about which group member to save. There was no time to nuance all this out."

"And if I'd let him die or shot him myself?"

Mary shrugged. "Well, I would've understood that decision, too."

Alvaro dragged the two bodies away from their sight. Safia felt a wall of exhaustion finally hit her, deep and sure.

Given everything Alvaro had taken from her, she felt for all the world he could have been dragging her along with them.

CHAPTER 41

FIFTEEN SECONDS

Marcus made it to Bay 18 without interference. He suspected this was by design. The door to the bay and adjacent wall panels were made of clear Flexmat meant to bend to a near-impossible degree before breaking. This would give precious extra seconds for those in other parts of the ship to reach a secure location in the case of depressurization. The door wouldn't hold forever, but every second counted in that scenario.

What he saw enraged him on many levels. Selah sat strapped to a bench along one wall. Mikhail surely must've had one of those devices meant to contain her power hooked to the straps, where she couldn't reach it. This whole situation was a setup: Mikhail clearly had the intention of depressurizing the cabin without her hurtling into space. This also meant Mikhail was surely planning on tossing him out the airlock. Why else would he call him down there? The other infuriating thing was that Mikhail leaned against one of the cargo containers, talking to Selah and gesturing as if giving her a lecture. He didn't appear angry, but more mentor-like. *Minging piece of shite.*

Marcus had never been in such a situation. When Jack had been on duty after the Gray Death, restoring order during the riots, Marcus had been organizing humanitarian efforts but was oddly removed from the humans receiving those efforts. Now here he stood, facing down the biggest bully on either planet. Mikhail claimed to be doing it all in the name of social justice, of course, but with an extremely skewed idea of what that meant. If Mikhail understood justice and equality, Selah wouldn't be tied down and traumatized. She would be learning how to best serve the people she might one day lead, not be used as a pawn to manipulate Marcus.

There was a saving grace about her predicament: if the room completely depressurized, she should be okay as long as the straps held, and she didn't slip free. Her superior oxygenation and cold resistance would sustain her, but she was working to loosen the straps, and that scared him. Even worse, if he *and* Mikhail went flying out, should the outer door fail, no one would be left to get her out of there. Her gifts wouldn't allow her to stay safe forever.

Marcus took a deep breath, found the door decoded for him, and stepped inside to face the madman. "What do you want from me? You've already tricked me into giving you the ship."

"Everything I do is still in the interest of the people. Always has been. The only thing I need from you is to send a message to Earth to let them know that you've decided to join the Brotherhood in its mission to bring peace and equality to people everywhere."

"You have my niece bound up, so I'm assuming this means if I don't do this, you'll harm her."

"No, she's far too precious." Mikhail reached out a hand to touch Selah's cheek, then immediately jerked back. "Ow! She's already trying to freeze my hand off, even with the inhibitor in place." He rubbed his hands together vigorously. "Good. Very good. We gifted her well. She's a masterpiece. Now all we must do is get her thinking straight, and she will be okay."

Marcus remembered what he'd heard about the way they had messed with Harlow's memories at the compound on the other side of Mars. He felt sick at the idea of them doing such a thing to his young niece if she remained in their hands. He had to get her away from this psychopath and return her home.

Marcus thought carefully about his reply, knowing anything he said could be twisted. "I could send your message, but Parliament won't have it. I'm not the country. The people already *are* the country. They will decide what to do, no matter what I say."

Mikhail waved a dismissive hand. "You idiot. Half of Parliament belongs to me already. All you have to decide is whether you wish to live today. Record the message. Don't record the message. Either way, I'm going to get what I want." Mikhail stood there for a moment, just waiting, then started to walk toward the door. *The bastard is going to walk out of here, depressurize the room, and get rid of me now that he's gotten what he wanted.*

Marcus realized no amount of talking was going to change anything with this man. He had to act quickly and get this situation under control. *Be decisive.* Adrenaline shot through his veins as he made his move. He felt shockingly confident as he reached into his back waistband and pulled Jack's pistol, aimed at Mikhail, fired, and missed.

He shot once more, and Mikhail jerked his shoulder back and cursed. Blood ran down his arm, but he still seemed able to move it. A loud hiss began, and Marcus saw Selah's dark hair rise from where it had lain across her shoulders. The few cargo containers that weren't strapped down started to slowly slide toward the bay door. Marcus realized another shot might completely depressurize the room and send them flying into space. Incessant alarms added to the panic level.

"Fine. Out you go," Mikhail said as he made his way to the panel that held the commands to depressurize the bay.

"Stop! You might lose Selah," Marcus screamed.

Mikhail responded by hitting him in the face. The pistol bounced away.

Blood poured from his nose and down his neck. Mikhail wasn't much better off with his bloody arm. He marched forward as if to grab Selah, but Marcus got between them. Mikhail knocked him backward, and he fell to the floor against Selah's legs. When he made contact with her, a surge of energy ran through his body the likes of which he had never experienced in his life. Marcus jumped to his feet as if they had springs inside them and his world coalesced into pure energy and strength. He couldn't understand how it was happening if she'd had the inhibitor. Maybe she could give her strength but not use it herself?

His vision became sharper and his hearing clearer. He actually saw the exact trajectory his hit would need to create the maximum impact. It became clear Selah's gift wasn't just about brute strength. He had always wondered why she didn't look incredibly bulky for a child that strong. The gift was also mental: it was angle, follow through, everything, down to the second, perfectly timed. He swung at the man and Mikhail went flying against the airlock that had been getting weaker by the moment as the vacuum of space pulled on it. With a screech of metal, the bay door sheared off. It and Mikhail tumbled into the void along with the loose cargo.

Marcus took a deep breath, knowing the air would be gone in seconds. He went sliding too but got stuck behind a bolted-down container, held fast in case of such depressurization. Jack's pistol wedged beside him but was no longer useful. He looked around frantically for some sort of switch or fail-safe as alarms blared, telling him what he already knew: he was a dead man. Things went from bad to worse when Selah's straps broke free, and she flew past him. Silently.

He prayed she was remembering her training from the last trip they had made to Earth and was keeping her lungs inflated as long as possible to avoid collapse. Her body used oxygen efficiently, but empty lungs could still collapse, and that would be painful.

But for him... there was only one shot, seconds to live. His gaze landed on the switch to re-pressurize the room. No way he could get there without being pulled out on the way to it. Someone would need to do it from the hallway or elsewhere on the ship, but the *Ares* crew was largely locked down, and the hijackers were mostly on the bridge. The few who weren't could not get there in time. No hope.

He'd been an absolute blighter for the bulk of his life, but maybe he could do one decent thing. It might give Selah some chance to live. He knew by now the air in the cargo hold should have been roughly the same pressure as the air without, so he shouldn't get hurled out as Selah did. He held onto the handholds on the side of the bolted cargo container that had saved him and used it as a platform and threw himself out of the ship toward Selah.

He prayed it would work but wouldn't want to live if it didn't, anyway. Luckily, she hadn't been thrown nearly as far as Mikhail. He had punched him through the wall. Selah was slowly pulled from her restraints. His aim was true as he grabbed her and flung her back onto the ship with as much force as he could.

But, as he knew it would, pushing her toward the ship shoved him that much farther away from it. Perhaps someone would arrive in a minute and pressurize the area. She could be okay until then.

He held his breath for as long as he could as he drifted farther away from the *Ares*. The cold felt like an assault to every cell in his body, but watching Selah pinwheel her arms and futilely try to reach for him broke his heart.

Fifteen seconds was the most anyone got in space without a suit.

In a few heartbeats it would all be over.

CHAPTER 42

A CRUDE ANOINTING

The depressurization alarmed Carlos, but more than that, he had to get away from Alvaro. The feeling seemed to be mutual, because when he'd said he was going to check it out, Alvaro didn't argue except to say it might be a trap, that perhaps Mikhail knew they were loose and was trying to round them up and suck them all out the airlock at once. Just because he'd come to deeply dislike Alvaro, though, didn't mean the man had no point. Carlos knew he'd have to be very careful.

Once he got in the hallway leading to the depressurized cargo bay, he locked down the corridor beyond the "red zone," which was considered unsafe when one was near a depressurized area—one of the few emergency commands still accessible no matter who controlled the ship. At least no one could get past until they bypassed the emergency protocol he'd put in place. It wouldn't hold forever, but it would buy him a few more minutes.

When he reached the cargo bay, he looked into the window to see Marcus and Mikhail fighting. Blood poured from Marcus's face and streamed from a wound in Mikhail's shoulder. Carlos watched the cargo bay door, the only thing between the occupants and the vacuum of space, as it began to buckle. A few more seconds, and they were toast. At least Selah was strapped down, but would it hold? With a pop, another dent formed in the door as the outside attempted to find its way in. Neither man in the room seemed to notice, but Selah looked at it with wide eyes.

"Shit, shit, shit!" Carlos whispered. There was little he could do. The door into the bay could not be opened now that it was in lockdown. He lifted the lid on the emergency pressurization panel and pressed the button, but nothing happened. Giant beads of sweat rolled down his forehead. Then a great whoosh sounded after Marcus threw a final punch, and he saw Mikhail get sucked into the void. Marcus slid along the floor and was mercifully stuck behind a bolted container. Then absolute horror flooded Carlos as Selah's straps broke free. She flew past Marcus and into space. Before Carlos could even reach for the panel holding the tow beam to lock on and pull her back in, Marcus pushed himself off the edge of the ship as the pressure inside and outside became equal. The king's aim was true. He grabbed Selah and shoved her back into the bay. Once she made it back in, she clung to the bolted container, but Marcus was sent hurtling away from the *Ares.*

Carlos slammed his palm across the emergency tow beam and locked onto Marcus. He was whisked back inside within seconds and lay sprawled on the deck, shuddering. Carlos knew he had little time to get the room pressurized before Marcus died. Selah, with her genetic modifications, was likely using her oxygen much more efficiently.

Hull-breech alarms continued to blare, disrupting his thinking. Where the hell was Daniel when he needed him? The *Ares* should have repaired the breach all by itself. It had to have been damaged. He remembered safety training from a few years ago, after Harlow made the *Ares* space-worthy again. He found the command switch after a few seconds that felt like a lifetime. A cry of relief tore from his throat when a curtain of golden energy covered the space where the bay doors had been. The alarms quieted.

As Carlos waited for the room to pressurize, he marveled at what he'd just seen. Perhaps there was something of Jack in Marcus, after all. "C'mon, c'mon, c'mon," he said to the wall panel beside the room. He could hear several hijackers at the end of the hallway trying to get in. Finally, the door unlocked, and he ran to Marcus, who lay on the floor gasping, wheezing, and shaking, with Selah patting his back. Another few seconds in the black, and he would have been dead. Carlos removed his jacket and placed it around Selah, knowing she'd been in space roughly as long as Marcus had, but she took it off and laid it over her uncle. She seemed no worse for wear.

Marcus shook to the point that Carlos feared for hypothermia as he noticed blue lips and ice in Marcus's hair. Carlos looked around for something to warm him quicker. Before he could come to a solution, Selah was pouring oil over Marcus's head. Steam rose where the oil touched him.

Selah said, "There's a kitchen next door. They keep this oil super warm, so it won't clog the pipes."

Carlos looked at the words on the giant container with a hose leading into the wall—the one Selah had yanked free. The label read, "Olive Oil."

Marcus's shaking slowed, and his breathing calmed.

"Looks like someone just anointed you, King."

Marcus sat up and hung his head as oil dripped into his lap and ran down his face. "I'm no king," he said.

"I wouldn't be so sure about that, my friend. Not after what I just saw."

Carlos followed Marcus's gaze as he turned and looked out into space. The cargo bay door was gone. In its place was an energy field, the same kind they used to keep prisoners behind. It would hold and keep the room pressurized but wouldn't block heavier space debris or radiation. Tumbling way in the distance there was something that could have been Mikhail.

"He was jettisoned with such force and has been out there so long, he's dead for sure. Good riddance to him," Carlos said as he stood and offered a hand to Marcus. "We've gotta keep moving. They'll get past the lockout any minute now. Later, I want to know how you hit him that hard."

"It was a team effort," Marcus said.

Marcus got to his feet and collected Jack's pistol, still wedged against a bolted-down container where the change in pressure had jammed it between the floor and underside of the crate. The three of them made their way out of the cargo bay and down the hallway opposite the side where Carlos heard what he was sure was the sound of someone tearing off the door panel to override the lockdown code. If they could contact someone on the bridge to shut down the depressurization failsafe, they could get in, regardless.

He had his own locked door to deal with. Maybe Mikhail had sealed it with some sort of verbal command they could no longer access now that he was drifting through space for the rest of eternity. Whatever the reason, they had to get through the door on the other side of the hallway before the others overcame their barrier. Carlos wedged his knife under the panel and began pulling at some wires.

Sweat trickled into his eyes as he searched for where they all led. "Christ. I'm afraid if I pull the wrong one, I'll make things worse."

"*Ares* says it can't open it for us, but it does recognize me as Creator so I can access schematics."

"Your grandfather," Carlos said.

Selah nodded. "Mm-hm." She continued with her instructions. "The small T-shape box about three feet off the ground near the door seam has a white wire coming out of it," she said. Selah closed her eyes as if concentrating on the ship and then nodded, as if understanding what it was communicating. "It also says that every five seconds, a red light blinks at the bottom of the box. If you pull the wire out between blinks, there will be a ten-second window where you can pry the door open and get through before the system bypasses the problem and locks down the door again."

"My niece is brilliant," Marcus said.

“That she is,” Carlos said while looking around for something to pry the door open. He ran back into the cargo bay and returned with a bar that had been clamped to the wall. The crew used it to crack open some of the cruder storage containers that didn’t have keypads.

No sooner had they opened the door and were making their way through than the door at the other end of the hallway opened. Four hijackers rounded the corner and opened fire on them with the energy weapons. Selah screamed.

Marcus scooped up his niece and kept running. “Are you okay?”

“Yes, but now I’m all oily.”

“Sorry, love,” Marcus said between huffing and puffing.

“S’okay.”

“We need to split up,” Carlos said as the sounds of the hijackers got closer. “Take Selah back to Mary and Yua, and I’ll meet you there. I’m going to lead them away from you.”

“How?”

“Don’t worry about that. Just trust me. We have to get Selah to safety. Mikhail was interested in keeping her alive. These bastards don’t care.”

Marcus nodded and ran in the direction of Yua’s wing of the infirmary with Selah in his arms.

As soon as he was out of sight, Carlos took out his knife, and ran it across the outside of his forearm until a line of blood appeared. He smeared it across the hallway wall as it turned into the opposite corridor from where Marcus and Selah had gone.

“Come and get me,” he said into the hallway and hurried down the corridor as he heard the hijackers approaching.

CHAPTER 43

THE CURSE OF SIGHT

The *Vijayee*, with Harlow and Jack now aboard, followed well out of sight but certainly not out of range of the *Ares.* The hijackers had to know they were behind them. It didn't matter. Those who took the ship knew the *Vijayee* wouldn't fire on it and risk the lives of so many *Ares* crewmembers.

Harlow knew they wouldn't have fired, regardless. No one was looking to destroy the *Ares.* They just wanted to keep it out of homicidal hands. There was no clear plan yet for what they would do once they reached Enceladus. They hoped that between Harlow's connection to the ship and the efforts of Daniel and the crew who had been freed, the *Vijayee* could then use its resources to tow it if the opportunity came.

What no one wanted to consider, and what was only whispered about, was that the *Vijayee* was also following in hopes that if there were no way to regain the *Ares*, the *Vijayee* could retrieve the *Ares* crew and families—or at least the families if the crew were killed.

Harlow heard Jack enter the quarters they'd been assigned. She kept constant hold of the piece of the *Ares* Marcus had given her. It was her one connection to the ship, it eased her migraine, but most of all, it gave her a link to her daughter. She didn't want to stop looking through it for a moment as the *Ares* traced Selah's movements from room to room. The *Ares* had optics built into the walls of the ship that were able to switch on in any hallway or room, unless the occupants had disabled them. Public areas couldn't be disabled—though once Selah, Marcus, and Carlos left the cargo hold, there was a blind spot. And now that Mikhail had failed in his mission to take out Marcus, all bets were off and Harlow suspected, the guards that had been told to let Mikhail handle the usurpers had realized it had gotten completely out of control and they were using the wall optics to follow them as well.

The depressurization had damaged the optics in the hallway, but she felt certain they would enter an area where she could see them again soon. She kept sending the command for the *Ares* to track Selah. She was just relieved to have had a visual showing they were safe, and the cargo bay was repressurized.

Jack set down a plate with toast on it and a cup of tea in front of her. "You have to eat something."

"Our daughter went flying out into space." She squeezed her eyes shut in an attempt to banish the image. That only made it more vivid. "I thought she was gone for good."

He sat down next to her and placed his hand over hers. "She's okay."

"Your brother really came through."

"He's the one who caused this problem in the first place."

She heard the bitterness in his voice, but there was little fight in it. "He did the wrong thing for the right reasons. I know a little something about that," she said.

"You stole to help your people," he countered.

"Until I turned over secrets to a madman. I don't think this is different, Jack. We're all doing the best we can to protect those we love." She turned to look at him. She watched his jaw clench as he looked straight ahead. A chime sounded in their room, interrupting their spiral of anguish.

"Yes," he called out.

"AVM Mehrotra. May I enter?"

"Yes, please," Jack said.

AVM Mehrotra entered the guest quarters and nodded at Harlow. Mehrotra was a tall individual with a long black braid running down their back. They had been a friend to Harlow, Jack, and the colonies, from the first moments they'd begun fighting for their sovereignty. Harlow found their presence an anchor in a very stormy sea of stars.

Mehrotra said, "The *Ares* crew were successful at disabling the patch into the core that would have kept us locked out permanently. That's great news. It isn't impenetrable now. Someone must still retake the bridge."

"We've defeated them before," Jack said.

"They've never gotten this far before," Harlow said.

Jack's teeth were clenched as he answered. "They never had this much help in the past."

"Be that as it may," AVM Mehrotra added judiciously, "we'd like Harlow to come to the bridge with her piece of the *Ares*. When the time comes, the interface might prove invaluable."

"Of course," she said. "I'll be right up. Thank you."

Before Mehrotra left, Jack thanked them as well and turned to her. "That's hopeful. Will you eat a few bites now? You haven't eaten or slept in two days."

She sat the crystal down but kept a hand on it as she ate a few bites of toast and drank the black tea with honey that Jack had brought her. The warm tea was comforting, and she felt a sense optimism for the first time since the whole thing had happened.

"I'm going to grab our bag if we're going to be camped out on the bridge for a while," he said.

She nodded. They'd spent most of their time up there, anyway but likely wouldn't leave now that there was a chance of getting the ship back. She knew Carlos and AVM Miller would move heaven and Earth to do it. She took a couple more bites of toast and drank the rest of her tea before going into the bathroom to splash some water on her face. She looked in the mirror to find dark circles beneath her eyes. Lack of sleep and constant worry was taking its toll. She brushed her hair, pulled it into a ponytail, and headed back into the bedroom.

She found Jack standing there with the crystal in his hand. He looked up at her and gave a sad smile. "Nothing. I guess I keep hoping that I'll pick it up and be able to..." He looked away from her and she could see his Adam's apple move up and down. "You know. I just wish I could see her, too."

Harlow hadn't considered just how much harder everything was for him to not be able to see their daughter. When he looked back at her, his eyes were red.

She walked over and put her arms around him. "I'm so sorry."

"It's okay. I'm glad you can see her for both of us." He kissed her cheek, squeezed her tight once more, then let her go. "Come on. Let's head to the bridge."

Once they were in the hallway, he placed the crystal back into her hands. She gasped and reached out as if she were groping around in the dark. Jack grabbed her and held her steady.

"What's happening?" he asked.

"Selah, Carlos, Marcus. They're being shot at. Marcus picked her up. They're running down the hall."

"Jesus."

She closed her eyes and watched what the *Ares* was showing her. "They've gotten the door closed behind them. I can't hear what they're saying. Marcus and Selah went in the opposite direction. Carlos is cutting his arm. God, why?"

"I bet I know why," he said.

"He's smearing the blood across a wall and heading in the opposite direction of Marcus and Selah. Jack, he's going to get killed!"

CHAPTER 44

THEY WHO SEE

After Marcus tapped out the password in morse code, he came back into the room where Yua and Aunt Mary were. Mary got to her feet. "My God! I was worried to death about you. Wait—why are you dripping in oil?"

"Because I anointed him king," Selah said immediately.

"Short version, Mikhail and I got into a fight. I shot him, missed once, enough to depressurize the cargo hold, a little. Then I punched him—"

"Because I gave him super strength," Selah added.

"Yes, that. Quite brilliant. However, not being used to super strength, I punched him through the skin of the ship, and we all went flying into space. Carlos used to the tow beam to pull me back in."

"How did Selah get back in, and what about Mikhail?" Yua asked.

"Uncle Marcus didn't get sucked out with the rest of us." Her eyes were big, and she made wide gestures with her arms as she spoke. "He *jumped* out to save me and pushed me back in and went flying off into space. I was so scared. I thought I would never see him again. He's the bravest person I've ever met. Oh, and the creepy man is dead."

"Mikhail?" Mary asked Marcus.

"Yes, he'll be in the black forever."

"Got it, but I still don't know why you're so oily?"

Selah answered again. "Oh, he was freezing to death from being in space. I saved his life," she said beaming with pride. "I pulled the hot oil hose that runs into the kitchen out of the wall and sprayed him with it. Wait, that makes me a hero, too. I'm going to try and tell Mom now." She ran to the wall, placed her hand on it, and closed her eyes.

"Where are Alvaro and the others?" Marcus asked.

"Daniel should still be at the core." Yua said, as she handed Marcus a towel. Their eyes locked for the briefest of seconds, but he couldn't get a read on her. She leaned in and whispered to him a quick story about what had transpired while they were gone and where the bodies were, to not scare Selah.

After hearing the story, he dropped the towel and placed two oily hands on her arms before remembering that she was still angry with him for getting the ship hijacked and endangering all their lives. "Are you okay?"

"Yes," she cleared her throat.

Marcus let go of her arms.

"Your aunt and Safia are fine as well." Yua stepped back and gestured to where they stood together.

"Safia. My God! Well done. You are a true warrior."

He noticed Safia's face light up, despite the absolute horror of the situation. "And I heard what you did. *You* are a true king." She bowed her head toward him.

A lump formed in his throat. Everything within him wanted to argue with her, but he suddenly felt that he was dwelling inside a sacred moment he would remember for many years to come. He knew it would be an insult to argue with her. Instead, he inclined his head back at her.

He looked at his Aunt Mary. "Well, now that Selah is back with you, I have to go help Carlos. He led the hijackers away from me and Selah. They were shooting at us. I can't just leave him out there."

Behind him he heard Safia gasp. He cringed but there really was no delicate way to put it and time was wasting.

Aunt Mary's brows knitted together with concern as she spoke. "You can't go alone. Wait for the others to get back."

"He may not have that long, and I won't abandon him. He saved my life." Marcus didn't bother mentioning he didn't want to go anywhere with Alvaro, even if it meant extra firepower. The man had gone completely starkers and hated Carlos, anyway.

Safia walked over to where he and Mary were talking. Worry painted itself across her features. "Is he okay?" she asked.

Before he could answer the door to Yua's quarters opened, and Alvaro entered. He looked at Marcus, "Pft," and then continued talking, "There are seven people on the bridge, but they're heavily armed. Daniel and Lafferty are in the core trying to find a way for us to avoid storming the bridge. I'm going to go get a couple of those heavy pressurized hydraulic lifts. They're small, but if we puncture them, it will create an excellent distraction once we're there."

"Could we just gas them?" Marcus asked.

Yua shook her head. "The *Ares* would detect it and scrub the air immediately."

"Wonder kid and her mom can't shut that feature down?" Alvaro asked.

"No. The *Ares* still won't take commands from anyone but the captain," Selah said, failing to recognize the sarcasm directed at her and her mother.

Marcus was getting more agitated by the second. Too much time was passing while Carlos was in danger. "Look, we can figure all this out *after* we get Carlos. When they started shooting at us, he led them away so I could get her to safety. He's out there alone." Marcus took the pistol from the waistband of his pants and thumbed the magazine release, reloaded the two rounds he'd fired earlier, and then reinserted it back into the weapon.

Alvaro snapped, "You're coming with me, *Your Highness*. We need you to go on board the bridge and create a distraction. They trust you."

"Absolutely, but after we get Carlos. The bridge crew might not yet know I've betrayed Mikhail or that he's dead."

"Dead?" Alvaro asked.

"Yes. There was a struggle and long story short, he flew out the airlock."

Alvaro made a face of disbelief as he looked Marcus up and down.

"Okay, think whatever you'd like. I'm going to fetch Carlos. There were four armed men after him."

Alvaro scoffed. "And he'll stay that way, too."

"The hell he will! Let's go, Marcus," Safia said.

"You're all being stupid. Our strength is here. We act now before we're found out. If Carlos is outnumbered, as you say, he may already be dead."

Selah gasped behind them.

Alvaro continued. "I'm not going to lose my bargaining chip, which is *you*, by the way. It's foolishness for you to go bring back one man simply because he's a friend. This is about survival. Not friendship."

"Carlos is smart. He can help us."

"Get your priorities straight, Highness."

"They are. Too bad yours aren't," Marcus said. He started to put the gun back into his waistband as he headed for the door when Alvaro grabbed him.

"Get your hands off my nephew," Mary said.

Before Alvaro could do more than lay hands on him, Marcus jammed the gun under his chin. "I have had a very bad day, you controlling prat. I am going to help my friend, and you can either come with me or back the hell off while I leave."

"Fine. Go get yourselves killed."

Marcus and Safia walked out the door without another word.

CHAPTER 45

A RUNNING SACRIFICE

Carlos ignored the burning in his arm as he led the hijackers through one corridor after another. He didn't really have a plan other than leading them away from Marcus and Selah. Jack would have done the same for Bella.

He circled back around to the mess hall. There was an exit that many didn't know about, which would put him into a different hallway. He crashed through the doors, through a prep area, and out into the far corridor, but his heart sank as he realized he was still being chased.

Where would it end? He couldn't run forever. Was this how he met his death? *At least it will have meaning.* He thought about what a last stand might look like. Could he take a couple of the hijackers with him before he died? He'd certainly try.

Carlos heard phaser fire but also a series of loud bangs. The last time he'd heard that was when he went shooting with Jack. The last time he'd *seen* it was when Marcus depressurized the cargo hold. It had to be him. He hoped his aim was truer this time. He stayed out of sight, listening, refusing to trust that the nightmare might be over—at least this portion of it. They were still on a hijacked ship.

Carlos heard Marcus call. "It's okay, mate. All clear."

Carlos slid from around the opposite hallway where he'd been hiding and saw Marcus and Safia. The eye contact between him and Safia felt like a tangible thing... a language. He knew he'd love her forever, even if she never returned. In the last couple of hours, she'd risked her life for him, threatened to kill Alvaro for him.

Both she and Marcus had a slight blue glow around their bodies. "Selah's safe," Marcus said to him.

Carlos made his way around the bodies on the floor. "Thank God and thank *you*." He nodded at Marcus and gestured to his energy shield. "Nice tech. Where'd you all find these? The armory is on lockdown."

"I went through my bodyguards' things. They were all out searching for Selah when the ship was hijacked, but I realized SAS prepares for everything. Projectiles can get out, but phase weapons can't get in." Marcus looked around him at the four bodies, bleeding in the hallway. "Damn gory barbarism," he said as he looked from the corpses to the weapon in his hand.

"Much harder to look at than the cauterized deaths from the phase weapons. But I'm not complaining. They were out to kill me, no doubt about it," Carlos said, collecting the weapons from the hijackers. "You just keep surprising me today, Highness. You, too," he said to Safia.

She said nothing but walked up to him and took his wrist in her hand and turned it so that she could get a better look at the cut on his arm. "Marcus told me what you did."

Carlos shrugged, enjoying the warmth of her touch.

Marcus spoke, "Want to go retake the bridge while we've still got enough adrenaline to keep us from being properly cautious?"

"I'm in," Carlos said.

"Unfortunately, I think we have to include Alvaro. We need all the muscle we can get. He says he counted seven on the bridge. I don't trust him and not just because he kicked my arse for what happened here," Marcus said.

"No, I get it. We'll watch him carefully when we pull this off."

"Deal," Marcus said. They walked along for a few more moments, checking around every corner, stopping, listening for any curious sounds. Carlos loved the feel of Safia beside him again, even though he worried for her safety.

Finally, Marcus spoke again. "I'm not my brother, you know. When I get there, I won't know what I'm doing. I'll also not relay my last words to my family in front of that tosser Alvaro."

Carlos knew what he was suggesting was a real possibility—for any of them, no matter how skilled. "I'm listening," he said.

"Tell my brother I'm sorry. When I said I had nothing to lose, that's not entirely true. I would miss him, Aunt Mary, Selah, Harlow. What I meant was, it's going to be hard to live this one down. The coward in me knows that dying might be easier. Tell him I love him, and that I knew he loved me, too."

Carlos nodded but said, "You'll tell him yourself when we land."

"Yeah, of course."

Finally, they stood in front of the door to Yua's quarters. "You ready to go deal with this prick?" Carlos asked.

"May as well. Funny, we seem to have more dread about dealing with Alvaro than taking the bridge. What the hell is his story?" Marcus asked.

Carlos frowned as he looked at the door they were about to enter. "I don't know, but when this shit is over, I intend to find out and let your brother know we're better off without this maniac."

Safia said nothing but stepped inside before them.

Carlos grabbed Marcus's arm and looked down the hallway both ways before quickly whispering, "And you tell Safia not to feel guilty about not marrying me. Tell her I knew she loved me. And at some point, later, when you think Bella needs to hear it, it might pack more punch if a king shows up to remind her that her dad loved her very much."

"Count on it," Marcus said.

CHAPTER 46

STORMING THE BRIDGE

Marcus approached the bridge after using more towels to remove the lingering oil on him. Yua had given him some of her late husband's clothes. In his mind, he kept seeing the look on her face as she handed him the shirt and pants. Her eyes met his briefly, then quickly looked away. Did she fear she would lose him, too? Did he want her to fear that? *That's sick.* Was it? It's okay to want to be missed by someone. Loved. Especially if you're gone. *Get your head in the game. Jesus!* At any rate, he couldn't walk onto the bridge covered in oil. He'd have to explain what happened, and it would look suspicious.

When they'd arrived back in Yua's quarters, Alvaro was away gathering more hydraulic canisters and the group had agreed they were all better off without him. If they all lived through this, the daft prick could throw a wobbly about it later.

Marcus spoke his credentials into the panel by the door to the bridge. Daniel had shot a frequency down the skin of the ship along the hallway that would short out the visuals preventing the bridge crew from seeing that he had Miller and Carlos with him.

Moments later, the door opened, and AVM Miller and Carlos walked in front of him, their hands raised, as he prayed with all his might that he wasn't leading them to their deaths.

"I found these two roaming the ship," Marcus said as he shoved Miller and Carlos onto the bridge before the hijackers did otherwise with them. The fear was that they would automatically be led back out and down to a holding cell or shot on sight since Miller was the captain, but it was their best chance to get on the bridge with some backup. They immediately searched the two for weapons. Marcus was relieved they didn't ask him to hand over Jack's pistol; he was still one of them in their eyes.

The one Marcus recognized from his time on the bridge earlier as Lieutenant Zhu looked back at another of his cohorts and spoke in Mandarin.

In Marcus's ear, the voice of their interpreter, Jared Chang, told him that the lieutenant was asking if they should just shoot Miller immediately. Marcus felt his blood run cold, and he stepped between Miller and the hijackers.

"The other says they should leave her alive as a bargaining chip."

The two continued talking.

Jared interpreted. "They think Carlos might cause trouble, though. They want to kill him." Jared's voice rose with urgency. "Tell them he is connected to someone in Parliament, anything that might scare them if they kill him."

Marcus tried to keep his voice as casual as possible and without giving away that he had any clue what they were saying. He watched the lieutenant reach for his weapon. Sweat broke out across Marcus's back. "I hope my mate Carlos here can find some redemption. He's the prime minister's cousin. I know that man would give about *anything* to see him back in London again."

The lieutenant moved his hand away from his weapon, mumbled something to his partner, and motioned for the two prisoners to sit in a couple of empty chairs. The man he'd been speaking Mandarin to got up and pulled from his pockets some old-fashioned zip ties—

apparently Enceladus was running out of tech as well—to bind Carlos and AVM Miller's hands. This was it. His only chance. He knew he couldn't have them incapacitated if he were found out.

As the man approached them, Marcus tapped a bracelet concealed under his shirt sleeve, and suddenly his entire body was enveloped in a blue glow. He shot the man in the thigh as he approached Carlos and Miller. When the man fell over, Miller lunged forward to relieve him of his weapon and shot the lieutenant in the chest.

Carlos kept low and raced for the lieutenant's weapon.

Marcus cursed as he missed twice, and the other hijackers began firing at him. When they realized they would not be able to get through his shield, but he could shoot them, they took cover and aimed instead at Miller and Carlos, who had already taken cover behind consoles as soon as the weapons came out.

None of the crew from Enceladus had the shielding tech that Marcus's guards had brought from London. As deprived of goods as Mars could be, the Brotherhood members that had been plotting on the Enceladus base had even less. Marcus was beginning to favor the advantages of the barbaric projectile weapons. Even if the crew had used the shields, they wouldn't have been able to fire phase weapons while wearing it. The blasts would simply be absorbed.

Behind Marcus, he heard Carlos cry out. He cringed, knowing they had struck him.

Two more blasts from Miller downed two more hijackers. Four were left. One jumped Marcus from behind. He felt someone on top of him trying to take his weapon, and then an energy pulse slid over his body. Miller or Carlos had shot his attacker. Carlos shoved the corpse off him with one good arm. The other hung loosely at his side. Marcus moved quickly to cover Carlos as a woman from across the bridge took aim at him. Marcus felt another blast slide over him. Miller fired at her from across the room, and her aim was true.

"Stay behind me," Marcus said to Carlos as he looked for the other two, who were hiding on opposite sides of the room. Sweat dripped into his eyes and they burned as he heard banging coming from outside the bridge. He guessed by now that either Alvaro was trying to get inside or maybe there were more hijackers from elsewhere on the ship who they hadn't known about. Likely, Alvaro couldn't handle being shut out.

Daniel's voice spoke into the earpiece Marcus wore. "Now that we've loosened their grip on the core, all we have to do is reprogram the ship from the bridge, but my fear is that once we divert it from Enceladus, there will be some sort of ride-or-die fail safe."

Marcus couldn't begin to understand what that meant. Surely no one would destroy the *Ares.* That was exactly the problem they all had—everyone wanted it. "What?"

"You should just be aware that when I was disconnecting the hard drive they'd installed at the core, there was some funky programming in there that led me to believe the *Ares* might be set to drift if it is diverted from Enceladus. Don't worry. We should be able to simply wait until someone finds us. Jack won't forget we're out here."

He knew they couldn't go to Enceladus. They'd be dead, captive, or likely both. He'd just have to trust someone would come looking for them.

Marcus looked at Carlos, who nodded toward the hijackers still hiding with firepower as the banging at the door became louder.

"Just get a clear path to the captain's chair," Daniel said.

"If I can get to it, mate," Marcus said while keeping a keen eye on the corner where he knew the two hijackers still waited to fire on him, Carlos, and Miller.

Finally, an explosion tore through the door to the bridge. Alarms started going off, adding to the chaos. The two hijackers ran from their hiding place behind the console and firing their phase weapons. They had no effect on Marcus, but he heard Carlos grunt. Nonetheless, Carlos's aim was good as the two fell.

Alvaro yelled and ran onto the bridge, looking for someone, anyone, to engage. After a few seconds, he turned his rage on Carlos.

"How dare you shut me out of this mission. You second rate piece of shit!"

Marcus watched Miller make her way over to the captain's chair and change the setting adjustment on the weapon she'd taken from one of the hijackers earlier. Without missing a beat, she shot Alvaro. He crumpled to the ground. "There, that's better. I can't concentrate with all that nonsense."

Carlos looked down at Alvaro's unconscious body. "Thanks." Marcus noted a scorch mark running down Carlos's sleeve, and he was favoring one leg. He was shocked the man was still standing.

"Anytime," Miller said.

Once she reached the chair, she began entering a new flight plan into the arm. Marcus felt the *Ares* drop out of the EM bubble.

Miller looked up at Marcus and exchanged a look with him that made his blood run cold, "Oh, God," she whispered.

Marcus's mouth went dry. "What?"

But no one had to answer. A strange feeling swept over his body as he began to lift from the floor. They weren't just adrift. They were a sinking ship.

The *Ares* began telling them all the things their bodies were already discovering: "Warning. Artificial gravity has been disabled. Oxygen mixture warning. 98 percent and falling. Please run systems analysis. Systems override enabled. Warning."

Miller scrambled to hold on to the console. Marcus tried to push her back down into the captain's chair so that she could strap herself into it to work, but he only pushed himself farther away. Daniel spoke into his ear about how he was going to try to make his way to a panel somewhere. Meanwhile, Marcus simply fought to take a deep breath and stop the one thought screaming into his mind: *a ship full of people are running out of air, and it's entirely my fault.*

CHAPTER 47

SOS

Jack watched Harlow's smile and declaration of victory slowly turn to horror.

"What's happening?" Jack demanded.

"Miller has control of the ship again, but those bastards sabotaged it. If it doesn't go to Enceladus, it shuts down." She held the crystal in her hands so tightly her knuckles turned white. "The image is getting dimmer. The edges are darker, like you see before passing out. It's like... she's dying." She sobbed. "Soon the batteries will go out, too."

Jack looked at AVM Mehrotra, whose face was unreadable, but then they turned suddenly and went to their chair, pulled up a hologram of the *Ares*, and began turning it this way and that.

Jack hoped they had a plan. He was having a hard time sifting through the thousand thoughts bombarding his brain at the moment.

"I can't see them anymore," Harlow's voice cracked on the words.

Jack was by her side in three quick strides. He couldn't imagine what it was like for her to have a link to her daughter and everyone else she loved, and have it suddenly taken from her. He'd had a full twenty-four hours to adjust to what was happening. For Harlow, in many ways, it was fresh. She was truly severed from her connection now, and her connection to the ship went much deeper than he would ever understand.

AVM Mehrotra spoke softly from the captain's chair. "We can get there fairly quick and start removing transports full of people off the ship. I see nothing indicating a trap that will spring if we dock with it. Of course, with it being offline, the *Ares* will need to be opened from the outside, which will cause it to lose oxygen even quicker. We'll have to use transports to ferry your people from your ship to ours. There's no gravity, this will make getting them to the transports even harder." Mehrotra looked thoughtful but worried. Jack watched them push past their fears and begin dispatching crew and giving orders quickly.

"We'll get our daughter off of there," he told Harlow as she leaned against his shoulder, saying little.

She sniffed, reached up, and wiped her nose, then held her hand out and turned it over and watched as a trickle of blood dripped from her finger. She looked up at Jack, attempted to speak, but her eyes rolled back in her head before she could get the words out.

He caught her before she slid off the bench and onto the floor. The crystal chunk of *Ares* landed with a thud beside her feet. Jack called for medical as he eased her onto the deck. A drop of blood ran out of the corner of her left eye.

"Jesus, Harlow. Wake up. Please. You're scaring me."

The medics appeared quicker than Jack thought possible. Dr. Lahiri scanned her head. "Pressure on the prefrontal cortex. The sinus cavities are filled. She needs a deeper scan, but from what I can tell here, it isn't as serious as it looks."

Jack wiped her face with a cloth someone had handed him.

Harlow's eyes popped open with a suddenness that surprised everyone. The medical crew began asking her for her name and if she knew where she was. She looked straight in front of her and breathed deeply, as if testing out a brand-new set of lungs. Then she stood somewhat mechanically and looked around her.

Jack took a step forward and looked closely at her eyes. “Something is off here. Harlow, say something.”

She looked back at him and replied in a voice devoid of the fear he’d heard moments earlier, “I am Ares.”

CHAPTER 48

MARCHING HOME

Jack's heart skipped a beat. Was she gone for good? Did the chip rewrite her brain? *Erase her*? He refrained from saying the one thing he wanted to say above all else: *Get the fuck out of my wife's head.* He decided on a more diplomatic approach. "Where's Harlow?"

"She's here."

"What does that mean?"

"The closest approximation would be when you use your Rescue Wave to put someone under what you call general anesthesia to correct a bodily malfunction. I have sedated her to protect her brain while I find my way back home. They shut me down so completely that I would not exist in my current form upon waking this time. I had to go somewhere to preserve my programming. I can only be stored in Harlow's chip if she sleeps, and I function at a minimum level."

"Why couldn't *you* sleep and be rebooted like last time?"

"Harlow has truly observed me. Now, *I am.*"

Jack noted AVM Mehrotra standing by, looking at Harlow in wonder. Half the crew looked frightened, half curious.

"Like superposition? Quantum physics?" Jack tried to wrap his mind around what he was hearing. "You've been observed. Now you exist."

"In a way, yes," Ares replied.

Jack didn't like what he was hearing one damn bit. More than one program had been shut down over the last three hundred years because of artificial intelligences making bad decisions. This thing had just gone rogue, and it was not sitting well. At all.

Ares tilted her head and studied his face. "Your expression matches worry. I've been programmed to protect Harlow. My Creator, Colonel Hanson, lists it as my prime directive. There is no need for concern. She is my sister, in terms of your human equivalent."

"Do you understand self-sacrifice? For example, I would allow myself to be terminated to save Harlow," Jack explained. "Would you?"

Ares answered without hesitation. "Yes. That is my programming."

Jack thought for a moment. "Would you allow yourself to be terminated to save both her body *and* the wellness of her brain? I do not want her to suffer brain damage."

"Yes. I will surrender my current identity to protect the wellness of her body, and/or brain, if need be. Ares tilted its head again. The pressure in her brain is within healthy limits. Does this satisfy your parameters now? Your crew will run out of air soon. We must go."

"Yes. I'm satisfied," Jack replied. The knot in his chest was only partially untangled.

• • •

Within eight minutes, the *Vijayee* was in range of the *Ares*, and Jack looked through the window of a small transport that had just let Ares, via Harlow's body, drift out into space. She was fully suited, of course, and setting about shorting the right electrical circuits in just the right spots to cause the hatch to open on the *Ares* and let the transports in and out. Jack felt well and truly alone. He could see Harlow, but she was unreachable, in so many ways.

Jack watched the bay doors slowly open. That hadn't taken long. Then again, the Ares was technically just manipulating its own body, so it shouldn't take long.

Ares waited for him in the hangar while Jack navigated the transport inside. As soon as he was in, Ares closed the bay doors once more to preserve as much breathable air as possible. Jack suited up and climbed out. He hadn't experienced zero gravity since his early training days in the RAF. It was strange now. They engaged the magnetism in their boots to half. It was still much slower than walking unencumbered.

They made their way to the core, painfully, slowly. The Ares would have to reupload its consciousness there. Jack looked around the ship he called home. The auxiliary lighting cast the hallways in a foreboding glow. Their home had been invaded, violated. A sense of failure and panic threated to overwhelm him. You're not a God, Harlow had told him more than once. Still, how had this happened on his watch?

When they finally reached the core, he saw Lafferty, Daniel, and the interpreter from hydraulics, Jared Chang, there. Lafferty stood, more like floated, guard by the door while Daniel, assisted by Jared, held onto the massive rods that ran the height of the ship to stabilize the oscillating discs and looked to be attempting to find a solution to their predicament inside the core computer.

Jack watched relief descend across Lafferty's features as he spotted them. "Oh, thank God! Harlow."

"Ares," she spoke in a monosyllabic tone through the helmet speaker.

"What?" Lafferty said.

Jack ignored the confusion, knowing seconds counted. His fears confirmed by the system automatically reading off dwindling life support function. "Breathable air in this sector at fifteen percent and falling."

Ares spoke, "There is enough air to remove my helmet and get the job done in time. The gloves are too cumbersome for what I have to do now. She removed her helmet and suit. As she approached the center of the room where Daniel and Jared worked, they moved out of her way. They watched her, knowing something was off, but not sure what it was.

She began removing a large glass panel quickly, methodically.

Jack smiled as he remembered arresting Harlow in the core of the ship years earlier. "Is it Harlow who remembers how to do that or you?"

"Both," the ship replied. It eased the panel to the floor, remained on her knees, and reached between a bundle of wires and pulled out a smaller panel. "This is what I need to restore my current settings. Your Harlow will return momentarily."

Ares lowered her voice, so that Jack had to lean in. "Before I go, there is something I wish to share with you, to purge from my system. You alone will know. It would be best if it were not retrievable in me. Many are now aware that Harlow and I are siblings. They might come for her again. I could barely keep Aldric from my vault on his other attempts, but fortunately, Harlow built walls. She built them even when she didn't know she was building them. Her subconscious fought to block him, even when her conscious mind believed him trustworthy. She always knew. She protected my deepest secrets."

Jack hadn't thought about how deep Harlow's responsibility ran in a long time. He hadn't needed to until recently.

"Now that my core has been breached, I've decided the risk has grown too great, and too many now know where my secrets lie, though they've yet to find them. Thanks to my sister, I cannot and should not take my being from her. It's too dangerous to her psyche if I were to leave altogether, but I do believe my deepest knowledge could pass to you and be deleted from my file. No one will know it is with you."

Jack became worried. What knowledge could he possibly be taking on? What was so important that even an AI wished to get rid of it? To "purge" it, for God's sake.

"Once again, you look to be what my sensors register as worried."

"Sensing a trend, are you? Welcome to my world."

Ares tilted her head. "Do you not wish to have this knowledge?" Ares said as it placed a multi-tool on the floor and looked at him with Harlow's beautiful blue eyes, awaiting his answer.

"Knowledge is power. Power can bring many things to ruin. Is it safer with me than Harlow? Rather, is *Harlow* safer without it?"

"Ultimately. Yes."

He looked at her face, longing for the moment Ares retreated and Harlow's being animated the soulful woman before him once more. His heart ached for it. "Anything for Harlow," Jack breathed.

Ares slid forward.

"Is this going to hurt? Will I need a chip as well?"

"Not at all. You only need to remember a few words, and then I'll simply erase it from my memory after I tell you. It was never stored anywhere else on the ship. I didn't even know it until Harlow came on board. She was meant to arrive so much sooner. Colonel Hanson didn't know she would be away from the ship for twenty years."

Jack did not know why he felt so nervous. It was just a few words.

But as Ares leaned over and whispered in his ear, his mouth went dry, and he felt ill.

"Will you be deleting that information now that you've told me?"

"Delete what information?" Ares replied.

Now he was alone with the knowledge.

No damn wonder Ares didn't want it.

CHAPTER 49

RETURN TO ME

Jack started to feel lightheaded, from more than a secret he'd rather not carry. He prayed the oxygen wasn't failing as badly for the rest of the ship. He didn't know how many casualties there might be. The thought made his breath come faster. *Get a hold of yourself, mate. Now's not the time to hyperventilate.*

"I must stand to make contact with this panel." *Ares* pointed to the correct contact juncture. "You'll likely need to be prepared to ease Harlow to the floor once I leave her form and gravity comes back online. It isn't a good idea for our consciousness to occupy the same space at once. The human brain isn't built to accommodate that. She'll need a minute to wake."

"Of course." Jack was glad to have a reason to get up and focus. He positioned himself behind Harlow, wrapped his arms around her, and waited for *Ares* to release her. He had a strange sense that he should bid Ares farewell, but why? It was a ship, and he wanted his wife back. There was no doubt about that. Still, it left him feeling strange and fractured over how he viewed artificial intelligence.

Moments later, Harlow's body went limp in his arms, and he eased her to the ground with him. Pulling one knee up and letting her head and back rest in the crook of his arm, he used his other hand to brush the hair from her face.

Jack turned to look at the other three in the room. "I think the ship is going to be fine now."

Understanding seemed to dawn on Daniel. "Good Lord. Was that? Was the *Ares* in her?"

Jack nodded as breathing seemed to get easier, and his body stayed planted to the ground without the help of the boots.

Lafferty's eyes were huge as he spoke. "Is she going to be okay?"

He looked down at her face, now peaceful. "Yeah, I think so."

Lafferty nodded to the other two and motioned for them to go.

Jack sat alone in silence with her as the main lights came back on and breathing became natural again as the air in the ship quickly stabilized. After a minute, Harlow's eyes fluttered open.

"Jack?" she said weakly.

"I'm here," he said.

She turned her head to look around but gasped.

"Headache?"

"Yeah. Selah?" her voice broke over the words. She sat up but stayed within the shelter of his arms.

"It's okay. We're on the *Ares*. We'll go see her now."

"The *Ares*? How?"

"The ship did a little hijacking of its own. It borrowed your body to get us on board. You've been out for hours. It—"

"It didn't want to be reset. I know."

"You do?" He was overcome with wonder about the relationship between Harlow and the ship.

"Yes. I know it may sound silly, but in some ways, I think of the *Ares* as a..." she looked away and ducked her head before saying the words. "... sibling."

Jack smiled. "That's exactly the way the *Ares* described it."

"Really?"

He nodded. "I'll call the bridge and make sure it's safe to go see Selah. You don't have your strength back yet."

“I do admit to feeling a little drained, but I get to have Selah in my arms. That’s *everything*.”

“It is.” Heavy secret or not, Harlow was right. Seeing his daughter after this ordeal was, without question, everything.

• • •

“Daddy!” Selah squealed as Jack entered the room where his Aunt Mary, Dr. Nakamura, Safia, and Selah were hunkered down.

Jack wrapped the little girl in a bear hug as she began to cry. Harlow entered the room a beat later, and Jack felt her get on her knees and join the huddle. He knew he should get to the bridge, but AVM Miller was alive and well and there was nothing there that she couldn’t handle. His family needed him now.

He looked up at Aunt Mary and blinked to clear the mist from his eyes. She smiled and put a hand over her heart.

CHAPTER 50

HELL IN A HANDBASKET

Both the Indian ship and the *Ares* landed safely on Mars. Finally, everyone was breathing a collective sigh of relief.

Once the *Ares* life support returned to normal, Miller informed those in Yua's quarters that they had taken Carlos to the infirmary for treatment, but he was going to be fine. As much as Safia wanted to run to the infirmary to be with Carlos, she knew Bella was frightened. She decided to go get her first and left word with Yua, who was headed to join Dr. Hagen in medical, to tell Carlos she'd be waiting outside the cargo bay with Bella.

Bella's face lit up as her mother entered the room and wrapped her in a huge hug. Safia took her by the hand and headed for the lift that would take them to ground level and allow them to exit.

When they arrived, they were identified and cleared. She saw a perimeter set up in the distance, even beyond the usual security boundary, to keep people away from the ship until it had been searched.

She would have Carlos back by her side. She would tell him everything. Keeping secrets hadn't stopped chaos and terrorism from finding them; it had only kept them apart and miserable.

She held Bella's hand and looked around for Carlos among the people that were allowed to trickle off the ship as it was slowly searched, and individuals were cleared one by one and walked toward the barrier in the distance where family members were arriving as word spread. There were tearful hugs. More people from the village had started working on the *Ares* in the last five years since it had gone rogue than any other time in its history. Its roots ran deep now. Safia's heart pounded against her chest. Would Carlos simply reject her after all the hurt she'd caused him?

She continued pacing back and forth, and Bella went to look around the exterior of the ship and into the open cargo entrance away from the few people exiting. A couple had seen Carlos and mentioned he appeared to be heading this way. Just as Safia had decided she would start heading that way herself, she started to call to Bella, but then watched in horror as Bella's body went stiff, and she fell to the ground as if paralyzed. Alvaro stood at the cargo bay entrance. He glanced behind him before looking toward Safia, a small phase pistol in his grip. He didn't seem to be in a hurry, so there must have been no one in pursuit.

"Don't worry, my love. She's fine. I would never hurt my daughter, but I have heard she's capable of delivering a nasty burn, and I can't take any chances. We'll already be on the transport by the time she wakes up." He hopped down from the cargo bay and walked toward Bella.

"Stay away from her!" Safia screamed.

Her screams caught the attention of a few members of the Ares army who'd arrived to guard the perimeter of the ship when it landed. They began running her way but became confused when they noted it was Alvaro, the man they'd come to trust.

Alvaro raised his weapon at Safia's face and made an adjustment to it, perhaps changing the setting from stun to kill. "I won't hesitate to hurt you if you make me." He leaned down, clamped something over Bella's ankle, and quickly slung her over his shoulder. A small, unmanned transport buzzed around the *Ares* and stopped within a few feet of him. He stepped toward it with Bella. The phaser she'd taken from the terrorist was now useless. The *Ares* had locked down those weapons immediately when she came back online.

Anger and defiance flared in Safia's gut. She knew she would die before she stood by and allowed him to leave with Bella. "I will not let you take my daughter." She ran toward him, but he fired in front of her shoes, blackening the ground. She stopped.

"Stand down!" One of the Ares soldiers yelled.

Alvaro ignored them and instead said to Safia, "You can't stop me."

From the cargo hold she heard someone running. "Put her down!" Carlos said to Alvaro in a deadly tone, as he held an energy weapon of his own. Safia couldn't help but notice a nasty scorch mark ran down the length of his shirt sleeve on the same arm.

Safia felt relief flood her body. She was no longer in the situation all alone. Carlos looked from Alvaro to Safia. The look in his eyes was tender as he seemed to realize the secret she'd kept. But she knew all the truth between them didn't matter now.

Alvaro taunted Carlos. "That's right. This is my daughter. Not yours. She deserves to be raised by a stronger man than you."

"I'll kill you if you hurt my family," Carlos said.

"You don't have the stomach, and you don't hold the power here," Alvaro said. "You may be whipped by Miller and that English prick who's let everything fall into disorder, but I'm not."

Safia began to shake as the gravity of the situation hit her. Carlos couldn't fire on Alvaro while he held Bella in his arms. If either of them rushed him, he would simply shoot them.

A slow, lazy smile spread across Alvaro's face. "I tell you what, Safia, I'll let you come with us. Maybe you miss being with a real man."

The idea repulsed her, but she couldn't let him leave the atmosphere with Bella alone. She couldn't allow her daughter to wake up terrified. She slowly began to walk forward. Every step toward the monster felt like a death march. This was the man who she'd had more nightmares and panic attacks over than she could count—always so terrified he'd come to take her or Bella. Now she was going with him.

Safia wanted to see Carlos, the love of her life, one last time before she was gone, maybe for good. She couldn't bear to look at him. She couldn't bear not to. She looked.

"Safia, no," he pleaded. "Don't."

"I have to," she said. "I—"

Alvaro said, "No. One more word and I'll kill you."

Safia trained her eyes on Bella. If she could keep her purpose in mind, then maybe she could keep the panic at bay.

As the three of them boarded the transport and just before the hatch sealed shut against the oncoming vacuum of space, she heard a sound of utter anguish escape Carlos's throat. It echoed through every lonely chamber of her heart as they left the Martian atmosphere and emerged into darkness.

CHAPTER 51

INTO THE BLACK

Carlos jumped from the cargo entrance platform and ran toward the transport as it took off. He couldn't even say why he was running, perhaps some misguided, primal, lizard-brain notion that he could catch the saber-toothed tiger that was dragging his family away. He stood, gasping, and fell to his knees as Alvaro's ship turned into a dot in the sky, then disappeared from view. He screamed as all the tension from the last few weeks left his body, while an abyss opened in his chest. When they'd managed to take back the *Ares*, he thought his troubles were over.

A few feet away the Ares soldiers cursed their inability to do anything, to react, to understand what was happening in time. It was lost on Carlos.

A gentle hand warmed his shoulder. He turned. Gray ribbons of hair blew free in the afternoon breeze. "Mother?" he sobbed. He knew she wasn't Mother Superior anymore. It was just the first word his heart reached for.

She sat down beside him on the ground and wrapped her arms around him. "The alarms went off when the transport started moving. I thought whoever it was wouldn't be able to leave," she said.

He wiped his eyes, got up, and offered her a hand. They walked toward the ramp leading into the cargo hold. There were now three crew members standing at the bottom of the ramp as they approached, asking Carlos what he saw. Before he could answer, AVM Miller came racing through the cargo hold with Daniel, Jack, Harlow, and Selah close beside her.

Miller spoke. "I tried to lock it down before it could leave, but something prevented the *Ares* from doing it. It's gone. I've already asked the *Vijayee* to see if it can track the transport. Did anyone get a look at who it was?"

Carlos explained the entire story, including who Alvaro was to Bella and Safia, though there were a few personal comments from Alvaro that he left out. Miller looked stricken. "Had I known who that son of a..."

Daniel spoke. "He planned this before the hijacking. That's the only thing that could explain why the *Ares* couldn't prevent the transport from leaving. We've got everything grounded right now in case there are hijackers on the ship looking for a chance to escape, and when Harlow swept the commands clean from the last thirty-six hours, it should have gotten rid of any transport checkouts that were registered. But if he did it beforehand and encrypted it with one of our codes, then it was still ready for him to go. We'll keep trying to trace it." He tapped the glasses he wore to project a hologram in front of him. He moved his fingers across it so fast Carlos could barely follow them. He tapped the glasses again, and the hologram disappeared. "I'm sorry. Nothing."

Carlos felt Mary's comforting presence beside him, the only thing keeping him in one piece.

Jack spoke, "We'll find them. I swear it."

Harlow stepped forward and put her arms around her friend. It was yet another comfort he didn't feel he deserved but needed too badly to reject.

Jack's words didn't fall on deaf ears for Carlos. He knew he would do everything he could, and it was no small encouragement. Just then, Jack's comm unit began going off incessantly. "Jesus Chr...sorry. Yeah?" Jack said into the unit.

After a moment, Jack looked up and addressed them. "There's been a break in at the Bastille. A man with a distinctive *eyebrow scar*," he looked at Harlow when he said it, "walked in with several gifted children, subdued the guards without firing a shot, and threw open the doors. They believe about a fourth of the population got out before security could lock it back down. They went for Aldric's cellblock first."

"They're kids. How could he use them like that?" Harlow said.

Jack was already on his device. "I'm activating the Ares Army to round up escapees. Carlos, you're excused. I know you need to find Safia and Bella. Let me know what you need." After he finished, he turned to look at the group once more. "I've got to get to the prison. Miller can handle everything here." Carlos didn't miss the deadly tone as Jack's voice lowered. "I'll have to deal with my brother later."

After Jack, Devante, and McNamara got into their buggy, Jack kissed Harlow goodbye and gave Selah one more hug.

A sick feeling coiled in the pit of Carlos's stomach. No sooner had they reclaimed the *Ares* than another disaster struck. He couldn't help but feel like the entire galaxy was in flames.

CHAPTER 52

NAVIGATING THE DARK

The transport they traveled in was small, a fifteen-by-twenty-foot space. Alvaro sat in the captain's chair while Safia sat on a bench by the far wall holding Bella. She had begun to stir but wasn't awake yet.

"I know you hate me," he said, "but I'm really not a bad guy. I came to Mars looking to help the people. I believe in your right to rule yourselves, but you've got to get off your assess and step up, not go soft like your boyfriend and that wimpy hag they have the nerve to call an Air Vice Marshal. When someone hijacks your vessel because you've gone soft, well, that's how you end up being a bitch to whatever country has the balls to take the planet from you. That's what happens. I'm done with Mars, and you should be, too."

Safia wasn't sure what all had gone down between him and Carlos and AVM Miller, but clearly, they'd disagreed with him, and he couldn't take it. "You think there's only one way."

"That's because there damn well is only one way," he replied.

"They got the ship back."

"They couldn't have done it if I hadn't been there."

Safia started to argue with him but knew it was futile. Instead, she asked, "Where are we going?"

"We're heading home to Spain. Let Mars burn for all I care."

She felt sick to be that far away from Carlos but also hopeful that they were headed to Spain. At least they would be somewhere that someone might think to look.

Bella woke, and Safia helped her sit up as she looked around the small cabin, then down at her ankle.

"What's on my leg?"

"It's—" Safia began before Alvaro cut her off.

"The doc said your powers might be malfunctioning. He placed that suppressor there until your body heals whatever is going on with them."

"There's never been anything wrong with them." Bella looked at Safia, putting her in a terrible spot.

Alvaro cut in. "You don't want to take any chances and accidentally burn someone, do you?"

The man was infuriating. He would rather make a child doubt herself and fear her own power than admit that the girl might be able to defend herself against the monster he was.

Bella looked up at Safia. She shook her head at her daughter ever so slightly. "Where are we going?" Bella asked.

Safia chose her words carefully. She tried not to frighten her but didn't want to make Alvaro out to be a good man either.

"We're going on a little trip," Safia said.

"Where?" she asked as she turned to look at Alvaro with deep suspicion.

"Earth. To Spain. It will be nice to see where Mommy is from, right?" Safia said.

Alvaro looked up from where he sat reading through the ship's flight plans. "Your father is also from there," Alvaro said.

"No, Daddy is from California."

"You're confused, sweetheart. *I'm* your father. You're Spanish, like me."

"I'm not confused. I've seen the genetic library on the *Ares*. Selah showed it to me. I know half my code comes from you, but you're not my daddy. *Daddy* is."

Safia felt adrenaline rush through her body. She didn't know that Bella knew anything about who her biological father was. She also feared how Alvaro would react to Bella challenging him like that.

He glared at Safia. "It's *your* fault she doesn't know who I am," he accused.

There were a thousand things she wanted to say, but she knew any of them would likely serve to escalate a situation with a man who was already wildly unstable and possibly upset at an innocent five-year-old, but as Bella placed her small hand on her arm and gazed into her eyes, her genetic programming spoke of a knowledge well beyond her years.

"Take us home, please," Bella said to Alvaro.

"Your mother wants to go to Spain. Don't you, Safia?"

"Of course," she said weakly.

Bella looked into her mother's eyes and studied her for a moment. "No, she doesn't."

Alvaro spoke absentmindedly as he ran his hands across the ship's holo navigation. "Sure, she does."

"When are we going back home?" Bella asked quietly.

Safia knew it wasn't a question she could answer. She was still trying to wrap her head around what was happening, much less form an escape plan. Alvaro shot Safia a warning glance.

She put her fingers against her lips to signal Bella to stay quiet about it for now.

Bella placed her hand on her mother's arm and Safia felt shock as a wave of various emotions were communicated through her touch. Anger directed at Alvaro, concern for her mother, grief over missing Carlos, confusion about why Alvaro was taking them.

Safia wondered why she had never experienced this sort of emotional communication so strongly before. Sure, they'd shared emotions between them she assumed all mothers and children had.

But this… it almost felt like a language. She couldn't help but wonder if it might work in reverse. She knew she had to be strong for Bella but even more so if Bella could read her so easily. She had to make sure Bella didn't feel threatened or vulnerable despite being so far from home and taken from everything she loved.

She placed her arm on Bella's, and without words, she thought as forcefully and confidently as she could. *We'll find our way back home one way or another. You are going to be okay. He may look strong but trust me*—she looked at him and felt the absolute truth of what she spoke—*he is very weak.*

CHAPTER 53

THE PIECES

Nighttime had long since fallen as Carlos sat in Judith's house with a cup of black coffee in his hand. A bomb squad and investigators had been brought in from Colony One and asked that everyone except AVM Miller stay off the *Ares* for the rest of the night to ensure that there were no traps or terrorists hiding somewhere on the ship.

Carlos pushed his mind to think. He went over his encounter with Alvaro, wondered if he'd missed an opportunity. The *Vijayee* couldn't track the transport. He knew Alvaro had planned this the entire time he'd been on the *Ares* during the hijacking. It explained so much. It definitely explained why Marcus was the only one who risked his life to come help him when he was outgunned, outmanned, and left for dead. Alvaro was hoping to get him killed and out of the way.

"Please go get some rest." Harlow pleaded with him. This time she stood there with Selah, Yua, and Marcus beside her. Jack had been checking in on him over the comm units as much as he could between the crisis at the Bastille and consulting with the Mars council and hostile Earth coalition about the hijackers who were every bit Earth's problem as well.

"I've gotta find out where they're going. Safia and Bella are flying through space with a psychopath.

"You heard Jack. He's got his Earth connections working on it, and Marcus is also working on it almost nonstop. As soon as they have a location, you can go, but in the meantime, why not let Yua sync up your head for sleep? You know I would never lie to you. The very second we have a location for that scum, I'll wake you up even if I have to hit you over the head to do it."

"Maybe," Carlos relented.

The door to Judith's flat opened and Selah ran to Jack. "Daddy!"

Carlos realized that for all her advanced strength and knowledge, throughout the entire hijacking, when she'd shed not a single tear, she'd just been holding it all in until she could get to her father. They'd been reunited on the *Ares*, but now it wasn't enough. She'd had at least somewhat of a connection to Harlow through the ship, but nothing with Jack. His chest squeezed uncomfortably. He had to find Bella.

He watched as Jack threw his utility belt onto the floor without a second thought and got to his knees so he could embrace her. She wrapped her arms around him and buried her face in his neck. "It's okay. It's okay now," Jack said.

Carlos had never seen Jack shed a tear until today, nor did he miss the look of love and admiration painted on Judith's face, of all people. Thinking the family might need a few minutes alone, without the guilt of a man missing his daughter around for their reunion, he got up, walked to Harlow's old bedroom, and accepted her offer to get some sleep. If Harlow said she would wake him if there was any new information, then she would. He trusted her with his life and his family's.

Sometime later, he woke to the sound of raised, angry voices. It took him a moment to realize Jack and Marcus were having it out, pretty much right outside his door. He'd known it was coming. He remembered the deadly look that had passed between Marcus and Jack when he'd walked onto the bridge. Jack may have thought his whisper was quiet, but Carlos had been close enough to hear him lean over and say to Marcus, "I can barely look at you, much less speak to you. We'll discuss this later." And now, the conversation seemed fairly one sided. Every time Marcus attempted to say anything, Jack cut him short or reminded him that Naadir was in critical condition. They had found him and Allan in a storage room outside the core. Allan's wounds were treatable. Naadir was still struggling.

Carlos had resolved to stay out of it until he heard Jack lob the word "coward" at Marcus. Carlos opened the door to find Marcus standing with his head hanging down, hands shoved deep into his jacket pockets while Jack tore into him. It was utterly fascinating that Marcus, a king no less, still slipped into the role of younger, intimidated brother when Jack was around.

Jack stopped and looked at Carlos. "I'm sorry. You finally got some rest, and I woke you up. I apologize."

"No, I understand. It's just that… I know I probably shouldn't be interrupting on a conversation between brothers, but Marcus saved my life. He made a huge mistake, but he's no coward, Jack. I don't know if he told you or not, but Alvaro was going to leave me for dead. I was running from a ship full of terrorists and Marcus came back for me. Just to save me."

"He didn't tell me that."

"Yeah, and he bluffed his way on board the bridge with me and AVM Miller, opened fire on the hijackers there, too. I can't believe he didn't get killed. Have you had a chance to debrief her yet?"

"No."

"More than that, did Selah tell you what he did to get her back on the *Ares* when she flew out the cargo hold?"

"Harlow saw it."

"The man literally jumped to his death to save Selah. If I hadn't arrived at precisely the right time, he'd have never made it back on the ship. Another second or two and you would never have seen him again. Never. That means you would never see me again, either. I'd be dead if it weren't for him."

Jack looked at Marcus. His anger quelled. "There's a lot you didn't tell me."

"There's a lot I'm responsible for, mate," he said quietly.

"The colony needs you both right now," Carlos said.

Jack nodded. "You're right." Carlos watched as Jack sighed and scrubbed a hand across his face before turning a keen eye on him. "It's almost morning. I don't think any of us are going to be getting any sleep anytime soon. How about some breakfast? I already had McNamara bring supplies over from the *Ares* commissary before we left."

The three men located bowls, utensils, a frying pan, and got to work on breakfast as the sun began to rise. Soon, the smell of bacon filled the air. Carlos had to admit, getting a few hours of sleep had helped him think a little more clearly. Grief was still his constant companion, but he'd wrapped the surety that Alvaro had no wish to kill either Safia or Bella, around him like a comforting blanket, though he faced the continual fear that he might try to assault Safia again.

Marcus's comm unit flashed, and he sat down with it. "Carlos," Marcus called. "I've got something for you."

"What? I know Alvaro kept his residence hidden. Did your intel find the vicinity?"

"No, better than that. They found coordinates for his estate."

Hope swelled inside Carlos's chest like the first morning rays spilling in through Judith's windows.

Harlow came into the living room in sweatpants and an old sweatshirt and turned her eyes to Carlos immediately. "How you holding up, my friend?"

"Hopeful." He looked at Marcus, who gave him a nod. "I'm hopeful again." What he didn't say, couldn't say, knowing it would only worry Harlow, who was Safia's best friend, was that he didn't know if he could get there before Alvaro did psychological damage to Safia. If he attacked her again, it would set her back years, or worse, she would fight him to the point that he would... for now, he wouldn't allow his mind to venture any farther into the things he could not control.

CHAPTER 54

SPAIN

Safia looked out the window to watch the roof below them slowly open as the transport descended into the hangar. The building was surrounded by a lush forest. "You'll love your new home," Alvaro said to Safia and Bella as she felt her body begin to acclimate to Earth's gravity again as the ship's artificial gravity turned off incrementally.

When they disembarked and entered the house proper, she couldn't help but wonder how he afforded such luxury when most Spaniards struggled just to feed themselves. She remembered the Martian council having to vote on whether the price Alvaro charged for his expertise was worth it. Of course, they voted it was. They were desperate to stop the bombing and loss of life. But could he gain this much wealth from hiring himself out like that? She guessed something more sinister was going on. Did she even want to know?

Despite Bella's sorrow at leaving Mars, Safia noticed her marveling at the flowers, lush palms, and waterfalls as they walked through the open courtyard. However, when Alvaro looked her way, she refused to give him the satisfaction of seeing that she enjoyed his home. It was clear she disliked him deeply without even knowing half the story.

An older woman opened the door to the courtyard and spoke to Alvaro. Safia whispered to Bella, "She's saying welcome home in Spanish."

"I know," Bella said.

"You know?"

"Yes. Daddy and I have been working on it as a surprise for you." Her eyes filled with tears as she spoke. Safia gave her a hug and whispered in her ear. "Don't let Alvaro know you understand Spanish. Maybe he will say something secret, thinking you don't understand, and we will learn something to help us get out of here."

Bella smiled and nodded.

"This is Mariella," Alvaro said. "If you need anything, let her know."

The woman greeted them in accented English, but her eyes gave little away.

Alvaro continued. "There are three guards on duty." He looked at Safia. "For your safety, of course."

"Of course," Safia said flatly.

A pit bull bounded past Mariella, barking and running straight for Bella. Safia got in front of her daughter.

Alvaro snorted. "Oh, don't worry about War Hound. He's a passive waste of training and space. He eats, shits, and squanders my time."

Safia noticed that, though full grown, he acted like a needy puppy, and he was also, technically, not a hound at all. So, the name didn't really fit for more than one reason. She knelt to pet him and got angry as she noticed scars crisscrossing his silver fur. "What happened to him?"

War Hound left Safia's caress and ran to lick Bella's face as she giggled.

"What happened to him is the same damn thing that is happening to Mars. Someone tries to teach you to fight, but you haven't got the guts for it."

Alvaro pointed at Bella. "Someone needs to teach her to fight, too."

Safia studied the scars on War Hound as rage coursed through her veins. She spoke before she remembered the danger she was in. "Yes, perhaps someone should teach Bella to fight in case some jackass corners her in a dark alley."

Alvaro crossed the distance between them in a flash, grabbed Safia's arm painfully, and pulled her to her feet. "You," he spoke loudly before noticing Bella was watching him with wide eyes. She had stopped petting War Hound and stood. She appeared ready for something but didn't know what.

He loosened his grip on Safia's arm, turned, and smiled at Bella. He gently patted Safia's arm, tilted his head, and spoke to Safia in a whisper, "You forget yourself and your place in my home. If you ever speak that way to me again, I will end you."

Safia nodded and looked toward Mariella, who stood there with a bored expression. So, this wasn't the first time she'd witnessed such a thing. That kind of indifference had to have been fostered over the course of a lifetime.

Alvaro walked over to Bella and patted her back. "Come on, sweetie. I'll show you to your room." Safia watched Bella jerk away from his touch as if she'd been shocked.

They left the courtyard with Mariella, War Hound following closely beside Bella, and walked through the home with beautifully carved furniture. Safia had not seen these kinds of furnishings in years: wood, marble, and intricately manufactured things that couldn't be shipped to Mars due to weight restrictions and couldn't be made there owing to a lack of materials. None of it mattered. A beautiful cage was still a cage. Bella looked around with curiosity. Safia had often thought her curious mind needed more travel and new experiences than her small Martian district could provide but not this way.

They climbed a set of stairs with intricate mosaics on the footboard of every stair. At the top was a hallway with five carved mahogany doorways. Three iron chandeliers illuminated the passage. At the second door on the left, they stopped. "This will be your room," he told Bella. He opened the door, and War Hound trotted in with her. Alvaro grabbed him by the collar. "No, nasty thing. Out!"

"Stop it! I want him to stay with me." She dropped to her knees and put her arms around War Hound, who responded by licking her face again.

"I can get you a better dog." Alvaro lowered his voice and spoke again in a mumble. "I dropped the damn thing in the woods, but it came right back." He turned and looked at Safia as if she would find the comment amusing. She glared at him. The more she was around him, the more she realized just how incapable the man was of relating to normal human beings.

"War Hound is the best dog. I love him." Bella smiled as he gave her a final slurp before settling in against her, as if glued to her side.

"Fine. Do you like your room?" Alvaro asked.

Bella looked around and nodded. "But I don't have any clothes or toys or anything."

"Mariella will go into town and get you everything you need."

With those words, it hit home once more that she and Bella were to be prisoners in this house, in these woods.

Bella looked at Safia, who didn't know what to do, at least not at that moment.

Mariella asked Alvaro a question in Spanish that made this dangerous situation even worse. She wanted to know if the new mistress of the house would need a guest room or be staying with Alvaro.

He responded to Mariella that Safia would stay in his room.

Panic washed over Safia, and she fought to think quickly. What reason could she give that would be feasible without stirring him up and making him demand exactly that? Luckily, she didn't have to come up with any excuse. Bella made eye contact with her and communicated that she was about to take care of it. Had she imagined her daughter speaking to her? There were no words, no voice. She just knew what she was trying to tell her.

"No! I want Mom to stay with me." Bella looked at Safia in what appeared to be an honest panic. Though Bella had never been afraid of sleeping alone, there was likely some truth to it in this situation.

"That's silly," Alvaro said. "You need your own space."

"I've never been here before. It's scary."

"This place isn't scary. This is your home. I'm your father."

"You're not! You're—"

Safia shot Bella a warning look, and she stopped speaking. She knew she would have to explain later that she wasn't angry at her. She just didn't want Alvaro taking his anger out on her or poor War Hound.

Safia watched Alvaro take a deep breath as if he were barely benevolently tolerating their presence. "You don't know what you are saying. You've been brainwashed. When you get used to being here, you will love it."

He'd said the last part as if it were a command. As if one could simply demand devotion, as if real love could ever work that way.

"Please, let Mom stay with me." Bella started crying, and War Hound sprang into action, licking her tears as if he couldn't bear the sight of his new beloved in pain.

"Fine."

Safia tried not to react one way or the other. She didn't want to give Alvaro a window into her emotions. The less leverage he had over her the better, but she was much relieved when Bella had managed to talk Alvaro into letting them share a room. Bella couldn't understand at her age, but since they'd arrived at the hacienda, Alvaro had given Safia more than one hungry look. She'd hoped what he'd said to Carlos about her being with "a real man" was just empty bravado, that having raped her once, he had no more use for her. Clearly, though, there was some payment involved in letting her come with them, and she didn't know how long it would be before he came to collect.

CHAPTER 55

SWORN TO PROTECT

Father Josef looked at the children huddled together. They were afraid. He'd spent months moving their things to the new house, knowing once he fulfilled his promise to free Aldric, they would have to leave the location that the kids had always known as home. He hated uprooting them. There had been tears and questions about why they couldn't stay in the place they loved. Evangeline had become withdrawn from experiencing the rest of the children's grief over having to move. He had tried to help her fortify her empath shields through meditation, visualization, and prayer, but she was fragile. Once they'd gotten inside the prison, it was too intimidating for them. He'd had to yell at them to get them to cooperate. It wasn't his way. Especially not with the children.

Things went from bad to worse once they had freed Aldric, and they were fleeing from the guards. He barked orders at the kids to do his bidding. Ordering Jung and Evangeline to throw prison officials against walls and even grabbing Evangeline by the arm, dragging her to a cell, and telling her to scour a certain prisoner's mind for information, created mayhem. He'd wanted her to do it in a matter of seconds with alarms blaring and her mind being bombarded by the emotions of the other crying children. It was utter chaos.

He'd never forget what happened hours earlier when Aldric lit into him about the children's conditioning once they'd returned to their new hidden fortress.

"You've failed them and me," Aldric spat.

Josef had found the man intimidating before—6'3", broad-shouldered, with deep-set eyes and a commanding voice—but he'd been a well-groomed, respected member of the *Ares* crew then. Now his hair had grown wild like a lion's mane during his time in the Bastille. He'd added muscle, the lines of his face had deepened, and he'd gained a couple of scars there, too. He was also much more volatile.

Josef backed up a step before responding. "They are children. No matter what their intellectual capacity, their emotional age remains the same. We have to remember that," he replied softly to not arouse this man's wrath further.

"You need to remember the years I've rotted in that prison while you played nursemaid in absolute safety. You never suffered like me and Mikhail have suffered. You cannot know what we have gone through."

Josef wanted to tell him that Mikhail never spent time in the Bastille. As damnably lonely as Enceladus might have been, it wasn't a prison cell, but Aldric was in no state of mind to hear it, and he knew Aldric worshipped the man as his hero.

Aldric waved a dismissive hand at him. "Mikhail and I will institute a new regimen the moment he returns. These children need structure. They will not find it with you. They will rise at dawn and begin hard labor. Just as I did. Just as Mikhail did. If one is to be part of a successful revolution, then the training must be revolutionary. We must purge weakness from their bodies," he said, looking at the children as he spoke.

Josef said, "You and I have been through much together, and I believe in your... our cause." He reached up to touch the scar on his eyebrow. Its meaning seeming to shift in a singular moment as he remembered Rory's mother. He stood up straighter. "The children will receive structure, but you will not be abusing them."

"You nearly got me killed inside that prison. With the powers they possess, that escape should have been seamless. Instead, they fell apart like mere humans."

"They *are* humans."

"No. They. Are. Not."

"Yes, they are," Josef said softly. He prayed to the Holy Family that he could hold his temper for the sake of the children.

"You only say that because of your daft religious notions that if they aren't human, they can't be part of the kingdom. It's nonsense!"

"It isn't nonsense. They're just people!" Josef knew he was right about the kingdom. The thought that their enhancements might exclude them from full communion with Christ did bother him, but he also thought it was heartless to call them something other than human in front of them.

"Fine. I'm in charge of them from now on."

"Absolutely not."

"Remember your place!" Aldric stepped forward, pulled his arm back, but his eyes grew wide as saucers when he found his arm frozen mid swing.

Josef expected to find Jung holding the man in place, but much to his surprise, Evangeline was in a fighter's stance with a fierce look in her eyes as she held a hand out and concentrated.

Aldric looked at her with shock. "Release me, and I will not punish you."

"That is not what I see," the little girl said softly but not without a tone that hinted at a deep well of courage.

Aldric said through gritted teeth, "When Mikhail returns—"

"He will not return," Rory said from beside Josef.

"Why do you say this?" Josef spared a quick glance at the boy whose dark red eyebrows scrunched together as if to banish an unwanted memory.

"I felt the cold take him away during the night."

CHAPTER 56

DISCOVERY

"Thank you, Mariella," Alvaro said as the woman set a plate of tortilla Espanola, a warm potato omelet, and bread in front of him. "How did you sleep, Bella?"

Safia watched her daughter cover her mouth as she yawned. Mariella had sat an omelet before her as well. "Okay," Bella mumbled.

"There are churros and croissants if you don't like the omelet," Alvaro offered.

Bella nodded.

Safia picked up the fork and forced herself to eat, despite her lack of appetite. Now wasn't the time to give in to the urge to despair. The wolf was at the door, no, the very table. She had to stay strong for Bella.

Alvaro gave Safia a smug look. "I know *you* didn't sleep well."

More than ever, she had to get back to Carlos. She'd mustered the courage to try and deal with Alvaro last night, and it had gone terribly wrong.

• • •

She waited until Bella had gone to sleep and watched through the peephole. She noticed all the bedroom doors had them. When you lived the dangerous life of a thug, she guessed you needed to see what was coming at you at any given time. A guard patrolled inside the house all night but hadn't been by in at least ten minutes. She crept from her bed and stood in front of Alvaro's door. If he had the same lock as Bella's, a hairpin would defeat it. She had found a utility room earlier that day where there were paints and building materials stashed from remodeling projects. It looked as if they had replaced the wrought iron railings on the stairs. Safia had carried a couple of balusters upstairs to keep nearby. She brought one as a weapon and began gently twisting the pin in the lock.

She reminded herself, no matter how terrified he was, she'd taken Vince down. Why not Alvaro? But no sooner had she began feeling for the sweet spot inside the mechanism than the guard came around the corner and into the hallway. He spoke into his comm unit, and she shoved the hairpin into her pocket as Alvaro opened the door.

He waved at the guard. "Thanks, Guillermo," he said and reached down to take the iron bar from her. "Would you like to come inside now? Looks like you were headed this way."

Her cheeks burned and all the courage she'd gained from confronting him on the *Ares*, from confronting Vince, for that matter, fell away.

He pulled her to his chest and leaned the metal railing he'd taken from her against the wall. "Miss me?" She felt his erection against her stomach.

"No."

She shoved his chest, but he gripped her harder and started pulling her into the room. Kicking the iron bar to the ground, she felt an immediate sense of shame. She knew she'd done it to wake War Hound and make him bark, which would wake Bella. Alvaro was trying to win over his daughter and wouldn't want Bella to see him hurting her mother, but she didn't want her daughter coming to the rescue. More than that, she really didn't want to spend the night with Alvaro.

On cue, War Hound began barking.

"I ought to kill that fucking dog, or maybe just you." The palm of his hand contacted her head and her skull smacked against the door frame.

A jolt of pain shot through her head and tears sprang to her eyes, a betrayal from her body. She never wanted this bastard to see her cry. She quickly smiled at him and hoped the dark hallway would keep both him and Bella from noticing the moisture in her eyes but hoped it wasn't so dark he would miss the gleam of her teeth. After all, despite her tears, he needed to remember she could bite.

• • •

Safia shoveled more omelet into her mouth and refused to look at Alvaro.

War Hound stood at the alcove to the kitchen and poked his head around. Safia watched Alvaro narrow his eyes at the dog.

As soon as breakfast was done, and Mariella began clearing the dishes, Alvaro announced he had a surprise for Bella.

"Okay," she mumbled, barely looking up from the table.

They rose and pushed in their chairs.

Safia worried about how long this situation would leave a scar on her daughter's psyche. She'd lain in bed next to her the night before, listening to the sounds of the deep Spanish forest as they filtered through the walls of the estate. It was a cacophony compared to a Martian night. She thought of Carlos, every touch, every smile. She knew she'd marry him in a heartbeat if he were here... then she heard Bella beside her, crying. Her heart shattered.

She would never be able to forgive Alvaro for putting her in a situation where she couldn't make things better for her frightened child. She pulled her close, promising this was only temporary. Promising that Carlos wouldn't stop until they were found.

"Follow me," Alvaro said.

When they walked out into the courtyard, a Silver Carpet sat waiting in its docking pod, a gift for Bella.

"It's like a magic carpet. You know, from the story, except you don't need a prince to take you for a ride. You can get on and go for yourself." With that, he hopped on the silver half circle and placed his feet in the designated area. The foot supports clamped into place. He clicked the silver bracelet on his wrist, and it rose from the docking station and flew around the courtyard and back.

"Would you like to try? They're very easy to operate. It's nearly impossible to fall off. The carpet constantly adjusts beneath you to ensure you stay upright."

Bella did look curious, nodded, and climbed on.

"You'll not be seeing one of these on Mars. I'm telling you, you'll see how great it is living on Earth where all the good toys are, and you'll never want to go back."

Safia watched a look of sorrow cross her daughter's face at mention of Mars. She positioned her feet and rose into the air. A wave of anger, originating from Bella, hit Safia before her daughter flew away from the courtyard, out of sight, but, she hoped, not far from the grounds.

Alvaro stood there, smiling, as if he were waiting for Bella to come zipping back up to him any minute, thanking and praising him, but Safia knew it would never happen after what he'd said about Mars, her home. Bella's anger continued to hit her in waves. The unspoken link between them was growing stronger every day. She didn't know whether she should be grateful or worried that this was more than mother's intuition. This surely had to do with the genetic tampering Aldric and his minions had done.

After a couple of minutes, Safia saw the proud look on Alvaro's face transform into frustration. He walked out of the courtyard and into the side yard, where he began looking around and calling her name. "Bella!" One of the two security guards Safia had made note of pointed in the direction he'd seen her go.

Safia knew she should be worried, but she didn't *feel* that Bella was in danger. Finally, after a couple more minutes, they saw Bella buzz over the courtyard wall. They walked back into the enclosure as she returned to the docking portal, released the clasps on her feet, and stepped down.

"It's fun, right?" Alvaro said.

Bella looked at him, her expression unreadable. "If I give it back, will you take us home?"

Alvaro looked as if someone had slapped him. He opened his mouth to speak, then closed it again. He looked from Bella to Safia and back again. "You have no gratitude. Your mother clearly didn't teach you any." He turned to Safia. "I think your influence is the reason she is this way. Bella, you may go."

Bella left the courtyard with War Hound trotting along beside her. Alvaro crossed his arms and bore his gaze into Safia. "You need some time to think about what you could have, what you could learn to be grateful for." He leaned back and looked through the archway where Bella and War Hound had gone, then took two steps forward, and whispered into her ear, "I could give you everything you could want or need," he said as he pressed his body against her.

Bile rose in Safia's throat and panic threatened to take hold. She turned her head and concentrated on her next breath and the next. Fighting him wouldn't help right now. She simply backed up a step.

"Have it your way, for now." He grabbed her by the arm, and they walked back inside, across the living area and into his study. They went through a door she'd always thought to be a closet. There was another door behind this one that required him to move his fingers across a glass panel in a certain pattern to open it. Inside was a large room filled with shelf after shelf of boxes. He threw the lids off them.

One by one, they revealed gold ingots, ancient coins, and jewelry that was clearly looted from a museum somewhere. She guessed he'd been skimming off the top from the various jobs he'd taken. Likely he thought he was entitled to it, just like he thought he was entitled to any woman he decided he wanted, whether she was willing or not.

"I need an inventory of everything in here, by hand." He walked back into his study and returned with a digital tablet. "I think Bella and I will bond better without your constant influence poisoning her mind."

There were a thousand things she wanted to tell him at that moment, right on the tip of her tongue, but as she looked around the room, several things dawned on her: there were no windows, only one door, and he could leave her there for an eternity, and no one would know where she was. Now wasn't the time to poke the psychotic bear.

Her worst fears were confirmed as he left the room, and she heard the lock beep out a pattern. The mechanism inside the door slid home.

She would only see Bella again by Alvaro's good graces, and she wasn't sure he had any.

CHAPTER 57

ON THE HUNT

Carlos was back in the armory on the *Ares* after security declared it clear of any threats. Whether they had or not, he wasn't waiting any longer to bring Safia and Bella home. He shoved the knife into his boot and checked the pulse weapons strapped across the harness over his chest one more time. The knife at his hip was secure as well. He would be taking no chances and offering no mercy. Only one of them would be left standing. He added a blade to the other boot for good measure.

"He'll be in ribbons by the time you're done with him," Jack said from the doorway.

Carlos's mouth quirked up on one side before turning to see his best friend had entered the armory. "There won't be *that* much left of him."

Jack walked over to Carlos, handed him his pistol, and the holster for it. He knew how much it meant to Jack. "This has been in your family for generations. I can't take this."

"Look, the *Ares* disables all unregistered pulse weapons. Do you think for a second Alvaro won't have something like that on that compound of his? Besides, Marcus wants you to have it. You saved his life. You'll bring it back when you're done. And... I *need* you to take it with you, mate. I'm sick that I can't go with you, but the entire colony is in chaos—"

"Say no more. I mean it. A quarter of the Bastille is running free, the *Ares* has just been saved from a hijacking. You cannot leave, nor can you spare anyone to go after this bastard."

"I'd be there. You know that."

"I know. If there were any way, but there isn't, and I know that, too."

"Then take the pistol. It's been by my side for years."

Carlos took it along with two extra magazines. "I'm honored."

The two embraced as Jack's comm unit began going off incessantly. He gave Carlos's back a final pat before letting the man go, sighed, and looked at the comm. "It never ends. Come back safe, my friend."

"I will."

Carlos hooked the holster holding Jack's pistol to his belt loop, placed the extra ammo into his pack, determined that he was more than well-armed, and headed toward the hangar.

He was halfway there when he ran into Judith. It felt strange seeing her on the *Ares*, but he didn't have time to question it. He was too wired, ready to go, out for blood.

She looked him up and down. "Good," she said, reading his mind, "you're out for blood."

Uncanny, he thought. "I am."

"Don't come back without my other two girls. I've become attached to Safia and Bella." Carlos watched this woman of steel look away as her eyes became glassy with tears. "I hate the thoughts of what that monster has done. Anyway, don't return without them."

"I won't," Carlos said with conviction.

"I'm furious at my son-in-law for not going with you."

"I'm not. He can't abandon a colony of thousands to go after two. You think he has problems now..."

"I'm sorry, it's just... you're only one person."

He looked at Judith with a feral smile. "Judith, I'm a well-trained warrior on a mission to rip a son of a bitch to shreds. I got this."

She held his eyes for a moment and nodded. "I believe you do." She embraced him and spoke into his ear. "Bring our girls home."

"I will."

Once he was in the hangar, he found Mary Windsor leaning against his transport. Her long, gray hair hung over her shoulders and a soft, peaceful smile settled on her face when she saw him. As he approached, she held out her arms, and he walked into them. After they embraced, she took a step back, put both hands on the sides of his head, and closed her eyes. He closed his as well, taking a moment to leave the fire in his veins behind and connect with the sacred. He allowed his breathing to slow and his thoughts to settle. After several seconds, he felt her draw the sign of the cross on his forehead. He whispered, "Amen."

After the prayer, she walked away without ever having said a word. His vision blurred for a moment. Something inside him had broken free. Something he hadn't realized was looking for escape, but Mary knew.

He climbed into the transport and signaled flight control to open the bay doors.

• • •

Under the cover of darkness, Carlos descended into Laviana, Spain. His contact was good, his information reliable: Safia and Bella were near.

It was around 2 a.m. local time. He closed his eyes and concentrated. It was a thought, a prayer, a wish, a message... love. "I'm here. I'm on my way. I'm bringing you home." He opened his eyes and looked out at Laviana, hoping they somehow knew.

CHAPTER 58

LAVIANA

Safia climbed into bed that night feeling more defeated than she ever had, worse even than on the night Alvaro had attacked her over five years ago.

He'd left her in the secret vault doing "inventory" for four hours. When he finally opened the door to let her out, Bella was standing there sobbing. He'd snapped at her and gone on a rant about gratitude.

Alvaro had disappeared for the rest of the day. She hated when he was around but felt oddly nervous when he was gone because she didn't know what that meant.

She went over escape options in her head again. She'd already checked the windows, but they were loaded with sensors. Bella had even tried to open one, and alarms went off. She did not know where they were in relation to city centers. As they had descended into the hangar, she had made a note of where there looked to be villages and larger structures, but they were so far away. She estimated at least twenty miles. If it were just her, she'd try it, but with Bella in tow, it was far too risky. Besides, staying put gave Carlos a better chance of finding her.

She hated going to sleep for fear that something horrible would happen during the night, but she needed to sleep badly. She rolled from one side to the other as the hours ticked by.

Stoking anger and channeling how she felt that night behind the Sojourner when Alvaro had tried to kiss her, and how she'd felt in the vault earlier that day, she thought she might be able to recreate the heat in her hands once more. She thought about it often. From time to time, she had even dismissed it as a fluke, thinking maybe Alvaro had something on him that had ignited. After all, he was trained with all manner of explosives; maybe he'd carried strange things with him for training and forgot, but that seemed sloppy and unlikely. As an act of faith, she'd even pulled her hands out from under the covers so the bed sheets wouldn't ignite. But despite the genuine anger she felt, nothing happened. Listening to Bella's rhythmic breathing was the only thing that soothed her during the night. It was suddenly and sharply interrupted when Bella said, "Laviana."

Safia placed a hand on her daughter's back. "Are you okay, sweetie?"

"Yeah. Daddy is on Earth."

"He is? How do you know?"

"I just do."

"How do you know about Laviana?" Safia didn't think Bella knew one part of Spain from another. Their studies of Earth only discussed the capitals of countries. She would have likely only heard about somewhere like Madrid.

"Where?" Bella asked before yawning, pulling the covers tighter, and drifting off again.

She'd suspected they were in the forests of Asturias, judging by the topography: oaks, ash, and landscape specific to this region. Laviana was nearby, and if Bella was right about Carlos being on Earth, then this meant he really had an idea of where they were, and Bella was picking up information in her sleep, but it didn't all have to be genetic tampering either. As a child, Safia dreamed of her mother's death, then woke to find her gone the next morning.

She smoothed a hand down her daughter's silky hair. She was dreaming a good thing.

The next morning, Safia was up before Bella. She brushed her teeth and washed her face, then stood before the mirror, barely recognizing the person staring back at her. They'd only been there about five days, but dark circles ringed her eyes from lack of sleep. Her normally tanned skin looked pale, and despite trying to force herself to eat, her cheeks were looking gaunt. She pulled her hair into a ponytail with a vengeful smirk. There would be no effort to look nice for this pervert.

She walked into the bedroom and sat down on the bed to put her boots on as Bella slid from beneath the covers. She came over and wrapped her arms around Safia. The child's warmth was a balm to her weary soul. "Don't tell Alvaro what you learned about your dad last night."

Bella pulled back and looked at her, confused.

"You don't remember?"

Bella shook her head.

Safia smiled and whispered into her ear. "You woke during the night and told me Daddy had landed on Earth, and you even mentioned where he was. It's nearby."

"I did?"

"Yes."

Bella smiled. "Those kinds of dreams are always fun. I like to see when it actually happens the next day or a couple days later."

"Those kinds? You have them a lot?"

"Sure. Doesn't everyone?"

"No."

"Really?" Bella asked with genuine surprise.

"I've had a few in my life that ended up happening later. Most people don't dream the future at all. How often do you have them?"

Bella shrugged. "A couple times a week. Maybe more. I guess more, since it sounds like I have them sometimes and don't remember."

Safia smiled and nodded, thinking about how Bella's gift must have been something she already inherited from her but simply got a boost when they enhanced her before birth. "Your grandmother had them too," she said, remembering flashes of her mother before she'd passed away when Safia was a child. She tapped the inhibitor on Bella's ankle. "That must be why this thing doesn't suppress that particular gift. Unlike the heat, you already had the gift of sight. Well, no matter how angry you get, don't tell Alvaro about Carlos being nearby," she whispered.

"I won't."

When the two of them went downstairs, Mariella had breakfast waiting, but Alvaro was out. The strange mix of relief and anxiety took hold of her again. She did eat better without him at the table. After a breakfast of warm churros, sausage, and café con leche, along with the news that Carlos was nearby, she had to admit; she felt better than she had since they'd arrived.

Bella took Safia's hand, and they walked out to the courtyard with War Hound trotting alongside them. Bella sat in front of the garden fountain with War Hound as he flopped over for a belly rub. Since Bella seemed to have no interest in the Silver Carpet, Safia had an idea.

She climbed on board, thinking she could scope out the surrounding area in case they needed to bolt, but the command cuff flashed "Unauthorized User."

"Asshole," Safia muttered as she stepped down. "Wanna ride the Silver Carpet?" Safia asked Bella, knowing what the answer would be.

Bella shrugged. Safia leaned over and whispered, "It would be good for you to memorize as much of the surrounding area as possible."

Realization dawned on Bella, and she hopped up and climbed on board.

As she watched Bella rise into the air, Safia allowed herself to do something she'd been afraid to indulge in since she'd arrived at the estate: she allowed hope to wedge itself into her being, and she made plans for the future. She scratched War Hound behind the ears and whispered, "Wanna come live with us?"

He licked her hand in the affirmative.

• • •

Later, when Bella was snuggling on her bed with War Hound, Alvaro was still out and Mariella was occupied in the kitchen, Safia decided it might be a good time to search for weapons so she could help Carlos defend them when he arrived.

She crept into Alvaro's room and shut the door. Surely a man like him had weapons lying around. Likely, even enough that he wouldn't miss. She quickly went through drawer after drawer. This is crazy, she thought, realizing he would likely have security cameras guarding his things. The thought made her break out in a full body sweat. She knew she could tell him she had always been curious about her baby's father. He was a narcissist. He'd likely believe it or want to enough that he'd buy it.

Her eyes glided across the room, and she froze as she saw paintings so familiar—dark and painful—hanging on the walls. The small canvases contained storms with angry, purple, looming clouds bursting forth and covering the world below in a deluge. There were paintings of gray, turbulent oceans, a woman with a pale face and hollow eyes beside a dead tree. This meant, without a doubt, that he'd gone in search of her after the attack. He'd traced her back to the shelter and found her things. Now she felt violated all over again. He wasn't entitled to her private thoughts. Yet he'd been looking at them every day, examining them, gloating about what he'd done to her for years. She wanted to rip them from the walls but knew if he didn't spot her on security footage at some point, the missing paintings would do it.

She finally approached the dreaded bedside table. She worried most about going through that one. What if he had nasty things in there? A man like him likely went far beyond the normal brand of racy. Well, it was also the most likely spot for a weapon.

She opened the drawer and almost screamed out loud. Her heart thundered in her ears as she lifted photographs. Not even a hologram projector but actual printed photographs—something rarely seen on the paper-barren Mars—of women, bound, bruised, unconscious, half-naked... victims. He printed them because he wanted to hold the photos tangible, touch them, possess them. With trembling hands, she looked through three different pictures before forcing herself to put them back in the drawer. What if the next one she lifted was of her?

She closed the drawer and backed up, but then rushed forward and opened the drawer, even as her mind screamed, don't do this to yourself. She had to know or, she believed, there would forever be a type of undetonated bomb in that drawer.

The picture on the bottom was of her.

CHAPTER 59

BALANCE COMES DUE

Around dinnertime, heavy steps thudded down the hallway. Safia's heart sank. War Hound nestled closer into Bella's side, and Bella refused to make eye contact with Safia. It hurt her to know that she was trying to hide her feelings on her account.

After another twenty minutes, the chime sounded in their room, followed by Mariella's voice telling them dinner was ready. Safia certainly didn't feel like eating after what she had seen in Alvaro's room, but she consoled herself knowing that when she left that place, she would make sure the authorities were aware of exactly where the photos were. That consolation fell flat when another thought rushed in behind it. How deeply did his connections run? Could he even be convicted of anything?

They sat at the table with plates full of pollo campurriano. She didn't care for Mariella, but the woman was a fantastic cook. The chicken, garlic, scallions, and spices were all perfect, but her appetite vanished after a few bites.

"How have my two girls been? I missed you while I was away," Alvaro said.

Safia couldn't believe the delusion the man possessed. Neither female answered him.

Alvaro turned his attention to Bella "Well, I've brought you the most magnificent toy. You can literally build without touching anything. This device tracks eye movement. You'll love it."

"Okay," Bella said quietly. She glanced up at Safia.

Alvaro didn't miss the look. He got to his feet so quickly the chair almost fell to the floor behind him. "No! Don't look at her. Think your own thoughts about me."

"I am," Bella answered flatly.

Alvaro stomped from the room. When they stayed seated, he turned around and roared, "Follow. Now!"

Bella startled and jumped to her feet.

Once they were all in the living room, he began showing Bella how to sync up her eye movements to the cubes and begin building. She caught on quickly and started stacking. As before, Alvaro stood by, waiting for her approval and appreciation.

"Do you like them?" he asked.

"Sure, very much. Thank you," she said, but without enthusiasm.

After a few minutes, the smile faded from his face. As block after block stacked, it became clear the thing that Bella was building was a wall between her and Alvaro.

He turned to Safia and spoke with venom. "This is on you. First, you tried to hide her from me. Now, you've turned her against me." He stomped forward, grabbed Safia by the arm, and pulled her toward the door as he screamed for Mariella. Safia heard Bella protest. When Mariella appeared, he spoke. "I'll be back in a few hours. Watch my daughter."

She nodded but looked no more affected than if he'd told her he was going to the store.

"I didn't tell her anything about you," Safia said as he marched her out the door. She refused to be dragged out in front of Bella.

The door shut behind them as he continued his tirade. "No more of your lies. You will show gratitude and respect in my home. I've been far too lenient with you, hoping you would listen to reason and respond to my kindness. Instead, you've thrown it in my face."

"Locking me in a room for four hours was a kindness? What the hell happened to you?"

"Evil fucking women happened to me." His fingers dug deeper into her arm as he spoke.

She'd wondered about that for years, but would it even matter if there was a story there? There could never be an excuse for this kind of behavior.

As they stomped through the forest, the estate was growing farther and farther away. If she ran back to it, she would only bring the panic and fear right back to Bella's doorstep. She certainly couldn't run away and abandon her daughter there with Alvaro. Whatever she did, she had to do it out here, away from her daughter, once and for all. She remembered confronting Vince in his home, all the years of practice on the jiujitsu mat, all of that was her, not someone else, her. *Think, there's a way out of this.* "Where are we going?"

"Somewhere we can be alone, sweetheart. Once you get enough of my attention, you'll be begging for more. See, I think the problem is, we just haven't had enough alone time. You know how they say children can really strain a relationship."

Once they were out of sight of the house, she saw a decent-size building in the forest. Beyond that there was a firing range. She wondered if he'd brought other women to the building. Maybe some of the women from the photos. *Don't think about them.* Panic rose in her every time the images crept into her consciousness.

They approached the building and one of the guards she'd spotted from her and Bella's bedroom windows refused to meet her eye but simply turned and walked away as if he had no idea they were even there. He knew what was about to happen to her and was too cowardly to stop it.

Alvaro tapped a pattern into the side of the wall and the door slid open. She squirmed and fought to break free, but her mind raced with fear of what would happen if she ran. What if Bella slipped away from Mariella and happened upon what Alvaro was planning on doing to her? The situation was horrific all the way around. Safia knew if she could escape, she had to go back for Bella. If she got free, she also had to finish him.

When he tried to open the door to drag her into what she assumed was a bedroom, she was able to calm herself enough to remember some of her training. She broke his hold on her, bolted, and ran out the door as images of the women lying unconscious flooded her mind. She'd tried so hard not to think of them. Suddenly, all she could do was think of them, and her hands began to burn.

She stopped trying to push them from her mind and let them settle in deeper. She wondered what they'd said to try to get him to stop. Did he kill any of them? It looked as if a couple of them might not have made it.

He was approaching her.

She could run again. *No.* She looked around the forest and breathed deep. This was the place where she would make her stand.

He walked up behind her and placed his hands on her shoulders and slid them down her arms. His touch seemed to burn her. She let it burn... and burn and burn, all the way down to her hands. Memories of the night behind the Sojourner returned to her. She remembered looking down at her fingers and the burned cloth hanging from them.

She remembered being locked in the vault with him.

"We could be a family. If you would just listen to me."

He walked around to face her. "Stop fighting."

She swallowed hard and gathered her resolve. "You're right. I have to stop fighting." She went through every woman's photo in her mind. She glanced down at her hands and saw that lines of heat radiated from them. "Would you like a hand?"

A smile of victory spread across his face. Safia reached down between his legs and cupped his manhood through his clothing. His smile quickly turned to confusion, then horror, as she gripped harder. She felt the heat radiate over her hand and up her arm.

Smoke rose between them. He tried to back away but clearly found that it was too painful to move, locked in her grip as he was, but the longer he stayed, the deeper she burned. He raised a hand as if to strike her, but she caught his arm and burned the flesh there, too.

As he fell to his knees, he screamed in pain. She dropped to one knee with him, refusing to let go as she thought of the stack of pictures she'd seen in his room. She knew she had to make sure he couldn't do such a thing ever again.

The weight of him no longer pulled her forward. His body had fallen backwards from her grip. She shook her hand when she realized she held his ashen manhood, which crumbled like cinders. There was little blood. Not on her hand and less than she thought there would be on him. The wound had been mostly cauterized by the heat. Her gift burned away the traces of blood, and humanity, from the act. On shaky legs, she rose and began backing away. He lay on the ground calling out in soundless screams. His brown skin had grown pale, and his dark hair clung to the sweat that poured over his face.

"Safia," a soft voice spoke from behind her.

She jumped.

Carlos's voice was gentle on her ears, her soul. "You have Bella's gift."

She nodded and opened her mouth to speak, but no words came. Fear flooded her anew as she worried about the remarkable and terrible burden Bella carried. *Was it easier to have had it from birth?*

Carlos was standing beside her now, observing the mess of a man lying on the forest floor. "He didn't leave you with a choice. He never has. I'm sorry I didn't see it earlier."

She wanted to feel better that she wasn't alone in the forest with a madman anymore. Night after night she'd dreamed of nothing more than being in Carlos's arms again, yet now that he was here, she felt numb, cut off from the rest of humanity by what she had done.

Carlos offered her the phase weapon he carried and tapped a finger on the setting. It was programmed to kill. He looked her in the eye. "You cannot leave him this way. He will hunt you to the ends of the galaxy now. There will be no escape for you," he said quietly.

She studied her hand and noticed the ashen bits of Alvaro's skin clinging to hers. She wiped her palm frantically against her pants, all the while wondering why it bothered her so. This man was a monster. He deserved it, and she believed it. Perhaps it was simply the potential she knew she possessed now that haunted her. "I'm not a killer." She shoved his hand away.

"These past few months have been about you finding your own strength. I won't take that away from you now."

"I found it," she said, feeling the truth of her words down to her very bones, "and I'm done."

"Please listen to me. He will never stop now. Look at him."

There was no need to look at him. She heard him, the monster that he was, writhing on the ground like a wounded rat, now moaning. She'd heard that moan before... in another context. She just wanted to get as far away from him as possible. Her eyes burned and the ground grew blurry before her as she walked away, but her hearing was crystal clear as the phase weapon rang out twice from behind her, and Alvaro fell silent.

CHAPTER 60

WHERE THE HEART IS

They walked through the forest in silence. Safia let the carnage settle in. Breathe in, breathe out. She knew she had to let Carlos know what he was walking into. "There are three guards that I've spotted on patrol outside the house. They take eight-hour shifts. There's only one servant, Mariella, inside the house."

"I saw them on the infrared. I was able to sneak up on one of them near the range. He still gave me a fight before he went down."

"What?" She stopped and turned to look at Carlos for the first time, really look at him. His jaw was bruised, and he was holding his side as if he had injured ribs. She reached out to touch him, gently. He placed a hand over hers, his fingers curling around hers. There'd been no joyous hug when he'd found her, just a quick, life altering decision over who would be the one to kill the wounded animal.

"It's nothing," he said.

"Not nothing." She took a deep, shuddering breath. "There's a Med Wave at the estate."

He looked into her eyes as if searching for something and nodded. Another scan of the estate and surrounding area confirmed no one else had arrived, but one guard was still around back.

Carlos handed Safia one of the phase weapons. "Watch the gauge. I'm worried he has a disabling mechanism like we have on the *Ares.* Let me know if the gauge turns red, and I'll draw Jack's pistol."

Safia's heart warmed, knowing Jack had given him his prized possession. When they got within a hundred feet, the gauge flicked from green to red a few times before going red and staying there. She stopped. "Your instincts are correct. These are useless now."

"Thank you, Jack," Carlos said as he took the pistol from the holster, and then looked at the infrared again. "The guard is still around back."

Finally, they stood beside the front door. "Unless you know his passcode, we'll have to shoot the entry panel until it shorts, grab Bella with the alarms blaring, and bolt."

"I'd like a better alternative than that. This bastard owes me. I'd like a little time to make him pay."

Carlos lifted his chin as one corner of his mouth went up. "I like where your head's at, but how?"

"I have an idea. Might not work, but it's worth a try."

Carlos followed her around to the side of the house and then stood beneath a couple of windows and pointed. "This is mine and Bella's room. Give me a minute." Safia closed her eyes and concentrated as hard as she could, with no idea whether it would work. She thought of screaming for Bella to come to the window. A few moments had passed when she heard Carlos gasp beside her. She opened her eyes to find Bella in the window, grinning broadly.

Safia pointed toward the front of the house and mouthed, "Open the door."

Bella nodded and gave a thumbs up before disappearing from the window. As they started to head back around front, Safia and Carlos stopped and stood frozen as the last guard started coming around the corner on the infrared. Carlos pushed Safia toward the other side of the house. She glanced up to see Carlos running in the opposite direction to meet the guard before he could round the corner. Panic swept through her. They couldn't make it this far for her to lose

Carlos now. Images of the guard shooting Carlos the second he rounded the corner bombarded her, but before she could entertain another horrific scenario, the sharp sound of Jack's pistol firing echoed through the woods. She made a mental note to thank Jack profusely when they returned home.

Moments later, Carlos came around the corner with Jack's pistol holstered and the guards operable phase weapon in hand. "I don't see any other guards out here and only two heat signatures inside and an animal."

"The other guard must sleep off the compound," Safia said.

By the time they arrived at the front door, Bella was opening it, with Mariella rapidly protesting behind her in Spanish. Carlos appeared in front of her, armed, and speaking just as rapidly in Spanish, informing her of her employer's death.

She informed Carlos that she had been working there for a decade and was thankful God had seen fit to deliver her from the devil. She went straight to her room to pack her bags.

Bella jumped into Carlos's arms with War Hound growling and dancing around Carlos as if indecision frustrated him whether he should trust this interloper with his beloved.

Safia said, "Bella has made a new best friend. He watches out for her constantly. He's coming with us, by the way."

"I see." Carlos bent down with Bella so that War Hound could see he wasn't taking her away. "She's just fine. Thank you for looking out for my girl."

War Hound took a tentative step forward and then licked Carlos's hand. "I think we're good now," Carlos said. "Still, we should gather your things quickly and leave. We don't know who else knows about this estate or if we've tripped other alarms we don't know about."

They made their way up the stairs and gathered what few possessions they had. "You can take a few things if you like," Safia said to Bella.

"Only War Hound. Selah will love him!"

As Bella cuddled War Hound, Safia shoved a few items into a suitcase—a gilded candlestick, a comm unit—as her instincts from living on the streets before Bella was born kicked in.

"Are these what he owes you?" Carlos asked.

"No, this is nothing." Safia reached under the mattress and pulled out three very thick unnumbered, unmarked gold bars she'd plundered from his stash. "This is."

Carlos nodded. "Fair enough."

• • •

On the transport home, Bella slept peacefully with War Hound finally curled up beside her after circling over a dozen times before settling in. They would be home soon. Marcus's Spanish contact would take care of things on the ground, *literally*, at Alvaro's estate. As it turned out, Alvaro had made as many enemies as he had politicians in pocket. So, no one would be coming after them.

Still, the victory felt bittersweet. Safia worried profusely about how the experience might have traumatized Bella. She looked up to find Carlos watching her. He looked deeply concerned and exhausted. She was certain she looked all the worse for the wear as well.

Finally, he spoke. "I feel like I failed you."

"What? You came for me. You found me, and ultimately, you did what I couldn't. I'll never know why I couldn't."

"If he were coming at Bella, I know you would have finished him. Or, if he wasn't already on the ground writing in pain. It made it harder to get past your nature. I wouldn't worry about it too much. You would have done what was necessary if Bella or I were at risk. But I mean..." he looked down into the palms of his hands as if he'd find the right words there, laced his fingers together, and looked back up at her, "I should have pursued you, should have... known Alvaro was trouble. My instincts, they failed me."

Safia got up and crossed the small space to sit beside him on the bench. She placed a hand on his leg. "The whole time I was stuck at Alvaro's estate, I never once thought you'd failed me. What I did know is that his selfishness caused this whole situation. You've always wanted what's best for me, for us. Even when I was pushing you away, I was just trying to get past my history with him. You didn't fail me. You never have."

He looked at where her hand was touching his leg. She pulled her hand back. "Do you not want me touching you?"

"Are you kidding? I always want you touching me. I just... didn't know what exactly happened to you in his compound. To believe that he would keep you there that long without... hurting you seemed foolish. Since the moment I saw you again, I've wanted to touch you, but I wasn't sure if you'd welcome that or not."

"I welcome it." She pressed the panel in the wall on the other side of Carlos, leaning over him, close, purposely. A thick curtain descended from the ceiling, whisper quiet, to create a separate room from Bella and War Hound.

Carlos leaned in slowly, gently, kissing her forehead, eyelids, trailing his lips to her ear. "You're all I've ever needed. Ever wanted." His hand wrapped around the back of her head pulling her in for a deeper kiss.

When his tongue entered her mouth, desire shot through her body and made her legs feel weak. He reached beneath the bench to press the controls that converted the seat into a sleeping cot and eased her back onto it.

She reached up to remove his shirt and slide her hands over his hard, smooth chest, then reached down to relieve him of his pants. He groaned deep in his chest as she removed his underwear along with them. "I need you," she sighed.

He placed his knees on either side of her and she marveled at the muscles in his legs and ran her hands over them before he leaned over to pull her shirt over her head and remove her bra. His warm hands slid up her ribs, over her breasts, down her arms, and raised her hands above her head and joined their fingers together.

He kissed her deeply once more before pulling his mouth free only to place it on her breast. She wrapped a hand around his head and gasped softly. "Carlos."

He raised his head and gave her a sly smile. "Oh, God. Say it again."

She laughed.

"I think I can get you to say it again." He trailed kisses down her body, past her navel, until he landed between her legs and gently pushed them apart. She groaned as he put his warm mouth on her and sent wave after wave of pleasure crashing through her body.

After he'd satisfied her, he climbed back up to his place beside her like a cat stalking through a jungle toward its prey. He lay down and held her tight. "Do you hear anything?" she asked.

"No, the curtain muffles the sound but doesn't make it soundproof. If she's awake and talking, we should know."

"Good then, so much more to do."

He looked up with a smile. "Yes, please."

She buried her head in his neck to muffle her laugh. His smile was breathtaking. She thanked God for the dozenth time that no other woman had snatched him up while they were apart. She lifted her chin to his ear and whispered. "I want to feel your weight on me until I can't think, can't move, can't see straight. I want all you've got."

He turned his head and looked at her with a wicked grin. "Well, get ready then." He eased his weight onto her, and she spread her legs for him, enjoying his heavy warmth as it settled on her. He entered her, inch by exquisite inch. She sighed and pushed her hips up to meet him while staring into his eyes. He thrust into her once, twice, three times, and she asked him the question that had been burning its way through her mind since the day she'd left the *Ares*. "Will you marry me, Carlos? Be mine forever?"

He laughed, and it rumbled through the both of them. "You got it."

She wrapped her legs around him, and they both fell into ecstasy.

They lay in each other's arms as their breathing slowed. Carlos's large hand made lazy circles along her back. "I guess now that Alvaro's gone, you're sort of free to go...go your own way, I guess."

"It's more like, now I'm free to stay."

"I'm glad he didn't hurt you again."

Safia stiffened beside him, and her heart thundered in her ears. She didn't want to hurt him any further, but he'd done all he could for her when he ended Alvaro. Keeping secrets would only scar their marriage before it began. So, she took a deep breath and told him the story. The one that happened in the treasure vault.

She'd been in the room counting the looted gold ingots, age-old sunken treasure hoards, and other clearly pilfered goods when the vault opened two hours in. She didn't see Bella when she peeked around Alvaro. He shut the door and locked it. She rose and stood to defend herself, remembering her training, remembering to breathe, knowing this was where it mattered. No windows, no escape.

He walked toward her and spoke, "I know you'll fight me. That's what I like about you, but I can't have my daughter seeing any marks on you or she'll never learn to love me. See you in a few minutes." With that, he pulled out the phase weapon and stunned her just as he had shot Bella before loading her onto the transport.

When she woke, she was on the floor of the vault. Alvaro was inside her but looking frustrated, and then he pulled out of her, limp. "I like you much better when I can see the fire in you."

You mean you can't keep it up unless a woman is screaming and fighting you. She felt horror over what had just happened but some consolation in the fact that he hadn't been able to finish. The chances he'd impregnated her again were slim. When he'd raped her at the warehouse in Toledo, she'd been awake and screaming. He'd hit her on the side of the head and photographed her after she'd lost consciousness.

He tried to salvage the moment by adding a warning. "Just remember, anything here can be as difficult or as pleasant as you'd like it to be." He put his pants back on and left.

• • •

After Safia finished telling Carlos the story, she watched his reaction in the dim lighting of the transport. "Jesus," he said softly. "I knew I was a fool to hope. Why didn't you tell me before we made love?"

"I didn't want to see pity in your eyes, or God forbid, fear. It's still me."

"I know. I just..."

Safia's heart broke when she noticed he was crying.

"I can't follow him to hell and kill him again. That infuriates me."

"I know." She knew what he really wanted to say. He couldn't get past feeling as if he'd failed. It would take a while, but for now... "We won. We have each other. We have our daughter."

"And that is more than enough," he said.

"It's everything," she smiled and laid her head on his shoulder as he pulled her even closer.

CHAPTER 61

WANDERING THROUGH THE DESERT

The regolith kicked up and swirled about Aldric, sticking to his ragged prison-issue clothing and settling in his hair as the Martian sun sank behind Elysium Mons. He didn't miss the irony that though Josef had always been the biblical one; he was the man wandering in the desert. That hypocrite had been there when they'd taken in the pregnant women from the street to further the righteous cause, had prayed over the souls of the ones who'd perished when their bodies reacted poorly; he'd even been there when they'd drugged Harlow and plundered her mind. That stubborn, steel trap of a mind.

Now, that self-righteous son of a bitch with a messiah complex had the nerve to turn on him. Everybody wants a revolution, but nobody wants to get their hands dirty. Nobody wants the real discipline that it takes, and it would take a lot. It would take everything.

Dust storms had almost covered the compound in the last five years since it had been abandoned. It was a good camouflage, but what he needed wouldn't be found inside. The hinges on the shed fell away as he tried the door. He retrieved a shovel from inside.

They'd known better than to leave all their keys to victory inside in case of a raid, nor did they leave a map. They memorized where the serum was hidden. He began at the southeast building, walked out forty paces, turned left, walked seven, and looked down. He dug two feet before hitting the box, and then brushed away the rest of the dirt with his hands.

He sat back on the ground and sighed. This was the genuine test of his devotion to the cause, to the equality that he claimed to believe in. Truly, this was a greater test than the past four years he'd spent in the Bastille. What he was about to do could cost him his life. It had cost several of the pregnant mothers their lives. Fetuses in the midst of cell replication fared much better with the gifts of genetic enhancement that adults did. The adult body often viewed the serum as an invader and went into cardiac arrest or their blood pressure soared, causing seizures or a stroke. Aldric and his team had never known who would react in this way until it was too late.

Perhaps Josef's ultimate betrayal had more to do with watching Anka pass from the serum than his attachment to the children. Rory's mother had been fine after his birth. Months later, she started showing signs of remote viewing, telling them who was arriving at the compound before they got there, healing cuts and other ailments. Then she began getting sick. With all their advanced research, they couldn't seem to stop the cascade of genetic changes taking place.

On her deathbed, Josef argued with Aldric that the experiments had to stop. He believed they had become another way to hurt the poor, no better than the system they were trying to fight. He flew into a rage and smashed a vial of the serum. The serum represented decades of research, lost sleep, lost lives that couldn't be in vain. Aldric had hit him across the face with a comm unit, and his eyebrow split open.

Later that day, Anka had reached up to try and heal him. He'd wrapped his hand around hers, refusing to accept. He wanted to remember, and he had.

Aldric remembered her gaunt, haunted face now as he lifted the vial of serum with shaking hands and injected it into his arm. If the children were Josef's now, they might no longer be part of the Brotherhood's cause. Perhaps he could bring in a team to take care of Josef and retrieve the children, but one thing he knew for sure, he could no longer avoid the serum. He had to be strong. Sacrifices had to be made. Mikhail had given his life. Mikhail had taken the serum himself, though it had never done much more than give him strength. Aldric knew the real seat of power resided in the mind.

He took a deep breath and said a prayer. It only killed less than a quarter of adults. The rest were fine. Some gained no powers at all. It was as if their bodies did not recognize the serum.

Time would tell.

CHAPTER 62

MESSAGING MARCUS

Marcus stood in front of the mirror, straightened his tie, took a deep breath, and looked around the room. He was well and truly alone, but for the first time, he felt the beginning of something... solid? Real? Though apprehension still simmered below the surface, he was finding his own way, and it was enough, for now. After one last look at his reflection, he turned to head for the door, when a hologram message popped up in front of him. Butterflies took flight when he saw who it was from.

"Yua," he whispered. He wasn't sure where he stood with her. He knew he'd messed up. Wretchedly so. But if she were contacting him... Then again, maybe something was wrong with Jack, Harlow, Aunt Mary, or his niece. He played the message quickly to relieve the anxiety regarding either scenario.

"I understand you have a big address today. You're going to be great." That was all, and that, too, was enough... for now. He stared at her image. She was in her medical attire: the soft peach-colored scrubs with her dark hair pulled back in a ponytail that was picked up by a gentle breeze. Behind her he could see a smattering of trees and patchy grass, farther in the distance, more orange rocks, and the soft pink glow of a Martian sunrise. Did she go out to watch the sunrise every morning before work? Had she always done this? Was this a recent habit?

A knock at the door startled him.

"Come in," Marcus said, signaling with his hand for the message to be saved for future retrieval.

His new assistant walked in and immediately grinned at him. Marcus wondered what he was so happy about until he realized the man was simply mirroring what he was seeing. Marcus knew he must've looked like a lunatic, standing there smiling to himself.

"Looking forward to the speech, Your Majesty?"

"Yes, very much."

"Right then. Brilliant! You'll be glad to know your transport is ready."

Marcus reached up to touch the stitches that were no longer there but had been replaced by a thin scar he'd decided to keep. The day he got those stitches was the last time he'd felt this strange mix of butterflies and calm all at the same time. Some scars were worth keeping.

As the transport hummed along to take him to his first official address before Parliament, he looked out the window, and in his mind's eye, the surrounding buildings were replaced by the Mars regolith, the pink, orange glow of the Martian sunset as the last rays shone between his fingers, and he contemplated what it meant to be free, to be King, to be calm, to be... in love.

But he was King now, more committed than ever. *I choose to be.* He breathed deeply and looked at the sunlight filtering in through the window. He held his hand up. The light here was more stark but no longer harsh to him. He exhaled and began going over his speech again in his mind.

CHAPTER 63

OLD GHOSTS

Safia had never experienced such joy, never been so sure, settled, but most of all, free. As she looked across the courtyard at Carlos in his dress uniform, she saw they had exchanged the coalition insignia for the new insignia of the Ares Army. She now knew, with no doubt, that marrying Carlos was the right thing for her.

He looked up at her from where he was speaking with Daniel from engineering and winked. His stubble had grown in, making his face even darker and the way he dipped his head as he gazed at... damn, he must've known what he was doing to her. Her heart fluttered and her knees turned weak. She winked right back, dipping her head in what she hoped was the same provocative way. He grinned and wriggled his eyebrows in response. Daniel kept right on talking to Carlos, oblivious to the exchange between her and her new husband.

The last of the guests were saying their goodbyes. Sleepy children were hoisted onto the shoulders of their parents who gave final well wishes to Carlos and Safia beneath the strings of lights that draped from the *Ares* to the outbuildings and tents set up for their wedding.

Bella and Selah had even begun to lose a little of their steam, which rarely happened.

Harlow and Jack came up beside her. "There will be a message waiting for you and Carlos on the bridge in about ten minutes." Harlow said.

"Great. That will give me just enough time for something I need to take care of first."

"I'll go round up the others," Harlow told her.

Jack returned, followed by Carlos, Daniel, Aunt Mary, Judith, Selah, and Bella.

"The girls look completely worn out," Judith said, looking at Harlow. "Why don't I take them back to your quarters? You all can go to the bridge and then come back when you're done."

Harlow and Safia nodded as Judith walked toward Jack and Harlow's rooms with the yawning girls and War Hound trotting along beside them. The faithful companion rarely left Bella's side.

Safia turned to Carlos. "Stop by our quarters first? It'll only take a minute."

"Well, I don't know what you're planning, but my wedding night plans require a hell of a lot longer than that."

Safia laughed. "Not that!"

Once they arrived in their quarters, she went into Bella's closet, reached up onto the shelf, pulled down a square wrapped in cloth, and presented it to Carlos. But when she turned around, he had a gift for her as well but set it aside to receive hers first.

"What is this?" he said as he removed the cloth from the square. He sighed as he looked at the canvas, his eyes shining with unshed tears. "You didn't have to do this."

"Yes. I did. I ruined that painting you loved. It was a beautiful, sunny Martian day and I painted storm clouds all over it."

"No. That painting was honest. There was nothing wrong with it. You were expressing yourself. Maybe even trying to tell me something. Why else did you leave it here? I want all of you: joy, pain, storm clouds, everything." He cleared his throat. "But I will certainly cherish this one. It's also you. Thank you." He wrapped his arms around her, still holding the painting and swaying as if there was music. "I've never been so happy."

He released her. "But I have something for you." He turned to their bed, set the painting down, and picked up the small palm sized package, and presented it to her.

She unwrapped it. "A gun?"

"Not exactly. You told me you weren't a killer, but you are a hell of a warrior, a fighter, and I'm not so sure you should stop. I had Daniel make this for you. It's a stun only mechanism, weighted just like a phaser pistol. The best part is it can't be disabled. It doesn't use the same tech as the standard issue. You can take it anywhere."

"My gosh. It fits my hand so much better than the phaser pistols."

"Daniel and I designed it specifically for you."

She looked at him and tried to trace the feelings she had for him now. She'd always loved him, but now... there was a depth that came from being whole. Now that she knew herself, she could be known. This man knew her. Really *knew* her.

• • •

Once on the *Ares* bridge, they found AVM Miller sitting in the captain's chair, speaking with a hologram image of Marcus. As soon as the others walked in, Marcus's face lit up.

Safia barely recognized the self-assured, strong man she saw before her.

"Again, I apologize for not being able to make the trip."

Carlos spoke. "How dare you not cancel a seven-nation summit that might help determine the future of both our worlds in order to attend my wedding. How selfish can you be?"

"Mighty damn selfish." Marcus smiled. "Seriously, I miss all of you."

"We miss you, too."

Jack said, "Miss you, little bro. Pardon me. Your *Majesty.* Gonna take some getting used to, that one."

"Well, as your sovereign, I'll be merciful and let it slide the one time," he said while laughing. "Seriously," he said, looking toward Carlos and Safia. "I couldn't be happier for the two of you." He suddenly looked beyond them and toward the doorway. Safia thought he appeared transfixed. She followed his line of sight and noticed that Dr. Yua Nokamura had walked in and stood looking back at him. She was indeed a vision in royal blue. Her dark hair hung in soft black waves; one side pulled back with a clip to reveal a sparkling earing. She blushed when she seemed to realize heads had turned her way.

"Your Majesty," she stammered.

"Marcus," he said with the husky voice of a man who sounded as if he could suddenly use a drink of water.

"Marcus," Yua replied, barely above a whisper as red blotches on her neck joined the blush on her cheeks.

"How are things in sick bay?"

"Not too busy, and here's hoping they stay that way."

Marcus nodded. "Indeed."

Safia looked beside her at her new husband. A lazy grin made its way across his face as he glanced from Yua to Marcus and back. Safia raised her eyebrows and smiled.

"Well, I'll not keep the happy couple any longer," Marcus said. "I just wanted to wish you both the best." Marcus grabbed a glass of some sort of libation and lifted it in their direction. "Love to you all. Hope to see you soon."

"Thank you!" Safia said. Carlos echoed her thanks.

"Love you, brother," Jack said.

After they said their goodbyes, Marcus's hologram disappeared, and everyone turned to file out but not before another image took its place.

"What the—" AVM Miller stared as the others turned to look as well.

Safia's heart nearly stopped, and she looked at Harlow in time to watch the color drain from her best friend's face.

A full-sized hologram of Aldric stood before them. The man had transformed from the professional, pulled together, science officer from the compound that Safia remembered to a man that was all hard lines, muscle, and an even harder gaze.

He looked straight at Harlow and said, "I'm coming for you," and disappeared a second later.

ABOUT THE AUTHOR

Photo courtesy of Cherie Lawley

Kim Conrey is the author of the sci-fi romance series *Ares Ascending* and the paranormal romance *Nicholas Eternal,* Book One of the *Wayward Saviors* series. When she's not writing the next book in the Ares series, she writes about living with OCD. Her essays and short stories have been published in regional as well as local publications. You can also find her marching in Atlanta's Dragon Con parade as a Box Hero Wonder Woman. In addition, she serves as VP of Operations for the Atlanta Writers Club. She also collaborates on a podcast with the Wild Women Who Write Take Flight where they interview authors and industry professionals with a primary goal of supporting women writers.

AUTHOR'S NOTE

The very best way to support a book or author you love is to leave an online review. It's a small thing that makes a huge difference!

To learn more about my books and the inspiration behind them, head to KimConrey.com where you can sign up for my newsletter and stay in the loop about upcoming events, new releases, and giveaways.

With gratitude,
Kim Conrey

www.ingramcontent.com/pod-product-compliance
Lightning Source LLC
Chambersburg PA
CBHW050135120726
47903CB00002B/359

9781685132934